THA' IN ALBANIA

A ROAD TRIP TO INTRIGUE IN THE BALKANS

LUZIA:
HAVE A GREAT TRIP!

PETER J. MEEHAN

outskirtspress
DENVER, COLORADO

That Weekend in Albania
A Road Trip to Intrigue in the Balkans
All Rights Reserved.
Copyright © 2016 Peter J. Meehan
v5.0

Cover Photo © 2016 thinkstockphotos.com. All rights reserved - used with permission.

Outskirts Press, Inc.
http://www.outskirtspress.com

ISBN: 978-1-4787-7709-0

Library of Congress Control Number: 2016910694

Outskirts Press and the "OP" logo are trademarks belonging to Outskirts Press, Inc.

PRINTED IN THE UNITED STATES OF AMERICA

Albania: Locations (approximate) mentioned in text

1

"WHY CAN'T WE just take the coast road both ways, down and back?" I bent down to look more closely at the nearly featureless map of the countryside. It was the only available guide to roads in Albania. How could this country, located between the two greatest empires of Europe's ancient world, be nearly unknown?

Ariyan, a local colleague, was watching me pore over the map on my desk. He leaned over to speak and the odour of stale tobacco tinged the air. "Is possible you come back same way by this road on coast, but"—he extended his nicotine-stained index finger upwards to make his point and then tapped a spot nearly halfway along the route, not far from the coastline—"here." He continued tapping it. "Llogara Pass nearly two thousand metres. Very steep." He stood up as I looked at where he had pointed. "Maybe, going *once* over is too much," he added. "But, better you come back inland. This way you have less problem." It was a conclusion, and he started for the balcony to escape for another cigarette.

I continued studying the map. His logic was unclear to me, but I was only just getting a flavour of the mentality in the Balkan countries, though Albania was even more unique. The mountains butted right up against the coast, but the route's steepness aside, how could returning on the same road be a problem? The only way to find out was to make the trip. How bad could it be? I loved driving any coast; there was just something about looking out to sea that resonated with me. I could still remember approaching the ocean as a child in my parents' car, though what country we were in was vague in my memory—anticipation filled the air as we came over the final hill and I saw, for the first time, the sun reflecting off water stretching out to the horizon. It was love at first sight.

This trip would be an adventure for the whole family. A coastal drive from the Adriatic to the northern reaches of the Ionian Sea had great appeal, much like a rougher version of the Cabot Trail or the Southern California coast. The big difference would be lack of infrastructure or modern conveniences, or so I presumed. Our big Nissan Patrol SUV was built for seriously rough driving and should be able to handle the roads. I'd seen the UN use them in desert convoys and for nuclear plant inspections on the back roads of Iraq. The principal route south to Saranda was reported as being in decent shape, but I'd recently discovered that there was a coastal alternative. The scenery: it should be fantastic at two thousand metres. One of my work colleagues, the finance manager, had taken the inland route a few weeks before, so it was generally assumed I would do the same. I wanted to handle the challenge differently. The coast route might have more rough spots, but this would all be part of the adventure.

It would be our first tour outside the broken city in which my family had been living for the last three months. I'd been in Albania longer, nearly six months, and despite the difficulties was really starting to like the complete change in lifestyle and situation. Some would say this attitude adjustment was the sign of a midlife crisis, but the need for change was something I went through every few years. (Wasn't "denial" the longest river in Africa?) My wife had yet to be convinced that it had been a good move, but before accepting the new job, I'd visited our consular office in the capital—always good to see the office, the city environment, available housing, and the school before committing to any job, particularly one in the poorest country in Europe. The consul had assured me that the family would be as safe in Tirana as in any European city, now that the country was opening up.

"Of course," she'd said, "there are bound to be isolated incidents, as there would be in any major city." Earlier in the year two gang members had shot each other not far from our office. "Travelling outside Tirana is usually fine, but driving on some of the poorly maintained roads can be challenging. There are no guarantees that conditions beyond the main highway to Durrës will continue to improve, but I don't see any real concerns now, other than in the isolated mountainous regions where blood feuds are still a concern for the locals." I'd heard about these multigenerational conflicts; they'd been outlawed by the former communist regime but were now being rejuvenated. Maybe they were viewed as an honourable tradition—however misguided that idea was—to be passed on from father to son. Or, she'd said, criminal elements could begin back-and-forth revenge killings, like the shooting in the city, to increase their credibility. She'd also advised against any travel to the northeast, near the border with Kosovo, where cross-border smuggling still hadn't been eliminated and weapons were prevalent.

Now, nearly six months later, travel had likely improved substantially—at least it should have, since available family housing and the schools were both steadily improving. I knew that road construction and restoration had continued around the city, so my wife and I had decided to take the family to the ancient site of Butrint on the upcoming weekend. She was becoming more comfortable in our "new" apartment and wanted to see just what kind of country we'd agreed to live in for the next few years. Our eldest daughter, who was transitioning to young womanhood at a French school in Vienna, would be visiting us for the weekend. There'd been concern from friends and relatives that we were asking for trouble, but we were confident our eldest could handle the pressure of boarding school, as long as she came home frequently. So the road trip would be just right for the family: it would allow us to visit Albania's most important historical site, and we'd all benefit from the time together.

I was eagerly anticipating the trip to the massive multicivilisation ruin—the most significant ancient site along Albania's coastline—just south of the small port of Saranda, near Greece's northern border. The ancient Greeks had enlarged an Illyrian encampment, followed by the Romans, who crossed the Adriatic Sea and developed the site into a major stopover between Rome and Athens. I'd tried to get our two boys excited about the Romans and Greeks by watching a few bad movies with them. The results were mixed, but we now had our youngest daughter ready to take on the invading hordes to defend the Empire of Rome—or Athens.

"The Greeks are the side with the pretty pink things sticking out of their helmets, right, Dad?" The videos were used copies I'd gotten from friends at various embassies, so the faded colour wasn't quite the Romans' imperial red on the small video-player screen.

Butrint's strategic position on a peninsula, guarding the northern Ionian coast and the channel to an inland lake, ensured its continued importance as a Byzantine fortress after the fall of Rome. It was largely abandoned by the Venetians prior to the Ottoman invasions that brought Islam to the region, starting in the fifteenth century. Day visits to the "forbidden shores of Albania" and the Butrint site had become increasingly popular with adventure tourists from the offshore Greek island of Corfu, after Stalinist communism ended in Albania in the early 1990s.

We were nearly prepared for the trip when the consulate called me Friday morning and asked me to come in. I agreed to be there just before noon. I'd already paid them a visit on Monday to inform them of our weekend plans, as they recommended filing any overnight trips outside the capital. Perhaps there was a new travel advisory or something. Maybe they'd provide a nice lunch. It was only a few minutes' walk from the office, just past the garbage heap that spilled onto the road, nearly blocking it. Large rubbish bins were only just being distributed in the city, but not all were being looked after on a regular schedule. I'd been sure to include several pictures of them for family viewing after my initial look-see in advance of getting the wife's agreement for the move; it was a fine line between keeping expectations to a minimum while praising the Mediterranean lifestyle we'd be able to enjoy—eventually. So far it seemed this health benefit was mainly outside the country, though small vegetable markets were springing up in several back alleyways not far from our apartment.

I walked faster as I approached the garbage trying to hold my breath, but I still caught the smell of a giant overflowing ashtray—the mix of cardboard, plastic, and discarded food was smouldering on one corner. My foot came down on something soft as I tried to step carefully over the worst part, and my shoe slid as it squeezed a nearly fresh patch of shit. The awkward movement to regain my balance startled a cow upwind of the smoke—so at least it wasn't *real* shit—and her head came up to look at me. She was wary of the disturbance, but there was no one with her that I could see. Her cowbell clanged as she swung her head back down to search for other edible tidbits in the spillage behind the bin, away from the street. I looked for the nearest green patch on which to wipe my shoe, but even a few blades of grass were rare in the dusty street—why else would the cow look in the garbage?

These city cows were usually led to the bins by small boys or old women. My wife now avoided buying all dairy products, unless we brought them into the country in our luggage. The packaging on the milk locally available in the few stores identified a European origin, but the indication of an Italian or Austrian source made no difference to her. Though it was unlikely that the milk boxes were counterfeit, I couldn't disagree with the family dairy boycott after Ariyan told me about the fake cigarettes: the containers were genuine but the contents were locally produced.

After I entered through the main gate and awkwardly slid my tainted foot onto the *real* grass growing at the edge of the path, the attendant checked my passport, and I was led into the waiting room. The events of 9/11 were only two months past, but I didn't have to wait outside for a consular staff member to escort me into the building—the guard, who nearly smiled, remembered my visit on Monday. I sat down and waited, trying to ignore that I was the source of the slight odour, while thinking about the conversation I'd had with my Austrian employers eight months previously. They had contacted me about a "highly interesting position in Albania." Some of my colleagues had referred to it as the "toilet bowl of Europe," so I followed up the offer by calling my cousin who worked for the Foreign Service. Her opinions were biased, but whose weren't? And who else might know about Europe's last remaining WC country, previously an isolated and paranoid backwater with a Muslim majority? The last bit had surfaced when Islamophobia briefly dominated the world press following the September attacks on New York.

"Well, Tony, that's quite a coincidence," my cousin had said. "We've just received a report that the country is finally undergoing significant, *fundamental* changes." As if "significant" weren't enough. "Ever since the collapse of the pyramid-banking schemes chased off foreign investment and caused rioting, the European Union has been hesitant to get too involved, despite reduced tensions next door in the ex-Yugoslav states. But recently we've had visitors returning with really positive reports, and the consulate has noted some good developments. Tirana's new mayor is taking on the corruption and making some headway, so it might be a great place for a posting, being close to Greece and Italy." She knew I liked the Mediterranean. "Even the northern border with Serbia and Montenegro may improve over the next year."

By this she meant Kosovo in the northeast, still officially a province of Serbia (which itself had been part of Yugoslavia) and about which I was learning more and more. My wife and I had recently met a crew of landmine clearers in the main Tirana hotel one evening. We'd exchanged social pleasantries and then one of them, who was busy enjoying the local wine, mentioned they were just back from a "regular" sweep of the inland Kosovo border area—I wondered if an "irregular" sweep was something to be avoided. They talked about it as if they'd been picking up garbage in a field.

"Of course we have to adhere to a strict methodology to ensure our safety, but we *are* professionals," he'd said. I wondered about the local professionals. There was a tendency to cut corners here, as I'd seen with the city's rubbish bin pickups. But mines are a bit different from garbage. Nothing like a little too much excitement to liven up the job.

The ongoing unrest in Kosovo also encouraged human trafficking and prostitution, and gun running continued to be an issue, even as relations improved nearer to the coast in Montenegro, further to the west. My Austrian general manager hinted the Americans were the cause of the unrest, but he also blamed them for many other problems in Europe—I think he just envied their success and wished the Hapsburgs and the good old days of the Austro-Hungarian Empire would return, so that Vienna would be the centre of the world.

My cousin had a final word of advice. "I'm an optimist, Tony, but there are no guarantees there won't be setbacks. Remember this is the Balkans we're talking about."

Ah, yes, the ass-covering, just in case things didn't quite turn out the way she predicted. Or was I being overly cynical? Maybe a wee bit of both.

"The Greek border is stable, and an Italian presence in the country helps, but the northern border with Serbia is the issue, at least for now. Montenegro is fine—being on the coast helps keep them honest, and they're well on the way to becoming independent from Serbia—but east to Kosovo, away from the tour groups and in the mountains? That's where we've been focusing our efforts."

A knock on the door brought me back to the present, and the consul entered. I stood to shake her hand. *It must be important if she's greeting me herself*, I thought. But could she smell my shoe?

"Mr. McAtee, I apologise for keeping you waiting. How good to see you again. Please come this way."

She led me through a hallway to a small conference room, where two people sat deep in discussion. I assumed they were both diplomats—I knew at least one of them was.

"Tony, great to see you!" My cousin jumped up and shook my hand.

The consul seemed eager to get away. "If you'll excuse me, I'm due to make an important call. Let me know if you need anything else." So it wasn't my shoe? Maybe she was being diplomatic.

I turned back to my cousin in surprise, not entirely

believing she was here in the country. Why hadn't she told me she was coming?

"Please, come in, have a seat. This is Mr. Brown from our ...overseas department."

Mr. *Brown* from the *overseas* department? I raised an eyebrow after shaking his hand and welcoming him to Tirana, but she ignored it and continued.

"We've only just gotten in this morning. Interesting drive from the airport."

Yes, an economy midway between collapse and progress provides many interesting sights, I thought.

She started to speak again but stopped. Then, "I didn't know it was only a ninety-minute flight from Vienna."

I sat down and looked at her, the career diplomat. She'd become very successful as an Eastern Europe specialist after being posted to many of the former Soviet Bloc countries. The last time we'd talked, she'd mentioned more trips to Vienna, but I certainly hadn't been expecting to see her here.

"We've been reviewing budgets for various developments and programs in Eastern Europe, particularly now with the signing last year of the Stability Pact for South Eastern Europe. The first big payment is due. Last night I realised you might be in a position to help us out, and it was just as easy to come in person as to call."

So she had known it was only a short flight.

Mr. Brown's phone rang, and he got up and walked over to the other end of the table. My cousin leaned over to me. "You're wondering why I didn't call in advance. I should apologise." A moment of silence, then she added, "How's Michaela making out in Vienna?"

I was regaining my composure, and took a sip of the bottled water that was on the table. I hadn't replied when my cousin looked over to Mr. Brown as he returned.

He sat down across from me and said, "Yes, well we only just decided last night to come. It's a matter that we felt would be better handled in person." His accent was hard to place: Harvard American English or pretentious Canadian?

I waited for more details on "the matter." What could this have to do with me? Mr. Brown paused, likely for effect, and Celine jumped in.

"Listen, Tony. Albania has made some tremendous advances since the last disturbances ended. Our government is very keen to support them in every way possible, but . . ."

Mr. Brown was more direct. "There are elements in the support lobby willing to fund a number of infrastructure investments here, but unfortunately, at any cost."

Getting the job done using the local mafia, for instance? I thought, as he continued.

"You probably noticed the state of the airport."

The small terminal had a dirt floor, no security to speak of, recycled French buses with worn seats and barely visible *Defense de fumer* notices, and landing forms inscribed on low-quality cardboard "paper" that I had last seen in Libya ten years earlier. Yet modern, world-class airlines waited on the tarmac: Austrian Airlines, Swiss, and Lufthansa were all prepared to use Tirana as a base, predicated on the belief that a stabilising economy would grow, as had the economies of other former Eastern Bloc members. Albania certainly had room to improve—the lower the level of development, the more significant the possibility of growth. It was the reason my employer was here and why I had been hired.

Mr. Brown elaborated. "We'd like to help out. The problem is, we aren't so sure that the ruling party here hasn't reverted to some of the old ways."

I wondered whom "we" referred to, but was aware of the dilemma facing donor countries. Albania's democratic government was now run by the Socialist Party. The Democrats, the first elected government after communism, had allowed private banks to invest in pyramid schemes, resulting in a catastrophic devaluation of the country's currency in 1997. Only the very rich had benefited, or those who had seen the inevitable collapse coming. The people had come onto the streets in the capital, and the situation had been bleak for a while.

"Let's just say that transparency has been lacking in some areas." Mr. Brown paused, and then said, "If we had another set of eyes on developments away from the capital—the south of the country, for instance, where you're going—it would be a great help."

There was silence as I digested the implications of his request, but finally Celine stepped in. "Yes, we don't want to end up supporting the local mafia chiefs." My cousin used the term "mafia" loosely; these were not Cosa Nostra, despite the close relations between Albania and Italy. They were family heads and local clan leaders who had taken control of shipping and transport when the Communist Party, which had seized power under Enver Hoxha in 1945, collapsed in the early nineties. There was a vacuum until Europe and the Americans became involved. The deteriorating situation in the former Yugoslavia a short time later brought NATO into the region. If the locals hadn't continued distributing food and everyday supplies when the government collapsed, how many families and children would have starved or died in the mountains? It was inevitable that there would be rivalries between clan leaders, and competition to control these now illegal organisations, resulting in confrontations and shootings.

Even after listening to both of them try to win me over for the better part of two hours, I remained unconvinced when I arrived back at my office. And I hadn't had lunch. My cousin was returning to Vienna, but her companion was staying behind. He hoped we could keep in contact. I wasn't so sure—even an observational role seemed suspect. Why had my cousin come with him from Vienna? Just to get my cooperation? I still didn't think they were giving me the whole story, and sensed they weren't quite working as a team.

I was home by 7:00 p.m., but not before finalising my family-trip itinerary with Ariyan—from the capital, Tirana, we'd head west to Durrës and the Adriatic Sea and then take the coastal route south through the port city of Vlora, and on to Saranda.

Ariyan had retrieved the only Albanian road map we had access to, other than the page-size drawings I'd seen of the main roads, and the country outline we used in presentations. He'd found the map on one of his trips to head office in Vienna, at a major cartographic supply centre, but it was hardly Michelin-starred quality. He finally convinced me that a return trip on the coastal route wasn't advisable—I realised that the time it would take to drive up and down a mountain pass and follow an unknown coastal track might be more than we could manage in a weekend if we wanted to visit Butrint. Looking more closely at where the red line of the road thickened and wiggled on the map, I noted little black chevrons marking the route he'd indicated. They didn't look like much, but I knew they indicated steepness, and since the nearly bare map had few other details, they had to be quite significant. *But it shouldn't be a problem with our Nissan*, I thought.

Then he pulled out a large-scale high-resolution satellite photo of the southern interior near the coast, one of a few that the company had ordered in advance of bidding on some work. The coverage included a portion of the shoreline, and he pointed to a beautifully shaped natural harbour in a bay some distance north of Saranda. A fortress had been built on a small island near the middle of the bay and was joined by a causeway to the mainland.

"This fortress was built by Ali Pasha," he said proudly. "You know of him, yes?"

"Yes." I had heard of this Albanian, a renegade from the nineteenth century who had turned on his Ottoman masters and become a cruel clan leader, committing atrocities within the local population for his entertainment.

"The Britisher, Byron, stayed with him." Ariyan had many stories to tell me, and some of them were true. "Byron come first here before he get to Greece." I knew that Byron's writings indicated he was secretly horrified by the Albanian's methods. I looked closely at the fortress and its shape, having seen quite a few castles and fortifications around the Mediterranean during my earlier youthful wanderings.

"But Ariyan, this fortress looks much older than nineteenth century. Just look at its shape." To me, it looked Venetian, and I figured it was likely built after the city state of Venice expanded south along the coast into Albania, early in the fifteenth century, before the Ottomans came north.

"I don't think so, Tony. I have been there." The discussion on the fortress' origin was now finished as far as Ariyan was concerned. He did have firsthand knowledge of his country, having travelled to most parts of it with his father under the old regime, but his visiting the fortress hardly proved it was Ali Pasha's.

He drew his finger around the bay and island. "This bay is Palermo. Is very beautiful area. Resort companies try to develop for tourists, hotels, restaurants. It would be much money, this plan."

"Really?" I asked. "Has it gone ahead?" This would be of interest to Mr. Brown, if I decided to help him out. "Will we be able to stop and see it?"

"There were problems." Ariyan looked at me and smiled. "No approval." He got enthusiastic. "You can still visit! Is why I show you." He was proud of his country, but he was getting fidgety—time for a cigarette. But first he said, "You can go north from Saranda. No need for Llogara Pass." I didn't answer. He shrugged and stepped out onto the balcony.

I would have to see this bay and fortress myself, after Llogara Pass. Maybe they hadn't paid off the right people, or the locals hadn't wanted the development. The people in the most need of employment and opportunities just didn't have the access to resources and money. It might be worthwhile helping Mr. Brown if he was supporting them.

My wife and I spent the evening talking to our daughter. She'd arrived that morning on the same flight as my cousin but hadn't seen her. Celine must have been keeping a very low profile. Near the end of her update, Michaela casually mentioned that she'd made friends with an older male, but not to worry, as he was Canadian. Well, I was totally relieved—Canadians could never do anything wrong. Ariyan's logic came to mind. My daughter and I were going through a bad phase. It wasn't just teenage rebellion, though "midlife crisis" sounded a bit strong for my problem.

As we headed to bed, my wife gave me a questioning look. Michaela's news of her male friend had given us something more to sleep on. The trip couldn't have come at a better time. We'd settle everything over the weekend and live happily ever after.

2

I WAS HAPPY to see my family again after three weeks—
even my dad. Being nearly on my own in a big city was exciting, but living in Vienna wasn't like the adventures of the
girls I'd read about in my favourite books. And all those girls
spoke English—well, except maybe Heidi. Anyway, it was
always nice to see the family. My classes in Vienna were at a
school for French students, mostly. Their parents were living
in the city, and weren't we all so very lucky to be allowed to
live in the cultural centre of the old Austrian empire? A place
where nobody smiled and the buildings were all yellow like
baby turds. And then there was all that waltzing music that
put me to sleep whenever I heard it. The parents were always
going on about this cultural stuff to us, but we were just going to school, trying to do as well as we could.

The lessons in French were really hard at first—trying
to remember all the verbs and tenses—but after classes at
the lycée I could go back to my room at the Austrian boarding school and do what I wanted. I'd made a few boarding
school friends who could speak English, and we talked about
plans we had for parties and boyfriends. And eventually the

French I'd taken for a year of immersion at my old school started coming back to me.

Tirana visits happened every few weekends, but this trip would be longer because yesterday was a holiday. Three days was just about right for a visit—any longer and my parents started asking too many questions, giving me the lecture about being very careful, like "Don't hang around the subway when you travel between the boarding school and the lycée." As if the big bad wolf might get me. They didn't need to worry—the older kids who hung around the trains were too strange for me to like. I wondered what they did all day. One time a kind-of-hot guy tried to call me over, but my German wasn't very good back then and I ignored him. Maybe my German was good enough now.

The first day of the visit to Albania was always the best: seeing my parents, noticing how my little sister had changed in the few weeks I'd been gone, and catching up with my brothers. Last night after supper, I almost told them the whole story about my new friend. I caught myself just in time, when my mom's eyes got really big.

"Who is this you're talking about?" she asked. That's when I toned the story right down—for a minute I'd forgotten I wasn't talking to my friends in Vienna. I had the "first night happies" so was talking waaay too much.

"Oh just a guy I met at one of the embassy things." My dad was paying more attention now. "You know." I was trying to remember if I'd told them about some of the outings I'd had. "Giselle's parents take us to family events on the weekends."

Giselle didn't have brothers or sisters, and was boarding

at the Austrian school too, but she was going to the classes there and not the lycée. Her parents lived in Zagreb, which is in Croatia and up the coast from our Albanian home—I looked it up on a map at school—but they spent a lot of time in Vienna. Giselle said it was her mom's favourite European city. I also got the feeling that Switzerland was waaay too expensive for schooling, and maybe her mom liked to get out of Croatia whenever she could. I always wondered if it was like Albania.

"So you met him at an embassy party?"

Why did he always try to make it sound bad? "Father, it wasn't a party, it was a rugby match between the Canadians and the Romanians. Lots of the rugby squads are doing a tour of Europe to drum up support for their teams."

———※《◊》※———

I didn't know anything about the sport when Giselle and I found the Gösser beer tent the day of the match. We tried to find someone who would let us in to sample the Austrian beer because it was supposed to be really good, or at least that's what one of the French guys at school had said.

Giselle and I walked back and forth a few times in front of the entrance, speaking loudly enough so that anyone just inside the tent could hear us.

"I really think the team has made some major improvements," I said, and looked around. Unfortunately one of the bouncers near the entrance looked more interested than the beer crowd busy downing glasses.

"Really?" Giselle replied. "Isn't their captain injured?" We'd overheard this and hoped someone would tell us more and bring us inside the tent. Instead, the bouncer came towards us, looking to chase us away. We turned around quickly and ran back towards the stands, trying to stop laughing, and that's when we bumped into this really good-looking guy standing alone near the corner of the tent.

"Oops, sorry," I said, about to step around the end of the tent. But when I looked up I just about fell over 'cause I couldn't help staring into the most beautiful eyes I'd ever seen, and the owner of them was tall and dark.

"That's all right." He was returning my stare, maybe wondering how old I was, so I straightened up and turned back to Giselle, who was right behind me.

"I really think the better players should be more aggressive in their . . . attacks," I said, thinking that the man was probably watching the game closely, but was "attack" the right word? Giselle hesitated, her laughter cut short, and then she saw whom I'd bumped into.

"Yes, indeed," she said, "but my own preference would be for them to mount a better defence." Her father had taken her to quite a few hockey games when they lived in Quebec.

"Oh, so you girls are rugby fans, are you?" he asked.

Girls! That would need to be changed ASAP! "Well, of course," I answered. "But the view of the playing field from inside the tent just isn't quite what we expected. I was hoping there would be some seats outside here in the stands."

He looked more closely at me, then, but I wasn't quite sure what that meant.

When the rest of my family and I first joined my dad in Albania, I went to school in Tirana with my brothers and sister for a few months. It was a really small school, less than thirty students for all the grades. There wasn't much to do in Tirana, and I got bored because there were no other American or English expat kids in my class to talk to. The other high school classes had just a few Europeans and some Albanians—there were two who were a little older than me in my class trying to improve their English so they might get into an American university. One of them was sort of good-looking, but it scared me a bit when I saw that he kept looking at me from his seat near the back the whole time in class.

My teacher was an older Canadian who was doing a bit of teaching to support his travelling. He was the main reason my parents had sent me to the school—to see if having him as a teacher would be good enough. He was supposed to be a great teacher, and he was a big help, but he was quite old and got tired in class. I knew he'd talked to my dad about my not having any classmates who could challenge me. He said that competition was "essential" for me to keep up my standards, so my dad looked at other places, like an American school in Greece, or Rome, but none of them had boarding schools. And I wasn't so sure about going away for months to strange cities by myself. So he found the lycée in Vienna, where he would be able to see me whenever he was on one of his many business trips, and every once in a while my mom could come for a weekend of shopping to make sure I was doing okay. Her trips were what made my time in Vienna bearable, at least in the beginning. Sometimes seeing my father was good—at least we got on better than when I was living at home.

Now I found going home to Tirana a really good break to get away from all the studying and the different languages. The French I'd learned at my old school wasn't quite the same as the strict Parisian stuff they taught at the lycée—it was a bit of a surprise after I'd been there a few weeks when they told me that I needed to really improve my French—I'd thought I was doing pretty good, but they wanted it to be *perfect*. The science and math classes were also waaay ahead of what I'd been taking, but my dad tried to help me before I left, and we tried doing catch-up stuff on any of the weekends I went home. There was usually some problem when we had a talk—like he expected more of me or something—but the exercises had been helpful.

Most of the students who weren't in my class thought I was one of the Austrians. These Viennese students went to the school because their families wanted them to have a second language. I didn't really find any friends with either the Austrian or the French students. This meant I was even more alone at school—though my parents called it being independent—and I attracted the notice of some of the older guys who were always waiting outside the entrance near the tram stop where they could smoke. One time I dropped my ticket and didn't know until one of them tapped me on the shoulder and gave it to me. I just said, "*Merci*," and he went back to his friends. Most of them were smoking the really smelly French cigarettes. They weren't bad-looking guys, but the thought of kissing them—no way! It would be like licking an ashtray. It was while waiting for the tram back to the boarding school that I'd heard them talking about the rugby tour and the beer tents. I didn't know the French played rugby. I'd only heard about it in one of my books about England where the heroine falls for the captain of the squad and he turns out to be a twit.

3

MR. BROWN, AS he was currently known, sat in the hotel garden finishing his coffee in the warm midmorning sun. Reby, his driver, sat a few tables away—just another aspiring Albanian stopping for a coffee at the well-regarded hotel, hoping to be lucky and make some contacts—carefully watching everyone and everything at the little gathering that had just broken up between his boss and a few select businessmen.

Reby was from the old days, the only man still in Albania whom Mr. Brown could completely rely on. He was a stalwart that Mr. Brown, an American, had kept in contact with during his exile from the country. They'd talked occasionally over the last couple of years, but once Mr. Brown made definite plans to return, Reby had come back on board as his driver. Like many Albanians, he drove a Mercedes, but this model had a supercharged fuel delivery system, along with several other modifications that Reby had done himself—he knew he was much more than just another chauffeur.

His boss had told him that the meeting with the diplomats in Vienna had gone well—it helped that everyone was eager to assist the United States in the aftermath of the 9/11 attacks, rushing to outdo one another, so his expired credentials hadn't been too carefully scrutinized when he first approached the ambassador at an embassy function in the Austrian capital. When Reby picked up his returning boss at the airport, there had been another passenger with him—an embassy diplomat to pave the way for additional cooperation—and they had driven straight from the airport to the diplomat's consulate.

Reby sensed the atmosphere had changed when the two returned to the car. There was something about the way they approached, and neither of them said anything when they opened the passenger doors on either side of the vehicle. As Reby drove away and headed for the airport, the American finally spoke. "I thought you said he'd be happy to help out?"

The driver glanced in the rear-view mirror, expecting the diplomat to reply, but she remained stone-faced. The tension in the car eased only slightly when he turned off the highway towards the outskirts of the airfield and drove past the assortment of rusting aircraft that sat crookedly on what remained of their tires at the far end of the runway. She looked at the American and said, "I never promised anything except that I'd ask him to keep his eyes open. You have our support, but he's not a government employee." She paused as the car slowed to join the lineup for the passenger drop-off, and just before getting out she added, "It was up to you to convince him."

After she left the car and entered the tiny terminal building, the American said, "Yeah, goodbye, and thanks a lot." He got out and joined Reby in the front seat. "Well, Reby, anything is better than going back to our old friends at the American embassy—if any of them are still there, that is, or even alive. I'm afraid I carry a bit too much baggage." *Why would they care about his luggage?* Reby wondered, but he understood when his boss added, "That old Kosovo business means it's better to keep everything low-key—at least for now."

The American had spent the rest of the drive back into Tirana on the phone, confirming arrangements for the breakfast meeting the next day in the hotel garden.

Across from the planted roses and intervening tables, Reby watched the American settle a bit more into his seat, now that his visitors had left. It was good that he was finally relaxing. The hotel had been built around this garden enclave that Reby rarely had an opportunity to see, but even he could feel the calming atmosphere that made it difficult to believe they were in the very centre of a rapidly expanding third-world metropolis. His boss had talked about Reby's nearly undeveloped homeland as a place "on the verge." He'd explained, "It should be on track to catch up with the rest of the development boom in Eastern Europe." Reby had heard much of it before: Albania was ideally situated on the Adriatic, only a few minutes from Italy and just north of Greece, and he knew the importance of both countries' European Union membership. Reby remained alert as he recalled these discussions, and stiffened when he felt something brush against his neck. Turning carefully, he saw it was only a solitary red rose hanging down from the gardener's carefully tended trellis.

From his position, he'd had a clear view of the breakfast

business meeting, and it had gone well with many hearty greetings and some hugs, and the American had even given some cheek kisses in the Albanian fashion. Other tables took an interest as various successful entrepreneurs arrived in the warm atmosphere, but as it was an Austrian hotel, it was discreet enough that the American's former undercover associates were unlikely to be informed of his presence in the city. Reby had carefully scrutinised the other hotel guests while his employer laid out his plans to those at the meeting. The American badly needed to widen his circle of contacts in the country after losing so many after the incident in Kosovo. Reby's fellow countrymen were all smiling as they left, so it looked as though they had accepted his boss's plans.

At the prearranged signal, Reby left to get the car, and the American joined him within minutes, getting into the backseat. They had a long drive ahead; Reby appreciated having the front to himself, and his passenger would have more room to stretch out in the back. When their eyes met in the rear-view mirror, his boss said, "That went well. Lots of serious enquiries about our plans." For the next hour Reby heard him on the phone. Many of the same expressions were repeated with each call: "There's no lack of opportunities here for someone with drive." "We need to make our move, now!" "It's time to get back in the game." "Actually, I think we learned from the Kosovo experience—besides, that's ancient history."

Finally, about two hours south of the capital, his passenger put his phone away and said, "Okay, now I'm looking forward to an interesting drive, so show me the changes you were talking about—how many years has it been since

I was down here?" There was silence for a few minutes as they drove on, and then the American spoke again, but it was almost to himself. "There was a lot of talk this morning about my old partner's success." Reby had to strain to hear the last words. "So let's just see how his new ventures are turning out."

⸻ ◉ ⸻

Petro Bega looked out over the town towards the harbour and the sea through the picture window on the top floor of his house. It would be a busy day making sure all was ready by this evening. He sat his large frame down on his favourite seat, an old relic from his great-grandfather that was rumoured to have been the chair that Lord Byron had used when he first arrived in Albania. First off, there was the meeting with his investors, to give them details on the planned project's construction delay. He was confident the development would still go ahead, despite the new regulations. It was really a matter of distributing benefits to the right people, provided those in charge stayed around to follow through. Once funds were made available, there was a noticeable tendency for others to become involved, further postponing approvals. That would have to change. His new partners had expected him to react with violence because of his old reputation, but times were changing; best to take small steps to solve issues, even if it meant delays.

It had all been so different when they started. Bega had been the family clan leader in Tropojë, near the Kosovo border. For the communists in Tirana, the town was a pawn in the ongoing politics of the Balkans—a way to infiltrate and influence Kosovo when it became a nearly autonomous region of Serbia. Albanian communism had begun to falter in 1990, and party control finally collapsed in 1992, so Bega had taken control of the local fuel market to keep their businesses operating; soon they had a monopoly on all truck transport. He found himself and his clan getting further involved when one of his drivers, the son of his cousin, was killed during the Kosovo Crisis. As a patriotic duty, and to avenge this killing, he expanded into importing and exporting by collecting all the weaponry looted during the bank failure riots and supplying the Kosovo Liberation Army with it, which guaranteed him safe passage even as the violence increased. But that was before he found out that the KLA had allowed fundamentalist terrorists from Saudi Arabia and Egypt to join them. The Russian and Chinese munitions were effective, if somewhat dated, having been hidden in caches around the country due to the Great Leader's paranoia of an inevitable invasion from the west. Hoxha had been proven right eventually, but the invasion was one of consumer goods, and that was an American ideology the leader hadn't anticipated. The old ways of thinking needed to be revised to fit in with the modern world.

The border situation became increasingly difficult in which to operate once NATO bombed Yugoslavia; hundreds of thousands fled from Kosovo across the border into Albania. It was a tumultuous time, and then Bega met the American. The new man reacted quickly, showing Bega how to better manipulate the warring factions, and they did well supplying fuel and cross-border transport. The subsequent arrival of NATO'S Kosovo Force (KFOR) began well enough—the multinational force had been short on contacts, and Bega had the knowledge of the local region's many border infiltrations. The American arranged for Bega's company to transport and resettle many of the refugees throughout the country, but increasingly he demanded more of "the action," as he liked to call it. The work kept them busy and nearly legitimate for a time, but the commencement of military operations severely restricted their movements. Both KFOR and the Yugoslav forces didn't want an independent third party getting in the way and he was learning that some of the mafia in Kosovo had connections with the jihadists who had joined the KLA.

That's when Bega decided it was time to leave. He would move his base, even if it meant giving up control of much of his well-established territory. When everything settled down, he might return, but for now, the future lay elsewhere, away from foreign military activities and jihadists. He needed a new area for development, far from the capital with all its bureaucracy and self-serving lackeys. He'd always enjoyed visiting the coast and its mild climate, but had decided to go to the south rather than west to the Montenegro border. There would still be issues in Montenegro, with its Serbian countrymen wanting access to the Adriatic. His wife's family was from the south, not very far from Vlora, but they'd been relocated after a long-standing blood feud killed many of her brothers and cousins.

Vlora already had a well-established transport industry and so was off limits, at least for now, but a visit to the beautiful little port at Saranda during an inland trip to his wife's old family home had convinced him to look into resettling on this section of coast. It was nearly undeveloped, had a nice harbour with transport access, an emergent infrastructure, potentially great future hotel needs, and Greece was just across the bay. He would make his main backup and supply base further inland, but most operations could be run on the coast.

After some initial discussions with the local headmen, he'd arranged for a meeting with the American.

———— ◄(●)► ————

"So let me get this straight, Petro," the American said. "You're willing to let me take a major interest in your Tropojë operation provided I help you out with this other investment, sort of pave the way." He was looking at the map. Bega knew the American had enough pull to help with logistics and had been told by his informants that at the last regional meeting, even the American's Greek contacts had wanted a development proposal to get some of the money that was pouring into the Balkans. Bega's partner was making a name for himself and could be very generous. "What you plan on doin'?" the American continued with a grin. "Opening a resort on the coast?"

Bega recalled a comment that the man had made after the American had taken his team down this same coast and then to Corfu for some R & R. The coastal drive had been an adventure through wild and nearly uninhabited countryside, or so it had seemed to the American. "You local guys need to find out more about your own country," he'd said. "The only town we could find doesn't even have a decent restaurant, and the only thing to drink is the god-awful plum brandy."

Now Bega waited while the American excused himself to make some calls. The big Albanian knew his proposal to the American would make his partner wonder if there was a hidden agenda. The American returned after a half day of contacting his sources and, likely, some careful thought.

"Okay, Petro. I've had to pull a lot of strings but I think we can make a deal." Always the careful man he added, "I might come back to you, if everything goes really well down south, but how likely is that? I've arranged a monopoly for you and your new company on customs and harbour rights from Saranda south to the Greek border. In return you cede control of your interests in the north, first along the Kosovo border and eventually the entire area. Agreed?"

4

THE AFTERMATH OF all the meetings, first at work and then at the consulate over an extended lunch break, kept me awake. As I lay in bed, thoughts of the consulate gathering bothered me the most, but I was also reviewing the decision to return inland on the family trip. Depending on conditions and timing, we could return on the "main" road, where newly built stretches of wide, modern dual highway led south to the Greek border. The bridges weren't finished, so the route required vehicles to drive down onto, and over, each riverbed. The combination of major improvement and temporary fixes was typical of the Albania we'd been encountering these first few months in the country. How much longer before the bridges were completed? This led my thoughts back to the discussion with Mr. Brown. Were the incomplete bridges an example of misdirected funds?

One advantage of returning inland was that we'd be able to stop in Gjirokaster. The old city was Enver Hoxha's hometown, and here the Stalinist dictator had imprisoned political enemies in the ancient Ottoman fortress in order to consolidate his position throughout the 1950s and 60s.

He had ruled Albania in North Korean style, closing the country's borders to outside influence and outlawing religion with some success. His major contribution to the nation was evident everywhere—during the 1970s, announcing that invasion from Western Europe and NATO was imminent, he had mobilised the masses into building over seven hundred thousand concrete pillboxes throughout the country, one for every ideal family of three in his utopia.

Very few proper roads currently existed in Albania, so it wasn't just the maps that were largely barren of alternate routes. When communism's decline began to accelerate after 1990, the few original routes quickly deteriorated into potholed tracks as more and more vehicles arrived in the country. Road maintenance had resumed only recently, along with new EU-funded projects to make the main routes more efficient and safe. This involved straightening dangerous curves, adding extra lanes and sometimes taking a totally different route over sections: between the capital and the coast; near the Greek border; and on the main route east from Elbasan to Macedonia. Prior to that, only limited maintenance was needed for the military and ruling secretariat that used the roads. Private ownership of cars had been prohibited in the Great Leader's visionary people's state.

Road conditions were why we had our Nissan SUV—we called it "the tank" for its size and colour. The big metal cowcatcher grill at the front garnered respect in a country that valued strength and power. The vehicle itself was reliable, and reliability was a necessity when I travelled with Ariyan (and his cigarettes) to our other ventures away from the capital. The SUV had been locked away and hidden during the worst of Albania's most recent troubles. What I hadn't realised was that the vehicle had been stored in a corrugated steel building for more than two years, which included two long and very hot summers that might have seriously affected the rubber tires, though they had proven fine for driving around the capital city and for quick excursions on the new highway to the coast. Luckily one of the drivers pointed this out to Ariyan before our trip south, and the tires were changed after grudging authorisation from my boss, the country general manager. I knew he had a reputation for keeping costs to a minimum, but my insistence that this was clearly a safety issue convinced him.

Besides visiting Butrint, we hoped to find out if there was a vehicle ferry service from Saranda's port to the island of Corfu, which could save us considerable time when we visited Corfu in the future. Otherwise we would have to drive another two hours from the Greek border to the main ferry point at Igoumenitsa, on the northernmost Greek coast.

Sleep just didn't come, and I moved on to thoughts of the family. Were there any issues with the Vienna boarding school that Michaela was keeping from us? If not, would our eldest son also board there in the new year? Certainly they would benefit from exposure to different cultures and ideas, but would this compensate for being away from us? There was a different way of life here, but it was still important for a family to stay together.

Our daughter's continuing growth and rapidly increasing maturity was evident during her trips home. She was in the French equivalent to the middle of high school but had the vocabulary and superficial social etiquette of someone much older. Her quasi-maturity had always been an issue when she'd tried to form friendships back home.

Her view on the matter of the young man she had met at the rugby match was pretty straightforward: "I'm finally able to share my thoughts and interests with someone who understands me." She had given me a quick look when she said the last part, and then turned to her mother to explain. "He isn't intimidated by what I have to say."

But I guessed she wasn't telling us the whole story.

We got started early Saturday morning, making good time on the fifty-kilometre autostrada that began just west of the city. The locals referred to it as an Italian highway in the belief that they shared history and culture with Italy—the country was also preferred when emigration opportunities arrived, legal or otherwise. The newly built route headed directly west towards the ancient port city of Durrës, where the Via Egnatia, a major Roman road, had its origins in antiquity. There were still parts of the road visible closer to the old city of Elbasan, which the Ottomans had made their capital. Unfortunately, to get to the original Roman port north of Durrës, one needed to cross an industrial wasteland of broken buildings and smouldering garbage. I'd visited Porto Romano myself one rainy day—the intervening blackened landscape and low grey clouds comprised a ready-made movie set for Armageddon. Or a zombie apocalypse film.

As an expatriate yet to feel a strong connection to anywhere I'd been, I found the history between Italy and Albania quite revealing. Commercial and family ties had existed across the Adriatic for centuries, with several Albanian communities established in Southern Italy. Roman communities had followed the Via Egnatia eastwards, starting in Durrës, where a coliseum had been rediscovered in the 1960s. The site was uncovered not far from the city centre, having been abandoned after the fall of Rome. It was being used as the community's dumping ground. Over the centuries the massive amphitheatre had been buried, so now it looked like one of the many coastal hills dotting the shoreline. The central low point, around which the seating levels rose, had made an ideal dump.

We continued south on a wide, newly built highway that had replaced the asphalt and stone track that originally cut across the marshy coastal plain. Lane markings were yet to be painted, so vehicles were driving without much regard to their proper position on the tarmac. Despite our speed, new German sedans flashed by dangerously close to us, so I sped up to keep pace and minimise being overtaken while paying careful attention to the animals grazing near the unfenced roadside. Distant orange splotches broke the November dullness and grew to become mounds of carrots for sale. Despite the numbers of sellers indicating a brisk trade, it would be difficult to characterise this as money laundering.

The wide highway returned to a much narrower track closer to the towns we passed through, since traffic bypasses had yet to be completed. The tracks weren't so much roads as wide swaths of bumpy trenches where potholes had grown so large that they coalesced into low-lying passages. Several vehicles would try to outmanoeuvre and overtake each other through these warrens of holes and ridges. Our tank was superbly designed for this type of driving, and we made good headway. It was thrilling for me as the driver but seemed less enjoyable for the family; the boys needed travel sickness pills after getting through the first few towns.

The ongoing extension of the new highway ended near the town of Fier, known for its Greek/Roman ruins at nearby Apollonia. Hoxha's regime had converted the ancient site to an artillery base, but this had been abandoned. Broken and rusted heavy-gun pieces sat mounted over the solid base of ancient stone foundations. The Roman town had been one of Octavius Caesar's early homes. In addition to the pervasive smell of petroleum fumes from a partially functioning refinery, the town was famous in the expatriate community for having the one acceptable women's toilet on the highway, at a very modern-looking gas station. I pulled into the parking lot and we all got out for a break. I took the opportunity to join my daughter as she waited for the toilet—my first chance to talk alone with her.

"So your new friend will still be in Vienna next weekend. I guess you'll be seeing him?"

"Father, it's not a big deal." I had hoped to tread carefully, but she was still getting defensive. "We've met before at the big coffee house near Stephensplatz. Nobody bothers us, and we can stay all day." Her eyes took on a dreamy look. "It's so good to talk to him."

"Does he know how old you are?" It seemed the right time to ask the question. The night before, she'd begun breathlessly filling us in on her adventures *in Wien*, but had stopped when she sensed our disapproval. It had been difficult, but my wife and I had held off on any more questions, even after we learned he was a graduating engineer getting work experience at a Canadian-sponsored nuclear site in Romania. We wanted to wait until the road trip, which we hoped would create a more open atmosphere.

She took her time answering. "Sort of."

"So he doesn't know how old you are."

"Dad! Why are you so against him? Mom is younger than you, right?"

"Michaela, your mother and I met when she was twenty-five."

She tried a different approach. "Well, he doesn't drink or even smoke."

That was unusual over here, but then I remembered he was Canadian—or so he said. Still, it was unusual that he didn't drink a little, especially if he was living in Romania. Maybe he was a non-drinker because he was antisocial—a weirdo who picked up young girls and . . .

"He has such a lonely life living away from his friends and family," she continued.

It sounded too much like the situation we had put her in. "It's only temporary, isn't it? He still has to get his degree, right?" I was getting concerned.

But she had taken on his isolated existence as her own, ignoring the question. "Dad, you wouldn't understand, but everyone is so much older than him at work. He doesn't have anyone to talk to."

I understood too well! She thought he was just like her. "I'll be in Vienna on Friday. How about if we all meet to have dinner? You pick the spot."

"Yeah, sure, Dad," she replied in a monotone. It was pretty clear she didn't mean it, but then the bathroom became available, and in she went. We'd have to talk more on this.

My thoughts shifted to Mr. Brown's request to keep my eyes open for developments or major construction that he could follow up on. I had no intention of taking this too seriously—but was I trying to convince myself? Unless things had changed since my last trip with Ariyan, nothing would be of interest until we were closer to the coastal port of Vlora, so I could put off the decision until then.

The children's schooling needed to be my main focus, along with my job. Since my employer's head office was in Vienna, I travelled to the city frequently and had been able to visit the French lycée and the Theresianum, an Austrian gymnasium equivalent to a high school, that accepted foreign boarding students. But my wife and I were concerned that our daughter might be too young at fifteen ("I'm nearly sixteen, Dad!"), having heard what effect boarding schools could have on young girls. Vienna was still a sheltered city though, a place where young children sometimes made their own way to school. We were confident our daughter would benefit and that we could see her as often as we thought necessary. Now I just had to sort things out regarding her new friend—perhaps encourage her to be more forthcoming about their age difference? Without sounding too negative.

5

THE BATHROOM WAS waaay better than others in the country, and there was toilet paper! But I still wiped the seat before sitting down. You can find bad toilets anywhere, but southern Europe had them everywhere, even in a place like Italy, which we visited before on a weekend ferry trip. I'd thought that with all the nice clothes and expensive shopping in the neighbourhood it would be better, but the WC—Giselle told me the letters used to mean water closet, so go figure how that gets to be bathroom—was a trip down "poo lane" without any toilet paper. Even getting close to a WC door in Albania was often enough—the smell or the sight of a stand-up "Turkish" toilet was a big encouragement for me to try holding it a little longer.

My father had said the bathroom in this gas station would be different, and it was. I even enjoyed some time relaxing on the seat, enjoying some privacy—it was something I had really started to like now, after spending lots of time alone in Vienna. I needed to think over the last day or two. For one thing, my father was asking waaay too much about Malik. He thought he knew everything. Just because Malik was older than me, so what? Wasn't it a good thing for people to have important things to say to each other? It was something that we discovered after I met him at the rugby game.

———◆———

Okay, so I said we were looking for seats in the stands, and stood there looking at him, but neither of us moved, so Giselle pointed to the bleachers nearby. "Let's go sit down."

He hesitated. "Perhaps I can join you ladies?"

That was much better than *girls*. He sat down beside me, with Giselle on my other side. "I'm Malik, and you are?"

Giselle leaned forward to look at him when I didn't respond. I was still a bit overwhelmed by his looks, and now he was sitting beside me!

"I'm Giselle, and this is . . ."

"Michaela, I'm Michaela," I finally said.

The rest of the afternoon was a bit of a blur. We knew we had to go back with Giselle's parents but didn't want the day to end. I learned a lot about rugby, but I talked to Malik so much that Giselle might have felt left out. And Malik became a different person once the game resumed—I guess he got excited by the action on the field.

"Forward pass!" he yelled as he stood up and gestured to the nearby referee, who glanced over to us. Knowing a bit about football, which I thought was probably similar to this game—both had nearly the same ball—my first reaction was *no kidding*, but then as others joined in the call, I realised it must be against the rules.

When Canada finally scored a goal he called out, "That's a try!" and looked to me, his face beaming. While recovering from that smile directed *at me*, I wondered why he'd said it. I had to bite my tongue to keep from saying, *They didn't just try, they scored!* Good thing, because when I turned to Giselle, she said, "I know, it sounds funny, but scoring is called a "try" in rugby."

"How do you know that?" I asked, but Giselle was looking away from the game, and then she sat up really straight.

"Here you are!" It was her parents. Her father looked over to the beer tent, attracted by all the noise. "Why are you sitting here?" he asked, maybe suspecting we were trying to sneak in—Giselle had hinted at a few incidents she'd had with her cousins. Then he looked back at our new friend.

Giselle was quick to notice. "Ah, Momma, Papa, this is Malik, a friend of the rugby squad. He's explaining the rules to us."

Malik stood at the mention of his name and shook hands with her parents, both of whom had looked like they were ready to leave when we first saw them. The game was nearly over, but now Giselle's father was smiling and talking with our new friend. I looked at her and whispered thanks.

Her mother looked at us and then at Malik. She leaned towards her daughter and asked, "Where did you say you met him?"

"We met him here, at the game," Giselle said innocently, though I wasn't sure why we were feeling a little bit guilty— my dad made me feel the same way. If anything, Malik had made us forget about the beer tent, or at least I had, but her mother continued to look around to see if we were hiding anything, or if anyone else was with us in the stands.

"Really?" Giselle's father exclaimed. "Why that's very interesting, what a coincidence!" He turned to Giselle and said, "This young man is getting his degree at my old school." He turned back to Malik, pointed to the tent, and said, "Let's find a seat and I'll buy you a drink. It's a perfect day to sit for a while, even if our team wasn't at their best."

Malik smiled and stood. "Yes, I also thought they could have beaten the Romanians. I'd love a drink, but not beer, thank you."

Giselle's father looked disappointed but continued towards the tent entrance. "That's fine. I'm sure they'll have something else." And we all went inside, past the bouncer, who glared as I looked as innocent as I possibly could. Giselle's mother asked her why she kept giggling, sure that we had been up to something.

Her father was in a great mood, and allowed Giselle and me to share a small beer, while he had a half litre of Gösser. My dad would never do that, treat us like adults. Both her mother and Malik settled on Almdudler, an Austrian soft drink like ginger ale with added herbs.

"So, Malik, do you play rugby?"

"No, sir, but I did when we were living in Iran. There was no opportunity at my new high school when we came to Canada, only American football and soccer."

"Malik, enough of the formalities. Please call me Serge."

I thought it was unusual that Giselle's dad thought it was okay that his daughter and her friend were sitting with an older man, just because he was going to the same school that he'd gone to—but he was different from my dad, which had to be good. He kept talking about himself, though. "I always wanted to play more, but I got injured in my first year of senior competition. Rugby is such an important sport for building character. I mean football is fine, but it has all that protection, and that's just not how life is. And soccer . . . well, we can leave that for the plebs."

At the mention of "life" I hoped the conversation would become more interesting—maybe they would talk about Malik's life, not his? I just didn't know what "plebs" meant. Perhaps Malik didn't know either because he didn't answer.

"But you lived in Iran, eh? That must have been interesting. I didn't know they played rugby there. How long have you been gone?" Now Giselle's father was just like mine— asking too many questions.

But Malik was happy to talk about his homeland, and I just knew that he was lonely. He'd been standing all by himself when we bumped into him, all alone in a strange city. Maybe he was only trying to find some link to his past.

"Rugby used to be a big sport when the British lived in my country, at least in some schools. It was still a tradition when I was accepted at the prep school my father had attended, one of the few nonreligious academies left. He thought the sport was an important tradition in the country since everything else had become political, so he pushed me to take it up." Giselle's father nodded in encouragement. "Then, about five years ago, the government started cracking down on any schools that didn't have Muslim teachings, and enforced even stricter rules for anyone out in public. Before that, there had always been a certain amount of religious freedom, especially for us, but with the change in government leadership, even my father was starting to feel pressure, and we all knew the family was being pushed to convert to Islam." Malik stopped for a minute, perhaps thinking this wasn't the right thing to be saying, but Giselle's father looked very interested. So was I—I wanted to find out more about him.

"Your father must have had an important position in the government?" he asked. "I thought everyone had to be a Muslim."

"My father was an engineer high up in the science and technology ministry, so he was protected by the minister, who had been a family friend for years." Malik looked beyond us as he talked. "I still remember the day my father came home to tell us everything had changed and that we had to leave, all because of our faith. My great-grandfather was one of the first followers of Bahá'í."

Giselle looked up at me just as I looked at her. *Wow*, I thought as we both turned back to our guest, who was still talking. We'd discuss this later when we were back in our rooms.

"The next day we packed our small valuables and took a train out of the capital. I never saw my school again." Malik stopped talking and looked a bit embarrassed. It was a story from a fairy tale—how romantic! "And you, sir, uh . . . Serge, you played rugby a lot?"

"Up until my injury, at least. It was a great time." He looked up at the sound of the staff cleaning the tables in the tent. Our drinks were finished, and we all stood. "Can we give you a lift, Malik?"

"No, sir, but it was very nice meeting you. I'm here all this week on a course and my hotel is only a few streets away, but

THAT WEEKEND IN ALBANIA

thank you."

He shook hands with all of us, and I gave him a slip of paper with my cell number on it when we got to the parking lot. And waved to him as he looked back while we were getting into the car. I could hardly wait to get back so Giselle and I could talk about Malik. It was amazing! Our favourite religion and he was part of it.

———«(O)»———

I hadn't realised how much I'd needed to use the bathroom until I got back to our SUV. It was wonderful to finally be able to sit still. Must have been the orange Fanta I'd finished on the way here and all the water I drank last night lying awake, thinking about everything that was happening. I'd had coffee this morning, too—it helped to get me going in the morning these days. I did live in Vienna, the coffee capital. They claimed to have been the first European country to discover it after they took it from the Turks, while saving Europe from the Ottomans. It was a regular habit for me and Giselle, before I left for the tram to school.

In no time at all, we had entered the city of Vlora and then left it by driving up to the mountain pass on a really crappy road—but everyone was quiet for a while because of the amazing views. The coast road that led out of the city and up to the start of the pass wasn't bad, but it was like leaving by the back way because we passed quite a few half-finished houses and bigger buildings—the first one looked like it was old and falling down, but after seeing others with stacked bricks and some rusting machinery, I figured they had just stopped working for some reason—it was hard to tell if it had been for months or even years. My dad pointed out an old oil derrick not far from the seashore, just before the road narrowed and we started to climb up above the bay. It must have been tricky driving because we slowed down over long stretches and bounced around a lot. He was probably driving too fast.

That's when I started talking about what things were like in Vienna. I didn't tell my parents everything, of course, but enough so my mom wouldn't be worried. When I said I didn't always make it to church on Sunday, I could tell they weren't too happy, but what did they expect? I only got to sleep in once in a while. And besides, I was learning that the Catholic religion's history in Europe was even worse than I'd thought—Giselle liked to talk about some of the problems she'd heard about, since Austria was a Catholic country. It was kinda interesting talking about other faiths and knowing there were choices to make for anyone who really thought about what was important to believe in.

Religion wasn't really taught at the lycée, but one teacher held religion classes at lunchtime for those interested, and being curious about everything in Vienna when I first got there, I went to it my first week to see if it was any different from what I already knew. Austrians weren't quite like the Catholic people I'd known, but I think Austrian parents expected there would be some religious classes at a French school. That way, they didn't have to worry much about teaching their kids themselves. But somebody needed to because Austria had very sexy billboards showing nearly everything and all the magazines had at least one or two topless ads and pictures.

Back home, we'd gone to church most Sundays as a family, and I'd had my First Communion, but religion wasn't too big a part of family life. My parents drove me and my older brother to Saturday morning classes, and I still remember the day I came home to announce to my parents that I was going to be the first female pope ever—of course that was all over now that I was older and knew I'd been brainwashed. I think my parents had hoped I would go to church on Sunday in Vienna so that I'd stay busy, but lately I'd learned about other religions that sounded waaay more interesting. Giselle had told me about Bahá'í, an eastern religion that seemed really cool. The beliefs were that all human beings were equal, there should be no prejudice, and we should all try for universal peace and harmony, just like everyone wanted to believe in the sixties! It was just such a perfect idea, and we were both tired of going to a church where the sermon was in German—and now I'd found out Malik was a Bahá'í!

Besides, other religions didn't seem to work very well from what I'd seen at the lycée. The Austrians and the French students there and at the Theresianum were mostly Catholic, but it didn't mean much, when really, it should—they couldn't even agree on how their histories with one another had happened, especially when it came to wars. In the lycée textbook, the cause of World War II was written in French: it was mainly German aggression, and since Austria was a German ally, it practised the same aggression. One of the Austrian students, a big blond boy, stood up in our history class and said the French history book was wrong—Germany had forced Austria to join by invading the country just before World War II began. He also defended the Germans for going to war with France, saying they had no choice because the French had made them pay too much after they lost World War I in 1918—the German people had been starving for nearly twenty years, so they couldn't keep paying with money they didn't have and ended up fighting the French instead.

It was really interesting to me, except some of the French and Austrian guys got really angry and nearly started fighting. When I told Giselle about the arguing sides after supper that evening, she told me that her father had told her a lot about Austria before arranging for her schooling at the Theresianum.

"He told me the Austrians joined the German Nazis because the Nazis blamed the Jewish people for everything. The Catholic Church in Vienna had been telling them for ages that the Jews killed Jesus, so no Austrians liked Jewish people."

I didn't quite understand what she was saying, so she added, "The bishops in Vienna were supposed to be the experts on Christian history, and they told the Austrians that the Jews were Christ killers."

"Wasn't Jesus a Jew?"

"Yes, but so what?"

"Well, the way you said it, it doesn't sound like he was a Jew, or maybe the Austrian bishop was saying being a Jew was only okay for Jesus, but not for anyone else." Then I wondered if it was still true—could that be why no one ever seemed to be nice to me when I was on the tram? Maybe my really dark hair had people thinking I was Jewish?

Giselle thought that over for a minute and then said, "And Hitler was Austrian." Just then, our boarding supervisor walked by our room. She was really nice compared to the others and not as strict, but Giselle looked concerned and waited a minute before continuing in a low voice. "My dad said the Austrians made out that Hitler was German, but he wasn't." When she saw the look on my face, she added, "And they wanted Beethoven to be Austrian, but he was German."

"I thought Hitler was German," I said. "Otherwise how could he have been the leader of Germany?"

"My dad says that nobody wants to talk about any of that here. Maybe they don't want to know their own history, if it was that bad?"

I guess that's why her father had told her what really happened, if the teachers were teaching history to be what they wanted it to be, not what it really was.

We both agreed it was a mystery, but then I remembered the movie *The Sound of Music*. "The Austrians must know the story of the von Trapp family, where the singing nanny saves Baron von Trapp from the Nazis? She was Austrian and so was the baron and they hated the Nazis. Maybe we can watch that in our class so the French students can see what really happened." Giselle thought it was a good idea but added that it took place in Salzburg, which was far from Vienna in the western part of the country. "Maybe it's different there."

That night in Vienna, I started to wonder if the movie was partly fiction or if the lycée textbook was just giving a French version of history. The next day I went ahead and told the teacher about the movie after class. She just looked

at me, smiled in a funny way, and said she was busy getting
ready to meet some parents. I'd seen them outside the class-
room waiting. They all looked angry, but that was the way
most people were in Vienna, hardly ever smiling. I heard her
greet the parents in German as I was leaving. We still haven't
seen the movie—not that it's that difficult to find a copy
with French subtitles. The whole subject of the war was a
learning experience for me. Both sides think they are right,
so how could a movie prove anything?—it's just a story about
Austrians that made their side look like they were right.

Of course before I understood this, I spent too many
nights thinking too much about it, often staying awake for
hours, even when I was really tired. And the move to Albania
and then to Vienna after a few months had made my head
spin. It was hard to believe that only seven months before,
I'd been in a regular school. Well, kinda regular—late French
immersion. That hadn't been easy, only being taught in
French, but at least it had got me a bit ready for the lycée—
the big difference was when school was over, the language
was German, not English, in the city where I lived.

The country of Albania was unlike anything I'd ever seen,
so in some ways it was better to be in Vienna. My brothers
acted like they were just on a holiday trip. It was supposed
to be an Islamic country, but my dad said there wasn't really much religion because the communists had made all
religion a crime. And Islam wasn't really practised by anyone, except older people who remembered the old ways.
The only mosque that I saw in Tirana was in the central
square, but it looked like a tourist attraction, without any
tourists. There was a new Catholic cathedral, and Orthodox

churches were getting fixed up, mostly in the south where the Greek Orthodox religion was pretty strong. I knew that Orthodox meant "old" and that it was an older version of being Catholic—I'd seen Albanian Orthodox believers when we'd visited a restored church one weekend outside Tirana. They crossed themselves twice, and with the left hand, not the right hand like Catholics, when walking past the graveyard nearby.

I didn't know that much about Islam except the mosque was their church. In Vienna there was a French girl in my class who was a Muslim, and we started to sit with each other. Maybe it was because we were both outsiders, but she was happy to sit with me rather than by herself, and I felt the same.

Our SUV lurched and I looked over as my dad abruptly twisted the steering wheel to avoid another big hole. "Sorry, guys, that one nearly got us!" he said, and I saw we were getting closer to the top of the mountain pass. We entered into misty woods where the clouds were so low it was hard to see. The dark forest was suddenly just there—that and the murky road made me feel we were on a quest, like something out of *Lord of the Rings*. It was easy to imagine the Nazgûl flying overhead.

While I was thinking about Vienna, the school, religion, and how "Nazgûl" sounded like "Nazi," we came out of the misty forest to bright sunshine on the top of a mountain. My dad stopped the truck and I took my little sister's hand because the wind was blowing so hard, but it was really beautiful with the bright light and waves far below us. We didn't stand there for too long though—the wind was really cold!

6

BACK IN THE Nissan tank, we crossed Fier's two un-marked intersections. I continued straight through them and drove onto an old, elevated roadbed, hoping we were taking the route to Vlora, although there weren't many alternatives. We were traversing a low-lying flood-prone region with badly deteriorated roadways and bridge approaches. There were no shoulders on the broken, potholed track, the result of heavy trucks, but it had several wider sections where bigger vehicles could pull over or be overtaken.

We skirted across the countryside towards a far-off dark patch—tall forest against a backdrop of hills. As we got closer, the tall trees gradually transformed into the abandoned drilling rigs of the giant Patos Marinza oil field that Ariyan had previously pointed out to me. Tarry petroleum seeps had been an oil source since antiquity in the area, but as the nature of oil accumulations became more widely understood, drilling to develop the possibly hidden underground resource started in the early 1930s—the result was the discovery of the largest onshore field in Europe. It produced hard currency for decades until communism and the investment needed to continue production floundered in the 1980s. The easiest recoverable oil was depleted, so production declined, as did the country's antiquated industrial sector, and it eventually collapsed at the end of the decade.

The last major centre before the coastal mountains was Vlora, beyond which I had yet to travel. The drab concrete of communist buildings marked the city's centre, but new private dwellings, financed by the city's marine transport industry, overlooked Vlora Bay. It was the country's second port, where the flat coastal plain ended and impressive coastal highlands began, but the harbour and heavy cranes around the docks looked rusted, broken, and inactive as we passed by. The undeveloped Albanian "Riviera" began where the hills jutted against the sea, south of the town, and marked the boundary between the Adriatic Sea to the north and the Ionian Sea towards Greece.

Ariyan had told me that Vlora's proximity to Italy, the closest gateway to mainland Europe and the EU (Greece was too isolated from the Promised Land to count), made the city part of a major transiting route for human smuggling. The fall of communism, which had opened the borders, presented opportunities for entrepreneurs to start businesses, and people to own private cars, but there was also the downside—many families were left without security as old grievances resurfaced and locals started taking the law into their own hands. The mafia often coerced Albanian children and women into false promises of a better life, and men wanting to escape the cycle of blood feuds were ready to pay large sums for the hazard of being transported by this lucrative operation. Mr. Brown would be interested to know, if he didn't already, what Ariyan had shared with me and had been largely confirmed by the expats we met—that hugely overpowered rubber Zodiac craft, really not suitable for travel on the open sea, were being used to carry illegal migrants to the Italian peninsula. To avoid detection, these boats remained hidden during the day and waited for nightfall and poor weather to traffic Albanians, and others risking the refugee route from Turkey and western Asia, to Europe. Many migrants didn't survive the cold and exposure in these overloaded craft. Several police checks to detect this smuggling had been set up on the last stage of my and Ariyan's entry into the city, but Ariyan had given me a knowing smile when we were waved through on my last visit. And today was no different; whatever visual criteria were being used to stop vehicles, they didn't apply to us, and we quickly bypassed the lines of windowless transport vans being checked.

I was watching for an abandoned oil rig near the outskirts of town, near where Ariyan and I had turned onto a dirt track that had taken us up into the hills above Vlora. A horn blared, warning me to keep to the right, and a late-model Mercedes flashed by us. I glimpsed the driver concentrating on his car's high-speed progress on the poorly maintained section of road over which we were driving much slower. Mercedes were very common in the country, though most were much older models, popular because of their durability. This one reminded me of the red vehicle I'd seen and admired at the American compound the previous week. It had been in very good shape, despite being well used, and then there was the unique style—the unusual flat-red colour and black wheel rims gave it panache, and the AMG high-performance tag didn't hurt. It was a tough-looking car with class. I saw the blacked-out rear windows as the car disappeared in the dust, and wondered who would risk being driven in a vehicle at such speed.

We followed its disappearing dust trail out of the city and soon left Vlora's reputation behind, following the bay south via the coast road. A mix of new hotels and older villas, which included Hoxha's own private retreat (according to Ariyan), was nestled along steeper sections of the seaside cliffs. Hoxha's private residence in Tirana was a large modern compound in the centre of the business district, more Frank Lloyd Wright than Joseph Vissarionovich Stalin, but the flat-roofed and tiered elevations lacked windows and hadn't been maintained. Military police guarded the entry in Tirana, but I saw no military guards at any of these villas to indicate a special status, just impressive views across the water.

The road turned, from the south end of the bay towards the steep pass separating two mountainous thrusts, and we started to climb the western mountain's flank. The road surface grew dangerously uneven in places because of the poor foundation—at one point where the grade changed, a large section had shifted and slid down the hillside, so a makeshift track had been constructed, packed with stones to offer some support for the occasional heavy trucks we met. The vegetation became less Mediterranean on the ascent and more boreal, as did the weather. We stopped on the edge of a thick pine forest to look back at Vlora Bay. It was actually getting cold, although it was still early afternoon.

Our daughter became talkative on the ascent and gave us

a rundown on the goings-on at the lycée and her daily routine. Her boarding residence was in the old Hapsburg summer palace, the Theresianum, named after Maria Theresa. The former empress of Austria converted the building into an educational academy, initially run by the Jesuits in the 1750s. Michaela took the tram from the Theresianum to the lycée. Because she'd had only a year of immersion in French language instruction before leaving Canada, Michaela was finding the curriculum in the French language difficult. I thought the challenge would keep her busy in her studies—she had always been an excellent student—and out of any possible mischief. At the old summer palace she had companionship and had met some English speakers, including a Québécoise girl. The buildings were full of history and artwork, including magnificent staircases, ornate ceilings, and wooden carvings on many of the doors and entryways. It was becoming clear to us that our daughter's independence was developing, possibly too much, but I hoped to see what was going on when I met her friend in Vienna.

Michaela ran out of steam by the time we emerged from the forest in the clouds, and the last few hundred metres of potholed road. The road changed abruptly, and with it the background noise that we had become used to—the SUV sailed smoothly along a newly paved highway complete with alpine drainage ditches for the steep descent down to the coast. The painted lane lines sparkled on the black asphalt, courtesy of NATO or the EU—Albania was attracting both American dollars and euros, seemingly in competition.

We stopped at the crest to take in the spectacular view, but the wind nearly ripped the door off when I opened it.

It blasted up the pass, taking away our breath and drowning out conversation. The panoramic sight was quite impressive—north was Vlora Bay and the sun, reflecting over the Adriatic. On the horizon I could just make out the next bay, where Ariyan had hinted there had been a lot of mercury pollution from industrial sources. In the opposite direction, to the south, Corfu was just visible in the Ionian Sea. The wind was cold, even in the sunshine, so we got back into the vehicle and started the precipitous drop to the coast and warmer weather with layers of sinuous new road visible below us over the edge of the steep slope. As we worked our way down, back and forth along the switchbacks, admiring the spectacular views at every turn, I remembered the chevron markings on the map.

There was a lone red vehicle far below us—the Mercedes must have stopped after overtaking us, either for the view or a break—and then miles of beautiful and apparently empty beaches with no people. At the base, after a final turn, we crossed a bridge into olive groves, and the new highway ended.

Over the next hour we coped with the road/track while trying to see as much of the countryside as possible. Conversation about life in Vienna resumed, and our eldest son joined in occasionally. The two youngest were more engrossed in the views and I wondered if they noticed there had been no garbage since we'd left Vlora—less money meant less waste.

"How about if I meet you next Friday after school at the lycée? The two of us can meet your friend later, maybe see a movie."

Silence. Then, finally, "I'll have to see whether I get home at the normal time," Michaela said, "and I'll need to check with Malik."

What? Her busy schedule had her booked up? Was I dealing with my daughter or someone playing hard to get? But I held my tongue. The last time we met in Vienna, we'd seen a film together, her choice, and she'd been quite pleasant. I hoped she'd focus on arranging a good movie again rather than worrying too much about her friend.

We continued, passing the occasional rusting military wreck. These were partially hidden by roadside vegetation, so it was difficult to know if they were the older Russian or newer Chinese trucks. Military assistance and country of origin had depended on the Albanian regime's changing alliances; the Russians had passed on the squat brick "design" of their vehicles to all their communist allies, including China, which had once been their major partner. Barbed-wire fencing appeared on the roadside after a sharp bend, suggesting a military installation, and a tunnel opening was visible at water level—likely one of the hidden submarine pens of which I had heard rumours, something that James Bond might blow up if he could reach this isolated area. In fact, Commander Bond participated in a raid on the Albanian coast in one of Ian Fleming's short stories. A No Pictures symbol hung on the broken fencing around the perimeter, but no one was around to enforce the rules in the apparently abandoned area. Plenty of concrete pillboxes dotted the hillside facing out to sea, along with rusting vestiges of the Cold War.

Not far from the military area, we crested another hill. A grey stone fortress sat on an island hill near the centre of the clear blue bay. My wife noticed it first and saw the adjoining causeway. I slowed, and was rewarded with squeals of delight from the two youngest as I turned onto a dirt track leading to the causeway. We passed a windowless brick storehouse that looked unoccupied, but multiple vehicle tracks were visible, some fresh. Cattle and goats grazed nearby around the few trees and short clumps of grass. We drove on, and I parked where the causeway ended, in a clearing surrounded by olive trees and bushes that obscured the citadel. The boys rushed out and ran ahead along a path that headed up the hill deeper into the trees. We followed a trail until we emerged near the hilltop to the sight of the thickly walled stone fortress.

The boys were waiting at the open entrance. It certainly did look to be Venetian in design, now that I had a good view of the towers and battlements. The triangular shape outlined by the three towers was characteristic of the Italian city state's defensive structures. But most important, at least for Ariyan, was that I had been to see it; therefore, I had to be right in knowing its origins. I wondered if his logic would allow him to be right if he returned for another look.

The fortress was amazingly preserved and had been rigorously built to withstand any onslaught, though Ariyan had told me that none had taken place. The stronghold was still in use during Ali Pasha's reign in the early nineteenth century, when the Albanian despot's rule had extended over most of northern Greece. Anywhere else in Europe, there would have been an entry fee and cordoned-off areas, but here we were able to climb up, free of charge, to the stone roof—each of the three corner towers had stairs. We wandered through the dark rooms, avoiding the dried livestock droppings. The interior well, built in case of a siege, was now likely a water source for cattle. Animals appeared to be the only visitors.

We returned to our SUV nearly an hour later and drove back down the track and across the causeway. The two boys and our youngest were still chatting about the castle when I noticed a large vehicle parked outside the brick storehouse. The building's only door was open. As we came closer, a big man stepped down from the truck, while another stepped out of the doorway and stood in the track. One of them held up a hand, signalling us to stop. They both looked intimidating; the bigger one had a thick neck and was bald. They wore dark track suits, the everyday wear for Albanians who had come of age after the fall of communism.

I could have driven around them—we had a good vehicle for driving over or across nearly anything. Instead, I stopped and rolled down the window. The bigger man came around to the door. I extended my hand, and he shook it while looking into the SUV. The tension seemed to ease a bit.

"Ciao," I said, while reaching over for a pack of cigarettes in the glove compartment. I offered him one.

He took it.

It was good quality, not counterfeit or the local brand. After lighting mine and his, he exhaled, pointed at the road, and said, "*Privat.*"

"English?" I asked.

He looked over to the other man, who came around to my window. He'd been trying to see into the back of the vehicle through the darkly tinted glass.

"This is private area."

"Oh, I didn't know that."

"Why you are here?"

"Driving to Saranda."

"Other road is better." He turned to his partner, and they spoke quickly to one another.

I got my cell phone out to call Ariyan. He'd helped us the week my family arrived, when we were told the hotel in Durrës, at which we had a reservation, was closed. This was different though. The two youngest, in the rear seat, were giggling, but Michaela and my eldest son, in the middle seats, were quiet. I could sense that my wife was getting nervous, and looked over to her.

"Why are they stopping us?" she asked. "Can't we just leave?" She was watching the two men with distaste.

"Just a sec." I accessed Ariyan's number, punched the call button, and waited. Nothing happened and I realised there was no cell coverage—the mountains were blocking the signal in this sheltered bay.

My youngest daughter slid her rear window down. The two men looked up at the sound.

"Hello." She grinned at them. Her brother stuck his head out and made a noise. They liked how the Albanians fussed over them at hotels and the airport.

The English speaker looked back at me. "Okay, mister. Better you stay on road."

"*Faleminderit*," I said, thanking them, and both men stepped back.

We started off as my daughter waved goodbye to them out the window, then turned around to us and said, "Daddy smokes!"

In my side mirror I could see one of the men had raised

his hand in return, but the other's stance meant business. I threw the unsmoked cigarette out of the window and turned back onto the coast road.

We drove quickly over the next hill. I kept my eyes on the rear-view mirror as the dust trail settled. We could certainly outrun them if they changed their mind, but where would we go? We approached another rise and turned around a sharp bend that took us up a short, steep climb. My phone vibrated with a text message as we crested the hill, but I was concentrating on getting us as quickly as I could to Saranda.

✦

Reby eased off on the accelerator as he approached the pass after emerging from the forest. Bright sunlight pierced the windshield, and then the car's wheels abruptly quieted on crossing over to the new pavement. He geared down in anticipation of the steep decline ahead, and felt the buffeting wind as the car became more exposed near the crest.

He saw his passenger shift in the rear seat with the abatement of road noise and reduction of the powerful engine's modified exhaust. Reby had spent a lot of time and money but had finally managed to secure California-type exhaust headers to fit the Mercedes' own AMG specifications. And he had done much of the mechanical work himself. He was proud of his abilities and knew he was a good man to have around. His passenger looked up and their eyes met in the rear-view mirror. They could go far together if all the American's plans worked out.

Reby slowed and pulled over after the first section of switchback—stopping here, they would avoid the full force of the winds they would have encountered at the top of the pass. He needed a cigarette break and his passenger needed to stretch his legs. They stood at each end of the car, looking out over the vista. This was Bega's territory, but they were here to try staking a claim on some of it. The American would eventually make a move for all of it once he'd recruited the right staff to build his organisation. Reby could do very well for himself.

Reby lit his cigarette with the high-quality metal lighter he'd been given years before, when he'd finished the intensive months of specialised American training. He took a last draw, exhaled, and flicked his cigarette over the edge of the slope before walking over to his boss. He knew the American disliked tobacco smoke.

"Only maybe two hours, then Saranda."

"How is the rest of the road? Does it stay like this?" the American asked. "Or . . ."

The question made Reby a bit uneasy. How could the American think this improved portion would continue all the way to Saranda? The mountain segment had badly needed repair, but the good road would end when they got down lower, closer to sea level, and then they'd be back to avoiding pavement breaks and potholes. The old alpine track had been impassable in anything but a big truck, and even then had been extremely dangerous. This rebuilt section must have cost several million euros, even more with the extra payments needed to complete it without the normal local problems: work slowdowns for better wages, local mafia wanting extra payments, and even farmers claiming compensation. It was true that they were several hours ahead of where they would have been had they made the trip five years previously, but the American needed to remember that this was the heart of the Balkans.

The American was grinning, but was he trying to make it a joke and cover for his gaffe? Reby thought that something wasn't quite right, but it might have been that the upcoming meeting with Bega was on his passenger's mind.

"We go straight to hotel?" Reby asked.

"Yes, let's drive straight there as though we belonged. I want to be in the centre of his operation, and I hear he'll be showing off tonight." They'd talked about the gathering earlier. The American had first heard about the meeting when he was making his rounds in Vienna. He'd rebooked his flight to Tirana and called Reby to pick him up at the airport a day sooner, allowing them to get to Saranda in time.

Less than an hour from the mountain pass, Reby and the American flew by the fortress. The two guards looked up from their backgammon game but saw only a dust trail after running out to see who was passing by. Bored and curious, they jumped into their truck and sped off to see whether the vehicle was transporting anything significant. After a few kilometres the hanging dust trail began to disperse. They would never catch up. They were turning around when a Nissan SUV turned in towards the citadel.

7

MR. BEGA HAD shifted his business interests south by the spring of 2000, following several reconnaissance trips. Later in the year, the newly established Stability Pact for South Eastern Europe had earmarked nearly 400 million dollars to help restore peace and stabilise the region. The main focus was Albania's northern border areas, where the money would be spent rehabilitating roads, railroads, harbours, and power and water lines in the coming years. Bega had thought that Greece, a supporting European Union member country, might also be able to lobby for a larger portion of the fund to be reserved for infrastructure near Albania's southern border. He'd met with his Greek contacts there to discuss how best to implement this possible opportunity in the summer of the same year. He found out the Greeks had already insisted that the official map name for Macedonia be changed to FYROM (Former Yugoslav Republic of Macedonia), and Macedonia had agreed, provided Greece supported their application for EU and NATO membership. Greece had yet to support either application, but Bega told his contacts that infrastructure funding was more significant than insisting on a name change. Whatever transpired, by late 2000, he'd found out that the area would be receiving substantial investment. The road from the Greek border needed major repairs as did the nearest port at Saranda. Most of this infrastructure work was now underway, and Bega was planning other developments along the coast, provided improved access via the coast road was also forthcoming.

After this morning's business, he'd returned to his villa. He found the view had a restorative effect, and today he would need it. A knock on the door brought his thoughts back to the present.

"*Po?*"

A messenger stepped into the room. "Nothing serious, *padron*, but you wanted to know when anyone stopped at the bay. The men told me there were visitors to the castle."

"How did they get past the guards?" Mr. Bega hadn't been able to find enough reliable southerners—perhaps too much Greek blood. They got bored easily and would wander off to look for something to do. He needed to keep them busy.

"I think the guards have to leave the bay to get cell coverage to report."

"Both of them? Are they joined together?"

The questions were met with a shoulder shrug. "They asked the visitors a few questions, but the Englishman just seemed a tourist with his family."

"An English tourist on that road?"

"Well, he *spoke* English, *padron*. Remember the road down from the pass has been repaired. They have mentioned increasing traffic."

"Yes, of course. Still, it's hardly an easy drive in the

country." One of Bega's first forays into his new southern-area business had involved subcontracting a few of his trucks for the alpine upgrades to Llogara Pass, and the enterprise had done well with hauling gravel, cement, and sand, even though they'd had to deal with those bastards in Vlora, Italian or not. There had been lots of papers to file and bureaucratic meetings with various foreign agencies demanding safety standards and legitimised receipts for various ministries. He'd missed not having the American around, as he'd been an expert at the required paperwork. It turned into an opportunity—his former partner's absence had forced Bega to learn EU business methods, as well as how best to circumvent the new rules. "Are we ready for tonight?"

"Of course, *padron*." The messenger closed the door as he left.

Looking out over the sea again, Mr. Bega reviewed the plan for the evening before retrieving his cell phone. "I'll be down in five minutes. Take me to my restaurant."

⸻ ◉ ⸻

Malik called me two days after we first met, but I took Giselle with me to wait outside the coffee house where we'd agreed to meet. We arrived a bit early. If he didn't show up I was going to go window shopping with her. She wished me luck and left me at the entrance when we saw him coming down the sidewalk. When we went inside, he ordered for me, and we talked about lots of things—it was better than I could have imagined, sitting in a Viennese café while the waiter rushed around us and old men read newspapers attached to long wooden handles. He listened to what I told him about school and Vienna, and he told me about his work in Romania. He was in Vienna for a course on safety at work, and was hoping to come back again the following month.

"The work is fine, very interesting and great experience for my degree requirements, but the other men are much older. They just call me 'the Student.' It is difficult to talk with them, except for work instruction." Then he looked right at me and I felt myself blushing. He reached out for my hand and said, "I have really enjoyed this visit to Vienna, meeting you at the rugby match."

"That's great," I said, trying to sound normal. My hand was feeling a little awkward, but I tried to let it rest steadily against his. "Maybe we can meet again the next time you're here." I was hoping he'd want to see me again before he left, but Giselle had said that he should ask me, not the other way around—she'd had lots of boyfriends, or so she said—I had started to think all the ones she talked about were really the same guy, maybe one or two others, at most. My hand started to get sweaty, so I slowly moved it to my lap.

"Michaela, that would be very nice, but I would like to meet your family sometime, also."

"Of course," I said, but I knew that would cause some problems—even my mother would get concerned if she saw that he was in his early twenties. He hadn't asked me how old I was, but I'd hinted that I was preparing for university by taking a few French courses at the lycée. "You know, Malik, I really enjoyed finding out about your life in your home in Iran, and especially about your faith."

Something in his manner changed, and he said, "I think I said too much about my history on Sunday at the match. It is not so good to expose oneself like that to people one has only just met—and it has troubled me."

"But Malik, your faith is so wonderful. Giselle and I have admired it."

"What?" He interrupted me quite brashly. "You are talking about my faith with your friend?"

Oops! I really didn't like the way he was looking at me, and I noticed some old men staring at us. He had changed so quickly.

"Malik, please!" I surprised myself with my tone of voice—it sounded very mature and he looked . . . well, I wasn't sure what his look meant, so I said, "No, we had discussed the Bahá'í faith before we met you, and had both admired the teachings and its philosophy." He was totally listening to me! "It was a complete coincidence that we met someone of Bahá'í beliefs. I thought you might want to share the teachings with me, but if not, that's okay." I knew it would be the first thing Giselle would ask about.

Malik sat back and looked around the room with the high ceilings and ceramic-topped metal tables. "Did you know that Freud and Trotsky both came here to get away from their problems and distractions, and sometimes to talk with friends?" He looked straight at me and said, "It is the same with us, I think."

The tank hit a big bump, and I was back and we were no longer heading down the curvy mountain road but were much closer to the sea, going up and down small hills. The shoreline appeared and then hid as we went around one bend after another.

"Dad asked you something," my brother said, turning to look at me. He was the older of my two brothers, but still nearly three years younger than me.

"I asked you where you eat lunch at the lycée. Do they make something for you or do you have to take it?"

I wondered why he wanted to know all this but told him about lunch and other things and saw my brother was interested, too. My mom started asking a few questions as well, and I liked that that they were all listening to me and some of my adventures, though just my usual ones—I wasn't going to mention Malik again. But then my dad asked about meeting Friday after school. I'd enjoyed seeing the last movie with him, and he was a lot more like a friend when we went out for supper, but this time he also wanted to meet Malik. I said yes, but didn't say for which part. I wasn't sure what might happen if they met and talked. It might be waaay too much information for my dad to find out and I needed to have some secrets.

My younger brother and sister squealed from the back seat at the same time, and I looked up to see what they were getting excited about just as we turned onto a track and a castle appeared up the hill. Did I want to go for a walk? Maybe it would feel good to get out and stretch, but I decided to take my book along with me, in case my brothers started playing war and running all over the place—then we'd be here for a while.

As it turned out, the castle was really neat, except for all the animal turds around the well. I tried to avoid the dark corners where the smelly dampness had me imagining long-dead soldiers—anything that died here might not be buried—but up on the roof you could look in all directions at the beautiful harbour and the deep blue sea. My mom and I sat against the stone walls on the roof top, nice and warm in the sun, while the children ran around playing sword fights. By the time we were ready to leave I'd nearly fallen asleep leaning against her.

I got a bad feeling when the mafia guys blocked us on our way back to the road and started asking my dad questions. I'd never seen my dad have to handle a tricky situation where he was being questioned. Offering them cigarettes worked really well—he almost got one of them to be friendly. But what were they guarding? Nobody was around except some goats. Were they like new shepherds, thinking we might steal their smelly animals?

8

THE COAST ROAD continued through steep hills, olive groves, and mountains, from which we glimpsed the water and wild, stony beaches. I slowed down after hitting a bad stretch of washboard and cobbles that would have made for hazardous driving in a car. Eventually I relaxed a bit, enjoying the warm breeze from the sea, and started looking forward to a nice meal in Saranda. We were all getting hungry, and I thought the kids might enjoy a beach, but first we had to get there. The next bend revealed an old settlement that looked abandoned, and the road was partially blocked by mounds of building materials that had slumped across the track.

Albania's evolving state of disrepair was the culmination of its history. The people had survived the Ottomans, two world wars and, most recently, communism. The borders and boundaries with Greece had shifted back and forth, even before both countries had achieved independence from the Turks. During Ali Pasha's rule, northern Greece was part of the Albanian Ottoman enclave. Alliances changed after Albania was recognised as a nation, when the Ottoman Empire began to break up just prior to the start of World

War I in 1914, and its status was confirmed in the armistice agreements that followed four years later. Southern Albania came under Greek rule at the start of World War II, in 1939, followed by Italian and German occupation. By the end of that war six years later, Albania had gained confidence in its independence, but went too far when it deployed explosive mines in the Corfu channel off its southern coast. Two British warships were heavily damaged when they encountered the mines en route to Corfu, and Britain therefore withheld the transfer of gold deposits back to Enver Hoxha's newly created communist regime.

I was telling my wife about this continual border shifting, without getting into a lot of the details. The Corfu incident could wait until we visited Corfu, sometime in the future.

"So where is the border now?" Michaela asked.

"It's just south of Butrint, where we're going tomorrow. Saranda is the most southerly Albanian settlement and closest to the ruins."

"Is that where those mafia guys were from?" she asked.

I wasn't sure what the presence of guards in the area might mean, or where they were from—Ariyan had told me that the development plans for the bay hadn't been successful, but he also thought Ali Pasha had built the fortress. It was all a little too uncertain.

"Maybe," I said, "but someone seems interested in making sure the citadel isn't damaged. Those guards are a product of the power vacuum left by the collapse of communism. There are probably no reliable police forces in the countryside here in the south, and without any opportunities, that's what the young men do."

"So it's okay for them to be in the mafia?" she asked.

"Not really," I said, "at least by our standards. These guys do what their boss wants by acting threatening, as we just experienced. Anyone with that kind of influence should be accountable for his actions, but they only report to their leader, not someone who is elected. The lack of opportunity and freedom to live without intimidation forces many Albanians to try to leave the country, so hopefully they'll have better opportunities if the country develops in the future." Michaela was looking out the window and didn't reply.

I didn't want to start a big lecture on Albania's history of changing alliances when dealing with the many different invaders, as everyone was getting tired and hungry, but the country's past had strongly influenced Hoxha's methods. He was a leader who switched allegiance when it was profitable to do so, initially allying Albania with Russia and Stalin. During Khrushchev's rise in the 1950s, a Soviet submarine base—and likely the deserted facilities we had seen—was built in Vlora Bay for access to the Mediterranean. However, Khrushchev's subsequent denouncing of Stalin's personality cult conflicted with Hoxha's building of his own admiration sect. Despite an increase in Russian aid, the country drifted towards Chinese influence, and by 1962, Albania's relations with Russia and the Warsaw Pact nations had been broken. Hoxha replaced Russian investments with Chinese money, and the Chinese contributed to his next five-year plan of heavy chromium, steel, and concrete development. To an increasingly paranoid Hoxha, kicking out Khrushchev had an ideological advantage, but the remoteness of his new Chinese supporters did not facilitate success.

The local Albanian version of these events was more interesting. Ariyan told me that after the switch in allegiance, Russia planned to invade the country and recoup its military investments, but in 1962 the country was distracted by its Caribbean objectives in Cuba. The US strongly protested Russia's intercontinental missile deployment in a country only a few miles from Florida. The ensuing American blockade was the closest that the Cold War came to ending with a nuclear bang, instead of the later whimper of the USSR's demise.

Our midafternoon arrival in Saranda was a welcome stop. We sat on a glassed terrace in the afternoon sun and scanned the multilanguage menu as I guzzled a cold beer. I ordered another when I looked at the text message I'd received after leaving the fortress. Mr. Brown "just happened" to be in town and wanted to meet later at the southern port's newest hotel.

Fuck that. I'd had enough. Why would I endanger myself, or my family? We were just tourists visiting the ruins at Butrint, and I wanted it to stay that way.

My wife's mind was elsewhere. This was her opportunity to further discuss our daughter's new friend, and she had slowly worked the conversation around to him. "Do you like him a lot?"

"Mother, we enjoy talking together, that's all." Michaela's phone vibrated with a text message, which she read as my wife turned to me, looking for help.

I saw my daughter was getting emotional as she read the text, but it took my wife a minute to notice. The wine had arrived during their exchange, and she had just sipped it and discovered why the next table had added Coke to mask the flavour. We had experienced amazing wine in the country and were now drinking equally terrible plonk—apparently from the same label and vintage.

My wife took a large gulp of water. "Tony, tell me again about all the good Mediterranean wine here—this is one of those mythical Mediterranean places, right? And that 'hold-up' back at the castle—just how much longer are we planning on staying in this country?" I had nothing to say, but then our daughter provided a welcome distraction.

"Don't worry!" Michaela burst out. "This week might be the last time I see him." Tears started to run down her cheeks.

"Oh, honey!" My wife reached over to take both her hands.

Although Michaela took her message as bad news, I thought differently—it was better if she was no longer going to be seeing him alone in Vienna. But not knowing how he felt about their friendship, even if what Michaela said was true, I needed to find out if the young man might be planning to visit Vienna again—always a possibility if the relationship was getting serious.

The restaurant's manager came over to see how we were doing. We seemed to be the only tourists in the place that was now filled with locals. He ruffled the hair of the two youngest, and then turned to me.

"You will accept another beer? Maybe the kids have one more drink?"

I assumed he wanted us to stay longer and spend a bit more or give us the bill, but he gestured to the middle of the room, where a large man was sitting alone. As if on cue, the man looked over and raised his glass in our direction.

"You will accept a gift." Now the manager wasn't asking. "A bottle of wine, maybe, or a cognac for you and your wife. Some dessert?" He was talking faster and seemed to be getting nervous.

The big man was getting up and coming our way. His track suit was from a top German manufacturer. He stopped to tousle all the children's hair, but as the manager stepped back to let him move around the table, our new visitor hesitated near Michaela. She had assumed a more mature posture, nearly rigid, and her emotional outburst had been replaced by a determined expression. I exhaled when he didn't pat her head.

He looked at me and my wife, then the kids. "Please excuse my interruption," he said, looking again at my daughter and then back to me. "My best admiration for you and your family." As he returned to his seat, other patrons whispered and a few stared.

We finally settled for some dessert, which the manager delivered personally, and I enjoyed another strong coffee. He asked where we were going afterwards and told us that a new monastery overlooking the hills of Saranda was under construction. It was to be a new home for the local Orthodox monks. Then he asked where we were staying and offered to provide us with "a special price" accommodation, so we drove up to the monastery while he looked for the keys to our rooms. We could always decide on their suitability later. We hadn't been able to locate Ariyan's recommended hotel coming into town, and of course, the manager told us he didn't know where it was, either.

Mr. Bega had enjoyed seeing the family of tourists; it was a promise of future potential. He interrupted his meal again to answer his phone—he'd asked for an update.

"*Po?*" He listened carefully. The news was good. The hotel was ready and most of the guests had already checked in. He was looking forward to an evening of discussing business opportunities. He knew everyone would enjoy the entertainment. The concierge had assured him that the opening show would be a fitting start to the night—a Ukrainian group known for their eclectic performances and beautiful women. Bega had also arranged for a top-quality caterer to provide food service throughout the evening, and had managed to acquire some very good French wines and other premier alcohol brands for his guests. It would be a night to remember.

He expected a big return on the extravagance.

9

AN OLD MAN greeted us near the entrance to the new religious retreat and offered to show us around, but there were language issues. Albanian is one of the original five Indo-European languages, but my skills only extended to numbers and everyday greetings, particularly when ordering beer, wine (both frequently) and pasta. We listened as he spoke a mixture of German, Italian, and French with possibly some Greek mixed in, and he could see we were trying to understand. He was telling us how old and important the original Byzantine monastery was. I was translating for everyone, sort of, but was quite sure he'd said "more than two thousand years old," so I started to think he was just telling us anything, with the occasional grain of truth. He grew more animated as he showed us the old buildings and then the newer parts. We wandered from room to room and entered a large, partly covered circular courtyard built of stone. He seemed to be telling us that, as well as a new hotel for tourists, this was to be the disco—either that or a church. Both? For a moment he looked to be as confused as I was.

Probably because of the long drive and all that had

happened that day, I found this extremely funny. One glance towards Michaela was enough; she had also been trying to decipher what he was saying, and was likely capable of understanding more of it. I tried to cover myself with a cough, but it was no good. We both burst out laughing, and the rest of the family joined. Luckily, our guide also laughed, and we escaped, thanking him for his hospitality.

As we returned down the hill, my wife and I shared a look—this outing would be something to remember. We needed to stop worrying so much, to stop attempting to make the world beyond our family a safe place for them. Michaela was going to be just fine at boarding school in Vienna, and with anything else that came along.

Michaela and I hadn't shared a real laugh for a long time, except maybe at the last movie we'd seen together. That we had both laughed made everything better and renewed my confidence that having the family here would work for us.

Unless it didn't.

This little cynical voice usually spoke up when I came to a positive conclusion. It actually helped me realise that I was an eternal optimist—well, more like a realistic optimist, knowing there was always the possibility of a bad outcome.

The sun was low when we found our accommodation for the night. We had settled for the restaurant's offer, hoping we would enjoy the rooms more than their wine. The manager was gone when we returned, but a waitress handed us some keys and pointed vaguely down the road after writing the name on a piece of paper and stating the Albanian equivalent of "you can't miss it."

As we drove off, the little voice spoke again: maybe what

she had really said was, "Good luck in finding it," but we eventually did locate the place, after trying several doors in which the keys didn't fit. The building was a large unoccupied "hotel," and we explored the various floors. There was a bar area that had never been used, with many unpacked items scattered around, and finally our very basic quarters. The two one-star rooms had a three-star sea view—a portion of our adjoining rooms had been built out over the seashore, and the water washed quietly onto the rocks under our balcony. It was good enough after the long drive, and we settled in before deciding on a little stroll.

As the sun started to set we drove back into the centre of Saranda, past the newest hotel. I remembered Mr. Brown's invitation and saw that the parking lot was nearly full. We drove on and parked by the developing waterfront, where we took a saunter along the newly built promenade. It was "almost" completed, as were most new buildings in the town. The overhead lights flickered on along the walkway as dusk fell and we wandered along the Ionian seashore.

We were all enjoying the warm evening stroll, especially considering it was November. The two youngest started running up and down the boardwalk after I told them it was likely deep winter back home. And to think we had almost listened to our expat colleagues who would never venture outside the capital because of the poorly developed infrastructure in other towns.

We were just thinking that Saranda was different because of the tourism potential from northern Greece when abruptly, the power was cut and the lights went out—leaving us in the reality of an Albanian night away from the capital. It was not just dark; it was totally black, except for the lights far across the harbour. It took a minute to realise we were looking towards the island of Corfu. As we stood there accepting that our evening jaunt was over, a lone generator started up somewhere in the distance. We all knew that sound from the occasional power outages in Tirana, when the multiple diesel generators at the back of our building all fired up together and a black exhaust cloud rose slowly from the engines' vented covers—but out here there was just the single note of a diesel motor in the night.

After a few tries at retracing our steps to our Nissan, we found it and drove back through Saranda, where one or two of the bigger corner shops had propane lanterns. The generator sound grew louder as we drove towards the big new hotel. The area was well lit as we approached, and we could see a casino with colourful lights at the back and lots of people milling about. Once past the bright lights, it was difficult to see anything or anybody. I used the Nissan's headlights to illuminate our hotel's entrance, and we returned to our rooms. There was still no power by 7:00 p.m., so after a little bedtime reading by flashlight, it was lights out, and the sound of the seashore lulled nearly everyone asleep in a few minutes.

I was too addled to sleep. Just when things had started looking up—a good meal, family moments at the monastery and the perfect finish, strolling on a lovely promenade in a resort town—it had all ended in darkness. The restaurant coffee hadn't helped, and I finally crept into the bathroom to text Mr. Brown and agree to the meeting at the new hotel. The place had looked like it was hopping when we drove by, and I was curious to see the clientele more than Mr. Brown, but his text was a good excuse. The family would need to be up early to get going to Butrint, but I wouldn't be out too long—just enough time to tell Mr. Brown I couldn't help him out, and maybe to work out the many different options for the next few days running around in my head. I wouldn't be putting the family in any danger going by myself. *And there's very little risk in my meeting him*, I thought, perhaps trying to convince myself.

10

THE WATER SWISHING under our "balcony" had nearly lulled me to sleep when I heard someone in one of the bathrooms. There were still two sleepers in the other bed in my room, which I was sharing with my mom and my sister. A few minutes later I heard the front door of the room beside ours open and close, and heavy footsteps moving down the hall. I guessed my dad was going for a walk. I knew he hadn't been sleeping too well since our move to Tirana and was always up early. He'd even taken up running before work in the morning if he woke up and couldn't get back to sleep. At least we had something in common. I wondered if not being able to sleep was getting worse for him or better.

Saranda: well, so much for the nice beach and cosy hotel. The beds were all small—the room wasn't really big enough to fit a double bed without blocking the way to the balcony, but my mom hadn't made me share with my bed-hogging sister. The bathrooms were tiny and kinda gross—not that I looked too closely in the corners or anything, but the shower just had a cheap curtain that was torn. Hearing the beach was nice, though. It made me think of a poem from school, but the sound was hardly like a "grating roar"—the pebbles on the beach were just getting wet.

The stop at the restaurant had been really nice. Well, at least until I got the text message. Sitting there in the warm, bright afternoon light with my mom and dad made me think about how important the "feeling" in a restaurant can be. It was something like being in the coffee house with Mikel, but that had been exciting, while this afternoon had been calming. And the food was amazing, especially the frozen lemon dessert after the salad and pasta. The only problem had been that big creepy guy who'd come over to our table. Who did he think he was? If he'd touched me I would have screamed. When he looked at me I think he knew that—he must have a teenage daughter, maybe even a young wife. That happens a lot here, old guys with young wives, though they're not always wives, more like "companions," as my mom once tried explaining to me. Sure, Mom, whatever.

Actually, it had been a great day. If we hadn't moved here, I'd be walking to and from school in the snow right now and needing something stodgy for supper. The funniest thing had been that old guy up on the hill at the "monastery." He got his languages all mixed up, and then said the old church was built before Jesus was born. Good thing he didn't get angry when we all started laughing, even though it was at him. It's been a long time since my dad made me laugh. He didn't know that the old man had been expecting some money, unless he hadn't been. It's hard to know what to expect in this country, like the electricity suddenly blacking out.

The only thing to expect here in Albania is something unexpected—or something like that. When I first arrived at the Theresianum, I heard one of the supervisors make a comment about my living in Albania. I hadn't really understood it, but it sounded negative. My boarding supervisor appeared to correct what her colleague said, after she'd looked at me, and I'd understood most of her answer—that the Balkans begins on Kärtnerstrasse, a famous street in the old part of Vienna. So Vienna is nearly Balkan or not that far away, but I wasn't sure if she meant that Austria was partly responsible for Albania, which is part of the Balkans, or that the way people thought in Vienna wasn't that different from the way people thought in the Balkans. She was more understanding and didn't think Vienna was absolutely perfect—that was why most of the students liked her. Many teachers and most adults in the city thought Vienna was this fantastic place in the clouds and we were all like unworthy children—*auslanders*.

I should have expected a text like the one in the restaurant though, after the evening date with Malik. He had asked me out for dinner and hinted it was going to be a special occasion, but it hadn't gone very well. I'd known that we would be going to a nice restaurant but hadn't expected just how expensive it would be—I mean, where would he get the money from?

—◦◦◦—

The old restaurants in Vienna's First District, near the city centre, are famous for their standards. We went to one once as a family on a weekend visit to the city. The food had been really good, and pricey, but I hadn't remembered it had also come with a lot of snootiness. During the evening out with Malik, I noticed there was only a small sign hanging in front of the entrance, and as we walked in, the maître d' greeted us, or more correctly, he welcomed Malik—I was ignored. Did he know Malik from before?

"*Guten Abend, mein Herr,*" he'd said, and then when Malik was busy checking our coats he ran his gaze up and down me, around his large nose that stood out so much. My schoolgirl wardrobe included a churchgoing dress but not a dressy dining outfit, and his look really made me feel uncomfortable. The feeling continued when I saw others looking at me as we made our entrance. I decided that they were wondering if I was Malik's younger sister, or possibly his daughter.

Malik noticed the faces turned in our direction as we sat at a central table. "Is there something wrong?" he asked.

"Not at all," I said, hoping my stubborn streak would get me through this bad start, but my stomach was churning as the waiters in black-and-white-striped waistcoats flitted around us. Two really big fancy-looking menus arrived, but I was sort of disappointed to see they were in English. "I'd almost wanted to order in German," I said, still attempting to sound *very* casual, and saw Malik respond by raising his hand. What was he doing? It was just drawing more attention to us.

Immediately, our waiter appeared at Malik's side. "*Wie kann ich* . . . sorry, sir—may I be of assistance?"

"Yes, could my . . ."—I could feel my face colouring as he hesitated—"*companion* have a German menu?"

The waiter looked at me without any kind of expression

and whipped mine away, and there was another in my hand as quick as a magician pulls a rabbit out of a hat. As I looked it over, I realised it was in a formal German script that I wasn't used to seeing on fast-food menus, and I felt sweat start to trickle down my back. Hadn't Malik heard me say "*almost* wanted to order in German?" At least I recognised *kartoffel*, so I could order as many potatoes as I wanted.

A gentleman in a perfectly fitted tuxedo glided into the room and slid into a seat in front of the grand piano waiting in the corner. He began with some Viennese waltzes (I would not be falling asleep here!), and then played some other Austro-Hungarian music, which I recognised from my piano lessons back home. For a minute I watched him play expertly, but quietly, never louder than the murmur of conversation that continued around the room.

I had been looking forward to an enchanting fairy tale of an evening but now was trying to cope with the dreaded feeling of being out of place. The waiter was kind enough to help me with the menu, but I could tell that Malik was seeing a girl rather than the young woman he had expected to enjoy the evening with. I think I only made it worse when I made the mistake of telling him too many details about my school. I'd become so determined to show him—and the maître d' and everyone else who had stared at me—that I was completely at ease that I'd forgotten I'd told Malik I was only taking a few classes in French in preparation for university.

He looked at me, likely in a new light, as I rambled on and then realised my mistake. There was a silence between us when I paused, so of course I just kept going.

"One of the girls in my class is a Muslim," I said, but

then didn't know how to continue. I had originally hoped he would tell me more about his faith, but this comment was going nowhere. "Excuse me," I said, getting up to find the bathroom. I walked towards the entrance when the location wasn't obvious. Two employees were standing by the door with their backs to me. At least I knew how to ask for the bathroom. "*Wo ist die Toiletten, bitte?*" It was the maître d' who turned around, and he looked down at me and just pointed. *How rude*, I thought, hoping his nose hairs would grow so much they'd cover his face.

———•((•))•———

The text I received from Giselle in the Saranda restaurant had told me that Malik had been waiting in front of the Theresianum entrance when she left the grounds after class with one of our younger friends. Giselle said he'd looked at the much-younger girl and then asked if I was back yet. He knew I wasn't, because I'd told him I was visiting my family here for the weekend. It must have been an excuse to find out more about us, mainly how old I was. What was I going to say to him if he called? I'd been hoping he'd forget about the restaurant night out, but hearing that he'd shown up at the Theresianum meant the worst.

At least he'd rode with me back to my tram stop after the restaurant, but he'd been vague about meeting again, saying that it would now be more difficult arranging to see me because his course had been shortened and he wasn't sure how much longer he would be coming to Vienna. He was being real snooty, like he was talking to a child, when he told me he'd try to let me know, and then he ran away after a quick handshake.

Yeah, sure.

But I could still *hope* that things would work out. As I started drifting off again, it came to me that I didn't really know what I wanted—some warm kisses and a feeling of togetherness were important, but what else? My eyes closed, but the sound of the nearby sea lapping against the shore had me thinking of a bright sunlit coastline, and then it became an image of wooden ships crunching onto the sand, and there were shouts as soldiers jumped into the shallow water and made for the beach, just like in one of the movies I remembered.

11

THE VEHICLE'S TURBO diesel engine started quietly enough, and I hoped the car park's distance from where the family slept would muffle the sound. The coast road into town took me quickly to the brightly lit hotel. There were no places left in the parking lot, but I found a spot on the sidewalk that someone must have just vacated. A few pedestrians were walking by on the road, a normal route in a country where sidewalks were often broken and muddy. I got out and was walking towards the entrance, past the lot, when I saw a red Mercedes. Curious if this was the same vehicle I'd spotted on the road, I headed back to it and was nearly at the car when a bald-headed minder in a dark suit appeared between nearby cars and approached me.

"Hey, *ju!*"

Better to answer in English. "Yes?"

"What you want?"

"Just admiring the car."

"This privat party." He turned and straightened up as headlights swung into the lot. A limousine pulled up to him, and the driver's window whirred down. The guard leaned in, listening, and then turned towards me, gesturing towards the car.

"Get in."

I hesitated, but then walked over as the large car's door swung open; I bent down and looked inside. It was very new and well maintained, *German*, I thought, with a lot of interior room. The two back seats faced each other. There were three men in dark suits, all sitting in the rear seat looking forward, and the particularly large passenger who sat between the other two looked familiar.

"Hello, my friend." The man who had bought me and my family dessert at the restaurant waved me in to sit down.

I shook hands with him, and he introduced me to his associates. They only nodded.

"You want drink?"

"No, thanks." Nobody else was drinking.

He waited, watching me and knowing my situation would force me to say something more.

"I'm meeting someone," I said.

"You meet someone here? Is private party."

"Not at the party, outside the hotel. We were meeting here because it's the only place with light."

"Who you meeting?"

I couldn't think of anything to say.

He tried to encourage me. "Is good you don't have business in Saranda, just meeting friend. For drink? But you come with me, and bring your friend inside. I give special invitations to you."

"Let me call him first." I was thinking I wasn't dressed appropriately and also wondering, *Why the invite?* It was a rare . . . opportunity? No internal alarm bells were going off so far and I was naively curious—I really didn't have a choice but was sure Mr. Brown wouldn't want this man's scrutiny; it might lead to complications for us both.

They waited while I called. There was no answer. Maybe he was in the lobby and couldn't hear the phone ring. The party was very loud. Muffled thumping bass music pulsed more clearly as the hotel doors slid open.

I tried again as they watched. Finally, the three of them got out of the vehicle. My friend was second. He said, "Maybe he have delay." He stretched in the cooling evening. "Come." Now I was glad Brown hadn't answered. It would be too obvious that we had "business." I guessed all business had to have the big man's approval.

Several bystanders took notice as we walked up to the entry. The doors slid open again, and I was overwhelmed by the noise, bright lights, and smoke as we stepped inside. The generator we'd heard had to be very large to be supplying this much power. The big man pointed, and one of his henchmen indicated I was to follow him, but I was led only to the bar to get drinks. My host was busy shaking hands and kissing cheeks back near the reception.

It was a big room, decorated to the hilt, with a small stage facing many tables and two bars on either side. I scanned the space and saw many dark suits and a few well-dressed women, some attached and others wandering between tables alone. A circular metallic structure stood on the edge of the stage, the floor of which was littered with more than an inch of red flower petals. Jagged edges in the metal gave it an explosive look—it was probably an entryway for the female entertainers. The strewn flowers meant we'd missed the main event.

Drinks in hand, the henchman and I walked back to the big man, who was still busy meeting and greeting. I sipped my beer. The music blared but now seemed less intense—I must be getting used to the volume. Groups coalesced at tables, leaning in as discussions got more serious. I stood back, not nearly as conspicuous away from the host's circle, and despite my lack of a tie, I relaxed a bit in my dark trousers, white shirt, and dark jacket. Some of the men, clearly enjoying themselves, had dispensed with their cravats.

"Hello, mister."

I turned around. *I guess I do stand out*, I thought. The man addressing me was carrying a nearly empty glass and dressed immaculately in an expensive Italian suit. He glowed with confidence and alcohol.

"Where you from? American, British? What you drink?" He talked fast and grabbed a bottle off the tray passing by, then held it up to my glass.

"Moment." I finished the beer and held the glass out; best to go along with the festivities.

"You stay in hotel?"

"*Gëzuar!*" Another man joined us, addressing my companion as Victor. They both turned to me.

"Tony," I said, raising my glass and taking a small sip. Victor's eyes followed my glass. *Maybe not so drunk after all.* Was he looking for an American or a Brit? Could Mr. Brown be British?

"Antonio, your business?"

His attention was firmly directed at me, despite his

friend and the surrounding excess, but we were interrupted by the sound of breaking glass at a nearby table. Two red-faced men had pushed back their chairs from the upended table. They were shouting into each other's faces, not caring as the spittle flew. A young woman was backing away and bumped into my host, who had come over to see about the commotion. He pushed the men apart, and before they could resist, the host's two minders moved in to calm them down. After appearing to withdraw, one of them abruptly ran at the other—one bodyguard stepped into his path, knocking him over, while the other grabbed him and held him down until he stopped struggling. They escorted him towards the doorway.

The boss, seeing the party was back under control, approached us and greeted Victor and his friend, and then turned to me.

"Better you should go and see your family."

As I left, Victor was deep in conversation with the big man. His friend watched me head to the exit.

The heavies at the door quieted as I got to the hotel entrance. The bystanders outside went silent as I brushed past them, and I could feel their looks behind me. I passed by the troublemaker, who was sitting on the curb, head down. When I got back to my SUV, the guard was still in the parking lot, near the Mercedes that I was sure I had first seen at the American compound in Tirana, and probably the same one that had flown by us in Vlora. I remembered the bumper that was bigger than normal, as though an attachment had been added to minimise damage if the vehicle hit livestock. I'd been cautioned about driving at night in a country where livestock roamed freely. The guard looked over as my door light came on. I resisted the urge to wave, started the Nissan, and drove back to our hotel.

⟫⟪⟫⟪⟫

"Petro, are you going soft? Why are you inviting this *anglez*? He forgot his baseball cap and T-shirt."

"Don't worry, Victor. Everything is fine," Bega replied, but his eyes were elsewhere, scanning the room. It was crowded and full of motion. "You see anyone you don't know?"

Bega had watched closely as the family man reached the entrance. Maybe he was more than just a visiting tourist, but coming to the only lighted place for a rendezvous made some sense. Still, he wondered whom he was meeting; probably a guide for tomorrow, something small time. It was always a good thing to know who was in town though. He had been overly generous in inviting him in, but he was a generous man. So far he'd been able to keep tabs on most visitors, although the American had managed to arrive in the afternoon without his knowledge.

"Only that one," said Victor, waving to the door through which Tony had left.

Now that Victor had made the rounds to check that things were okay, Bega tried encouraging him to relax a bit. The big man turned towards the door and saw others arriving. *Good.* His Greek visitors. First, let them have a few drinks, then show them some girls and walk them around to see the results; so much power in one place. He took a deep breath and imagined the changes his new development plans would make.

The Greeks had been smart to arrive later, or had it just been the usual border holdup? That annoying delay would need to improve, but what could he do about it? It was good that he'd moved most of his business from trucks to water transport.

He went over and shook hands. There were no Albanian-style hugs, but he could smell anise. *So, a few tipples before arriving. Good.* He would remain sharp for his guests and let them have fun. There'd be enough time for him to enjoy the dividends later.

⊷⊷⊷⊷⊷⊷⊷ ⊶⟪◉⟫⊷ ⊷⊷⊷⊷⊷⊷⊷

Reby had crouched low in his seat inside the red Mercedes in the parking lot, hearing the crunch of gravel and the approach of footsteps. It was always best to expect surprises, though he assumed the man assigned to keep watch over the vehicles was just doing his rounds. Then he heard an exchange between an English speaker and the guard, followed by the arrival of another car. It had gotten quiet after that, so he'd had a quick look at the hotel and recognised the big outline of Bega walking towards the entrance with his bodyguards—the man stood out, even amongst his muscled cronies. He looked to be even bigger than when Reby had seen him near the Kosovo border, years before on his first job driving the American. He relaxed and closed his eyes, waiting to hear from his passenger, who must be meeting Bega

─ 99 ─

shortly. Reby was well experienced at "not quite" sleeping—
he was thinking about how to get friendly with the guard.

They had arrived earlier in the day, before the guard had
been posted. As planned, he'd stayed in the vehicle while the
American determined if he'd be able to check in. A few minutes later, Reby's cell had rung.

"I'm good, managed a room on the first floor, over the
party room so I can tell when it gets underway. Let's limit
our calls—I don't know if cells are being monitored, but just
in case. Wait in the car and I'll let you know how the meeting
goes. I'm going to call our friend now. If I don't call back, he's
agreed to meet in the hotel. I'll try and get back to you after
that, but it may not be possible—I don't want him knowing you're here, so you'll just have to keep watch. If it's safe,
find out who's attending. I'd really like to know where Bega
keeps his backup. This town seems too open for them all to
be here."

The guard was making his rounds of the parking lot
again, and Reby opened the door of his car as the minder approached. The man stiffened as Reby's shape emerged from
the low shadows and stood up in the darkened car park.

"Ciao," he said, quickly offering a cigarette. The security
man stopped and was reaching for his cell phone—he looked
slightly familiar but didn't react as Reby drew closer, except
to consider his phone. It would have been a long time ago,
high in the mountains east of Vlora. Reby's memory for faces
had served him well. Back then, he'd had to stay in his car
for most of the action, but he'd seen nearly all of the others
in the operation.

The guard reconsidered calling in after quickly looking

around, and then accepted the smoke. "*Faleminderit.*" He relaxed a bit. "Who you driving for?"

"Aren't all the big shots the same?" They laughed together, but Reby thought quickly, knowing he needed the man's trust to remain here without generating suspicion. "One of the new guys," he said, adding, "Bega contacted my boss in Tirana. He needed someone reliable to pick up some of the fellows near Leskovik."

"Leskovik?" The guard was obviously not familiar with the southeastern border with Greece.

"Yeah, go a bit further and you get to Korce." *Don't any of these southerners know their own country?*

"Oh, of course, Korce."

Reby hoped he knew where Korce was, at least.

"And how is it over there?"

Reby knew he'd better not underestimate the guard, and replied, "Road was fine. Well, maybe not great, but okay." Maybe the guard was really asking about salary, but Reby didn't know anything about business anywhere near Korce and continued to remain vague. "I only picked these two guys up and will drop them off when it's all over." The guard nodded, seemingly appeased, so Reby added, "I hear it's going to be quite a party?"

"Yeah." The guard remained tight-lipped. "Thanks for the cigarette," he said, and he walked on.

Reby got back into his car. The guard might not know much, but he knew not to talk to strangers. Reby decided he'd stay put rather than chance being recognised while mingling with the other drivers.

12

WE WERE UP shortly after dawn. I'd fallen asleep as soon as I'd gotten back from my adventure at the party, having had just enough alcohol to help put me out. We made it to Butrint in the early morning, but no coffee was available in the nearby cafés with the power still out. There was enough time to visit the excavations in the bright warm sunshine and still leave before noon for the return journey inland. No one had been able to help us find the mythical ferry to Corfu, although I'm sure we would have heard something from someone if we had persisted; our friend at the monastery might have filled us in on what he hoped the schedule to be.

There was always a chance that Mr. Big from last night could make some arrangements, but he might make us an offer we couldn't refuse. In any case, he hadn't been at the restaurant when we'd dropped off the keys and paid. I wasn't that keen on getting to Corfu in a Zodiac, even if our benefactor was willing to "look after" our vehicle while we were away.

Butrint was impressive, a romantic oil painting come to life, with huge ramparts, broken where the trees had grown through, amid a Byronesque setting and light. The massive limestone blocks on the south perimeter were identified as the Illyrian walls. According to the faded, ancient photocopy of the original guide sheet provided at the entrance, this construction predated the Greek ruins and Roman amphitheatre. The older Albania guidebook that we'd taken along focused on the pre-war Italian excavations, and suggested that the Illyrians had been largely confined to northernmost Albania and the Yugoslav coast prior to the Serbs' arrival; the Illyrian ideal appealed to the Albanians as a story of origin, but it was impossible to be sure of its truth in a country where historical revision was a way of life.

There were enough different sections for each family member to be interested in some portion of the huge site. The boys enjoyed their unsupervised romp, though we told them to stay in sight. Steep walls, hidden holes, and flooded sections of ruins extended across a significant hill and ended in marsh on the south side; we could view Greece across the watery lowland. A fresh-water channel once flowed to the Ionian Sea, but the waterway silted up after the Greco-Roman period and was a malarial swamp by the Middle Ages. The guidebook noted that Hoxha's grand idea to drain the swamp and build a major port open to the Mediterranean had caused it to become a saline marsh, which could not support an environment for mosquitoes. The plan was listed as a failure even though malaria was eradicated, indicating that history is indeed written by the victors.

"There's more over there," said my older son. Another fortified ruin sat on a nearby promontory in the old channel.

I could see the broken and jagged walls against the

faded-blue autumn sky. "Sorry, guys. It doesn't look very safe, and how would we get there without getting wet?" The map in our old guidebook indicated that this broken jumble of blocky ramparts was the Ali Pasha fortress, and that Byron had visited the site on his excursions to the region in 1809.

We climbed past the massive "Illyrian" walls, up the various paths, and emerged at the top of Butrint's central hill, where a restored Byzantine monastery overlooked the site. There were drinks for sale, and we sat in the garden on top of one of Europe's best-preserved ruins, surrounded by history. The site typified a country that remained largely unrestored, as did its traditions and institutions, but progress was slowly being made.

Michaela noticed the Albanian black on red flag fluttering at the top of the monastery and asked, "Why do they use the double-headed eagle on their flag?"

Referring to the old guidebook, I read as the others enjoyed their refreshments. "'The original Byzantine citadel was captured by the Venetian city state during Venice's Mediterranean expansion, when the conquerors moved south along the Adriatic and Ionian coasts near the end of the twelfth century. The Ottomans took over from the Venetians, but modern Albania reverted to the black double-headed eagle flag of the Byzantines when Albania revolted against the Ottomans.'"

Michaela looked doubtful. She'd always had a mind of her own. "I thought the double eagle head was for the two ruling countries of the Austro-Hungarian Empire. There's a huge black double-headed eagle carved into one of the doors at the Theresianum."

"Yes, there's also a huge one on one of the old Viennese government buildings. I've heard it called 'very two-faced'"—Michaela frowned at the bad joke—"but it just shows nothing is really new and original. Maybe for the Byzantines it represented the two halves, eastern and western, that evolved from the old Roman Empire." This still didn't address what it referred to in Albania, though the guidebook mentioned the two heads of the eagle were looking north and south, a stance described as watchful, though it had become more like paranoia during Hoxha's rule. But I knew several Eastern European countries used the double eagle in their coats of arms, as did Russia. Maybe two heads are better than one? How would it look if they faced each other, rather than away? Austria had been very inward looking, so this would have been fairly appropriate until it joined the EU. But for some of the Eastern European countries—Serbia came to mind—it would still be very fitting.

Before starting back to the car park, we had a quick look into the monastery. The ceiling and doors were being refurbished, but unfinished sections were a faded blue with some music notes painted in black, which my wife thought had been an attempt to liven up the place.

Michaela noticed other ongoing changes. "It's just like the other monastery yesterday. Didn't the old guide mention music and disco in that room they were building?"

Perhaps there was a whole generation that thought monasteries should have a blue room with music. We later saw other partly coloured monasteries being restored and learned that in his quest to eliminate religion, Hoxha had tried to convert religious buildings into nightclubs and discos, which seemed totally at odds with communism—so it was probably true, based on all the consistent inconsistencies I'd seen in the last few months.

By late morning we were heading east after retracing our route back past the hotels and through Saranda, taking the inland route at the major intersection, not the coast road. As we passed through a small village, the road became a track; at an intersection we chose the option that appeared more travelled. It was the wrong turn, we quickly realised, and the track ended near an old drilling derrick close to a hilltop. Maybe it was a picnic spot and could be another investment opportunity! We backtracked, and after some distance in the dry yellowy light of autumn, joined the main highway north to Gjirokaster by descending the windingly steep and narrow hillside road.

The highway from the Greek border was a welcome change, a new divided four-lane, where newer German sedans easily achieved autobahn speeds, at least between river crossings. But many older Mercedes were doing all the heavy work. Some of these vehicles were hauling an entire family, large selections of produce, or smaller farm animals. Occasionally these overloaded transports were travelling on the shoulder of the wrong side of the road because of limited access to the main highway—getting over to the correct side was only possible at river crossings, where there was no middle railing separating the opposing lanes. Bridge work had still not resumed, so we bumped slowly down each riverbed's inclined flanks and ploughed directly across and over the stones of the streams, sloshing past the new sedans as they chose the shallowest route. They caught up and passed us once we all returned to the tarmac and resumed highway speeds. Where was the money for the incomplete bridges and safe minor-road access?

Mr. Brown's failure to show up the previous evening had me puzzled. He'd seemed very keen to meet when I checked my phone again in the bathroom at our one-star hotel. He must have known about the private party in the big new hotel. Had he been planning to attend? I hadn't seen him, but he might have just ducked out when I arrived. Maybe he had contacts there—how else could he have booked a room? I had wanted to ask him how he'd gotten to Saranda, and if the inland route was better, but we'd soon find out.

I planned to call my cousin when we got back to Tirana, to get a little more information on Mr. Brown, or whoever he really was.

13

PETRO BEGA SAT in the hotel's breakfast room with a pot of tea as the sun rose. He had limited his alcohol intake at the party to initial welcomes and special toasts, but he still needed more caffeine after finishing two strong coffees, and thought the tea would help. The evening had flashed by after the Greeks' arrival, and he was hoarse from talking over the music. Someone had kept turning up the volume, despite how deafening it had been even at the start. In the early hours, as his guests left or collapsed, he'd gone upstairs to see his unexpected visitor again. He'd postponed questioning him in detail until he knew the gathering had been a success—with so much going on, it was best to take one step at a time.

The American had thought he could get in on some of the action, claiming that had been part of their original deal. Bega remembered that day—*I might come back to you, if everything goes really well down south, but how likely is that?*—but his ex-partner would eventually want control, just like he'd wanted it in the north. Taking over the Kosovo operation had been a disaster for the American, and Bega's timing to move south couldn't have been better, but so what? There had been no guarantee that Bega would prosper as he had, but he'd certainly been smarter than the American, knowing his countrymen and seeing that changes brought by the Kosovo settlement in the north might severely reduce, or possibly eliminate, their business in the area. Bega had last heard through his sources that the agency had terminated his former partner's contract—his activities became increasingly desperate once most of the ongoing illegal cross-border activities were targeted—but he'd heard nothing more about him over the last few years. And then he'd shown up yesterday.

The American had contacted Bega from the hotel, after enquiries at the front desk eventually put him in touch with Victor—the American did have a certain way of getting what he wanted. Bega had to admire his ability to talk past the normally unwavering manager to find the only available room. Bega had agreed to a meeting just before the big event last night, but it had become tiresome and he'd lost his patience. He'd even missed the main event at the party—the women making their entrance. He'd been curious to see if they were as good as promised. If the American had thought he could walk in using his no-longer-valid credentials, he was *dead* wrong.

It had taken some time for the drugs to work on his former partner, and fitting that the American had been instrumental in providing these particular pharmaceuticals in Kosovo when they'd needed information. Before the eastern sky showed any light, he'd revealed the names of many of his contacts and people he'd met with in Tirana. Bega would postpone any final decision on the American's fate until he knew how much of a trail the man had left since his arrival. The drugs worked wonders for a short period, but then made the subject become incoherent and pass out. There would have to be at least another session to find out more—who knew that he was in Saranda, for instance. Eventually Victor would take care of him. The men had taken him down to the car earlier, "another party casualty who couldn't hold his drink," and were driving him to Gjirokaster, timing the trip to avoid any checkpoints on the main highway—shift changes happened in the early morning, so it was unlikely the police had had time to set up on the roads again, yet. The time to avoid was late morning through early afternoon. They would wait in the old city before travelling the final leg into the mountains, where there'd be plenty of space and time to deal with the problem, away from any prying eyes.

Petro's head snapped up when he felt himself slipping into a doze. He got up and went to the bathroom where he splashed water into his face, then glanced down at his watch. The vehicle and its passengers should be nearly at Gjirokaster. Victor would confirm their position and departure from there. Bega was still evaluating what he had learned from the American when the first of his bleary-eyed guests arrived for strong coffee an hour later. He'd have to follow up on the information and find out how serious the American's contacts in Tirana might be—enough for someone to come looking if he disappeared?

Reby had been following the vehicle for some time.

Shortly after sunrise he'd seen them "help" the American get out of the hotel and shove him into the rear of a new black German SUV, which sped off. It seemed his boss had been overconfident, but Reby was convinced he'd eventually recover, if he got to him before they got to their destination in the mountains. He wondered if his boss would be able to walk, or if he'd have to carry him. He hoped to find out soon.

Reby knew the roads, so waited just long enough for them to get ahead before pulling out and driving quickly to the main intersection. He pulled expertly around a massive transport, and then tucked in behind another vehicle when he saw Bega's SUV a few cars ahead. It looked like there were three of them, including the driver. He maintained a constant pattern—speeding up whenever they disappeared around bends or over hills, and then slowing down and allowing them to gain some distance when he spotted them. He knew that it was unlikely he could make his move until after Gjirokaster. There'd be too much traffic before that to set his plan in action, but he'd have to do it before they joined up with others or got close to the mountains east of Vlora.

He'd had another conversation with the guard after midnight, when he knew the man would be feeling particularly left out, hearing all the celebrating from the hotel party each time the doors opened and closed. The festivities even had Reby wanting to forget all this business and join in the revelry, but he owed the American a lot. The special operations training had been critical in keeping him alive, mainly the lessons on anticipating your adversary's next move. The most important lesson, though, had been to expect the unexpected when carefully laid plans didn't quite work out.

"So where you from?" he'd asked, emerging from his car to share another smoke.

"Not from here." The man was still reluctant to talk but accepted the cigarette when it was offered. The door to the hotel opened and the music drifted over.

"Sounds pretty good in there," Reby said. "Someday I'm going to have a party—big tent, enough good food for everyone, cooked by real chefs, a live band—that's how we do it where I'm from."

"And where's that?"

"Just outside Durrës. We'll have it on the beach in the summer, so people can swim and cool off after all the dancing." He almost believed it himself, and looked up at the November sky as he waited for a reply.

"In the mountains, we wait until spring, when everything is green." The guard allowed himself to be caught up in the wishing game. "We'll slaughter a lamb, maybe a few depending on how the winter has been. Have you had lamb that is only a day or two old? So tender."

Reby ignored his revulsion and probed a bit. "Mountain spring comes late, no? We can swim in May, it's so warm."

"Not in Lapardha. But we're not that far from the coast."

Reby knew the place; it was near the site of one of his first operations after he'd been recruited. The town on the leeward side of the mountains above Vlora offered an ideal location for a base—isolated but accessible by the road north of Gjirokaster. Was that when he'd seen this man for the first time? He reached into his jacket and pulled out a small bottle, which he pretended to drink from. "Ahh, that's good." He looked at the guard. "You'll have to try some tomorrow when you're not on duty." He was about to tip it to his mouth again but saw the other man look around quickly and gesture for the bottle. "Really?" Reby handed it over. It was excellent Scotch, and expensive.

It was empty within a few minutes. Reby kept up the chatter, learning that the guard's brother was Bega's main driver, and that they kept a few cars in reserve up near his hometown, far from inquisitive passersby. The American would be very interested in this and some of the other details. It had been part of their original plan to find out as much as possible at the party—information was power, and all of it could be useful. If not for now, then maybe later.

As the SUV ahead turned onto the main road to Gjirokaster, Reby hoped he was right and that Bega's men were heading for Lapardha, likely their other operations base. A few stretches of road might be suited for his manoeuvre before the mountain turnoff. The road had been widened through this section, with shoulders on either side making it possible to pull over. He just had to keep those in the vehicle ahead from knowing they were being followed, and hope that there wouldn't be much traffic. There were enough places to choose from to allow him to bide his time. So far, they didn't seem to know he was tailing them, and no one back at the hotel knew that he was with the American. Even under duress, Reby knew the American had been well trained to withstand interrogation, and unlikely to reveal his presence. It was something he was counting on.

———— ⟫⟨●⟩⟪ ————

Bega smiled and nodded to his guests as they appeared, all going immediately for the strong steam-pressed coffee at the bar as the morning shifted to afternoon. He'd provided everything for his guests' late breakfasts, and wandered around the tables extending best wishes to those getting ready to leave. As he stood at the entryway and watched the Greeks make their way down to their car, it struck him like a flash. He was getting old and stupid. Okay, maybe he had a lot on his mind—the party, the meetings, and making sure Victor was keeping track of those guests he was still unsure about—but how could he have overlooked the obvious?

The American had told him a lot of things: He'd arrived from Vienna after hearing that Bega's plans to expand his southern investments involved meeting all the regional heads at a gathering in Saranda. He'd used his former credentials to gain access and the recent New York attacks to get assistance from other Western embassy staff. And he'd maybe even recruited some of the expats working for the Austrians and Germans. But Bega had no idea how the man had travelled down to Saranda. The drugs worked well, there was no doubt, but the questions had to be specific, and Bega hadn't asked about his trip! He might have driven himself, that was what he hoped, but how likely was that? Otherwise, he had to have come with a driver, and maybe a few extra staff, though more men would likely have attracted attention.

They would need to find the car.

He turned back into the hotel and retrieved his cell phone. "Victor, we might have a problem." He tried to think of the name of that driver the American had recruited when he'd first arrived. He was an Albanian who had shown his worth when driving for the American on an early outing. Then he'd been trained with the KFOR special operations group—there had been a fuss about training a local, but the American had had the authority to push it through. "Have you talked to your guys?" Bega got a bad feeling as he listened to Victor's progress report. "So they already left Gjirokaster? How far are they from the turnoff?"

14

GJIROKASTER CITADEL IS an imposingly massive structure, and our stop there would be a welcome break for stretching our legs and having real coffee. After this we'd continue on the main road back to Tirana, bypassing Vlora to rejoin the route we'd taken south at Fier. Then we'd just retrace the coast road back towards Durrës, and turn inland to the capital.

Construction of the castle and its encircling walls and towers was completed in the thirteenth century, and then the Ottomans captured it. The Turkish invaders made it a regional stronghold that would dominate the area for hundreds of years. The citadel plays an important role in *Chronicle In Stone,* a novel about everyday life from the 1930s until the end of World War II. The story—told from the point of view of a young Albanian boy from one of the major Gjirokaster families—is a cloaked critique of Hoxha's postwar communist regime, and was written by Ismail Kadare, a native of the city and the only successful novelist during this repressive period.

We walked up towards the main gateway and, before the

entrance, paid another small fee to see the "war museum." A dark entryway led to a damp central room, likely the fortress' dungeon. There were a few broken tanks and military hardware pieces, but no names, or specifics on their ages. Really they were just broken pieces of artillery; some might be World War I vintage, others fairly recent. At the very back, the daylight leaking through the doorway revealed a well-preserved seventies-era Maserati sports car, which was most interesting to me. It was dusty and hadn't moved for a while, but the tires weren't flat—possibly the local mafia chief's undeclared trophy?

⸺•((◉))•⸺

Ariyan had been telling me a little about the Albanian car market in Tirana, though his initial version of events lacked specifics—he thought that newcomers had to be "protected" from the realities of the local situation. The high-end German and Italian makes that appeared on the streets were often illegally obtained vehicles, but there was currently no problem driving them within the country. Eventually I learned that new cars were made available through insurance fraud and collusion with customs—this new information was gradually disclosed as Ariyan became more comfortable with me, knowing I wouldn't overreact. Revealing aspects of the underground economy was a long process for him, almost a confession about his country. He'd start a subject, but then stop just as it was getting interesting—"Sorry, Tony, I just remember something"—leaving me wondering how much was true until I received corroboration from another source. In the case of illegal vehicles, an article in the *Sunday Times* detailed a picture of the car market outside Durrës. Even when I followed him out onto the balcony, where he'd go after "remember something," he'd feign ignorance as to what we'd been discussing, taking deep draws on a cigarette and smiling weakly, often brushing ashes from his shirt. It turns out that Ariyan's own car was actually illegal, something I learned from our finance manager. The fact that he had survived Albania's recent history and still retained a friendly attitude towards outsiders said much about his contacts but more about his character. He was working in a much sought-after job with the Austrians, despite all that had happened to him and his family, but was still willing to help me out when needed, and in a friendly way. I was hoping he'd eventually trust me enough to open up on all his edited versions of events.

The best story he told me—he'd referred to the event off-handedly at first, and added more details later—concerned the Saudi financing of buildings in the capital. He'd previously told me about the nearly unused green mosques that I'd seen around the country when I'd asked about the Muslim population. It was shortly after the events of September 11, 2001, in New York, when we were travelling to one of our operation sites. En route he mentioned a financier who'd gotten Saudi money to build two office towers in Tirana.

Our office was on the third floor of a brand new twenty-storey building, the tallest "skyscraper" in the capital. Four months after my arrival in Tirana, my wife telephoned me and told me to find a television because live feed was showing the World Trade Center on fire from an airplane collision. Curious, I'd walked across to the general manager's office in time to see the second airliner strike the buildings. Ariyan was right behind me, and there was a brief discussion on our building height and whether our frequent flights to Vienna would be affected. As the days passed and the al-Qaeda and Osama bin Laden connection was made with the terrorist attack, I noticed Ariyan and some of the other staff talking and looking out of the back windows of our office, at another building's concrete foundations, which looked abandoned. I'd asked him about the water-filled concrete and re-bar structure when I'd first arrived, but he'd shrugged the question away. Stacks of bricks and bags of ruined cement lay haphazardly around the site, which penetrated just above ground level, though the construction footprint was nearly the same as our building's.

"Tony, this crap building you ask about," he said, as we drove on the highway to Vlora at the end of the week that changed the world, "you know, behind our office, much water and spills of concrete." Seeing my uncertainty, he added, "You ask me why no work to finish building. Is because big financier is from al-Qaeda."

He had my attention now, but I waited for him to say more. I'd seen no evidence of Islam in the capital, other than the central mosque that Hoxha had allowed to remain as a tourist attraction. Ariyan had also told me that nobody went to the mosques.

"Tony, you know Saudis send money for mosques. Saudi money also used for new buildings. Albanian business man gets Saudi money for making construction company, hires workers. They build our office tower."

"Yes, Ariyan, but what about the 'crap' building?"

"Can I smoke?"

"Okay, but open the window." Was he going to say anything more? I looked at him as he concentrated on the cigarette. We were travelling fast, and nearly all the smoke was drawn out the window. As I waited, the big wad of Albanian currency banknotes in my pocket pressed against my leg. Everything was paid for in cash here, since there were no credit card companies. I had withdrawn the lek money from petty cash for our trip, which meant enough for meals, diesel, and two nights in a hotel in Vlora. The two-inch lump was irritating and marked me as the money man when I walked around trying to conceal the wad.

"Tony, is criminal this man." He was making his best effort to explain. "Many terrorists come here because they think we are Islam country."

The general manager had told me that in 1998 the Americans had assisted in apprehending a few Egyptians working for Islamic charities in Albania, after they were charged with the killing of tourists at the Luxor archeological site in Egypt. "But that stopped, right?" I asked. "The Americans stopped them."

He looked over to me with a wan smile. "Now they go to Kosovo Liberation Army in Kosovo. Also, Americans and Saudis are friends so maybe they look away? Remember, Bin Laden is also Saudi. But maybe this changes now—after New York attacks." He looked away, and then back. "Yes, financier afraid because money helps al-Qaeda, then leaves country before Americans can make arrest. So building stopped, now only wet foundation and cement bags."

That explained why he was talking with the others in the office and all of them were looking out the back windows. Okay, but he believed that the builder was from al-Qaeda and was implying that our office was connected to bin Laden? It seemed a bit over the top, and I waited for more.

"Tony, we stop? I need toilet."

———— ◦((◉))◦ ————

Back outside in the fresh air and sunlight, after the dark dungeon "museum," we climbed up the rampart stairs to the central part of Gjirokaster's citadel, passing the remains of an authentic 1950s American fighter jet. The outer aluminum/steel shell rested on top of one of the walls, but the engine and most other internal parts were gone. The vaguely American markings were just visible on the delta-shaped wings. Possibly an early version of an F-86 Sabre, it was labelled as a spy plane, and provided proof for Hoxha that Western Europe and the Americans were readying for an invasion. At the top of the stairs, a few big-muscled concrete statues with tiny heads were scattered around a courtyard. There were several other monuments in the same socialist-realist tradition, but most were broken or defaced.

The ramparts looked out over the "city of stone roofs" as it was called in the few guidebooks available, but many of the stone rooftops we could see had partially collapsed. The major characteristic of stone is, of course, its weight, and a roof made of stone needs to be continually maintained using material of the right shape and size. Collapsed roofs in Hoxha's hometown mirrored his flawed logic that his ideas were more important than the realities—a lesson other idealists of the world needed to heed.

We backtracked to our vehicle after finding a kiosk for drinks and biscuits and soon were out of the city, heading north on a patchily surfaced road. The highway was now back to two lanes, and after thirty kilometres we passed through Ali Pasha's hometown, Tepelena. The district was famous for its spring, from which our locally bottled water originated. The archaic logo and pseudo-English description was unique but unclear: "Suffle as it gush from the waters of Tepelena." We wondered if "suffle" was an attempt at "soft." The new owners, Coca Cola, would soon replace it to match the modern look of other bottlers.

This was progress, at least on the commercial front.

The road weaved across the open countryside, and we followed valleys offering views of small plots of agricultural land, usually subsistence farms near small clay-brick dwellings, often with a small field set aside for tobacco. Careful driving was necessary in a few spots, the roadbed having settled into abrupt depressions, but it was generally fine. At one point we were overtaken by a black German sedan, and a few minutes later a familiar red Mercedes blew by, nearly running us off the road—it appeared out of nowhere and sounded as if it had lost its muffler.

When the black vehicle entered Gjirokaster, Reby was not far behind, and so he saw it turn off the main road several blocks past the citadel and drive down a long, narrow street. He parked past the turnoff in an empty lot that allowed him a good view of the turnoff and the vehicles on the road. He walked back to the narrow street and stopped by a gas station to ask the attendant if the premium gasoline pump was operating.

"I'll start the generator for you."

"Not yet, I need to bring my car over, but you can tell me where that street goes." Reby pointed towards the narrow road.

"Nowhere, it ends at the big stone house. There is only a path into the hills behind it."

"So a car must come out the same way?"

"Exactly."

Shortly after 1:30, he saw the black SUV nose out into the street and turn towards Fier. As it passed him, where he was parked in the shadows near the gas station, he saw the driver and a passenger in the front. Another man was in the back, likely with the American—Reby glimpsed a slumped head near the other rear door. He attached his seat belt and started the Mercedes. The gas station attendant looked up at the sound of the throaty exhausts. The motor was quiet at normal speed, but the tuned exhaust pipes would crackle if he pushed the accelerator all the way to the floor. He did this briefly, engaging the dynamic compressor to make sure the motor was primed, and then allowed several vehicles to go by before joining the road.

———— ⊙ ————

"Who is it?" asked the driver of the SUV. They had left Gjirokaster and were nearly halfway to the mountain road turnoff when the cell phone rang once. He looked over to his front-seat passenger.

"I think it was Victor," his passenger replied. He looked more closely at the phone before continuing. "Yeah, missed call, but the reception is terrible along here." He looked into the back seat at his partner, and then across to the slumped figure that was their cargo.

"Victor can be such a—" His phone buzzed with a text message. "That's interesting. Victor says to keep 'a very careful watch' for anything suspicious. It might be that our man here"—he gestured to the back seat—"has friends who might try something."

The driver looked in the rear-view mirror at the big Nissan they had just passed on a long stretch of nearly straight road. "That's interesting? What else does he think we're doing? Stopping to pick flowers?" He slowed for a sharp bend ahead. As they came out of the corner and picked up speed, he could see another long stretch, and then they'd just have a few more kilometres until their turnoff.

———— ⊙ ————

Reby came out of the bend and glimpsed the shiny black SUV entering another bend about two kilometres in front.

He'd been following for some time, and the traffic was finally lessening. He was nearly sure that the series of long stretches was ending, and then the winding road would begin just before the turnoff to Lapardha. It was now or never—catch up to them on a straight stretch before they could react.

Grasping the steering wheel firmly, he floored the accelerator and the supercharger came to life, forcing more oxygen into the engine to increase the burn of the high-octane fuel—the car jumped forward and exhaust erupted from the rear. The low-frequency throb reverberated up through the floor and into his legs and upper body as the sound bellowed across the landscape. He backed off for the corner and the car's muffler tone changed as the engine briefly took a breath and throttled down—but the motor exhaled as he jammed his foot back to the floor midway through the curve, and the blast returned. The car shot out of the bend and flew past a big Nissan that had meandered slightly into the passing lane. The blowback from the near miss and the crackle of exhaust noise stunned the sleepy driver, who looked up and nearly lost his grip on the steering wheel, but by then Reby was into the next corner.

Barely keeping the car under control as he came out of the bend, Reby saw the target less than a kilometre in front. He had to catch them just as they were going into the upcoming corner. He thundered down the last stretch knowing the vehicle in front would soon react to his presence.

PETER J. MEEHAN

The SUV driver looked up to the sky when he heard the rumble. He was about to look out the side windows for storm clouds—it had been a clear, sunny day when they'd left Gjirokaster—but first he slowed for the upcoming left bend. There was sudden movement in the rear-view mirror, and a flash of red coming up on his left. The thought of encountering some crazy young driver out for a thrill evaporated when he realised they were being forced off the road, and at considerable speed.

In the back seat, just before the impact, the American stirred from his drugged trance, recognising a familiar sound that he'd counted on hearing again, and he felt around for his seat belt. In front, the driver was overwhelmed—the deafening exhaust, and then the amplified grating scour of metal-on-metal contact as the red car's strengthened front bumper ground along the driver's side, forcing the SUV towards the shoulder. The vehicle's rear window burst into glass cracks under the strain. The rubber tires tore at the pavement's edge, screeching in protest before the driver felt the right wheels slide off the road. The intense shuddering subsided on the gravelly shoulder, and dust filled the air as the top-heavy SUV spun around, hit a broken concrete pillar, and banged back down on all four wheels after nearly upending.

15

AFTER GETTING THE Nissan back under control, I slowed down and made certain we remained on our side of the road's centre line, at least where the faded paint was still visible. I must have lost concentration for just a second, but the close call certainly woke me up. Minutes later, we saw the vehicles pulled over on the shoulder in a haze of dust, with the big black SUV turned around to face the red car that had just overtaken us. We passed them on a bend, and I could catch only a quick glimpse of the scene, but a determined figure was crouched behind the back of the red car looking over to the other vehicle. It was unclear what he was holding in his hand, but it was black. And he was holding it like he would hold a handgun.

We didn't slow down; I wasn't looking for obvious trouble, and a third encounter was overdoing it for a weekend. Still, the man hadn't looked up as we passed, so I might have driven back to have a better look if the family hadn't been with me. He might have been a plainclothes policeman, but I'd seen plenty of crazy driving and only rare police interventions in the country, usually involving heavy trucks or peasants in small vehicles with farm animals seemingly too large to fit through the doors. Most likely it was a meeting, either planned or spur of the moment; because I'd seen the car in Tirana, I wondered if any Americans could be involved, but that seemed far-fetched. It was also possible that a reckoning was taking place between rivals, similar to the Tirana shootout earlier in the year that the consul had told me about.

Reby backed off once the bigger vehicle slid onto the gravel—he didn't want it to flip, and there was always a chance that too much contact could lock the two vehicles, causing him to lose control as well. He jammed on the emergency brake as he watched the black SUV rotate and smack into a block hidden in the long grass before rocking back and settling in the dust, and he was out the door with his handgun by the time his car had slid to a stop. He left the door open and, using it as a shield, backed to the rear of his car, where he stopped to see if there was any movement in the other vehicle. There was silence except for the sound of hissing—a punctured tire or a cracked radiator leaking fluid under pressure. He hoped it was the other vehicle, but now was not the time to check.

He vaguely heard a vehicle pass on the road. He refocused and ran over in a crouch to reach the rear door on the passenger side of the SUV—the side where he'd seen the slumped figure when the vehicle passed him in Gjirokaster—and tugged at the door. It finally opened with a loud metallic scrape, and the American's head fell forward, but his body was stopped by the seat belt. Someone groaned in the front seat. The other rear-seat passenger, who was pitched forward, had blood across his oddly tilted face.

Reby reached back and shoved his gun into his pants. Then he leaned forward, undid the seat belt, pulled out the American, and proceeded to half drag, half carry him back to the red car. To his surprise, the man attempted to move his feet in step, and blathered something unintelligible into his ear. Reby opened his rear passenger door and pushed the American in before running around to the driver's side to better pull him into the back seat. He attached the seat belts to the horizontal figure as best he could, and quickly looked again to the other vehicle before doing a quick check of his car. The tires were fine, and he could spray over the scratches and deep scrapes on the passenger side at his next stop. It would be easy to patch the flat-red paint with spray cans he kept in the trunk.

They were on their way quickly, passing the turnoff to the mountains after less than five kilometres. As he slowed to his normal excessive speed, the engine quieted—*no sense in attracting attention*, he thought. He'd need all the gas in case he had to hole up somewhere for a bit. Right now, they needed to get as far away from Bega's territory as they could, before word got out. He might have an hour, at most, to get past Fier. Bega could still catch them there, but beyond Fier, it was unlikely he'd have the influence to bring them back, even if he knew where they were. But Fier might be more than an hour on this winding road where speed just wasn't a real option, and if they ran into any heavy trucks to slow them, they wouldn't be able to get there in time to go on to Tirana.

He rounded a corner and could see far ahead to a long, slow line of traffic. A black puff at the front of the line indicated a big diesel transport gearing down as it laboured up the hill. Well, his decision had been made for him. He'd have to turn east and avoid Fier, so there'd likely be no police, but there'd be bad roads—tracks, really. Thinking quickly, he realised that wasn't a good option either as it might mean getting stuck. *Okay*, he thought, *but what about all the old back roads around Fier?* These had been built for access to the oil-fields, and he was almost certain he could turn off before the city and get over to the main eastern road, which then swung north and would allow them to get back to Tirana. Maybe they should even avoid Tirana, cut east to Elbasan, and head for the border. There was a good road to Macedonia, despite its ongoing reconstruction, but it would take time to get to the turnoff and much longer to get past the roadworks. Would it be best to stop somewhere for the night and wait, or go for the border if he got around Fier? The roads had many unmarked dangers with all the construction, so night driving was usually to be avoided. There would also be wandering livestock, and people who didn't want to be seen, driving blacked-out vehicles, but he'd have to take the chance if it meant getting to a safe haven.

"What is it?" Bega looked up as the door opened. He didn't like to be interrupted in these meetings and had already ignored his buzzing phone.

Victor stood back from the partially opened door, his face lacking expression.

"Excuse me, just a moment." Bega stood and went to the door, which he closed behind him. He turned to Victor and said, "Bad news, I guess."

"Yes. They were driven off the road, and the new SUV needs repairs before it can be driven. Your driver called it in. He was the only one wearing a seat belt. One of the other two is badly hurt. The American is gone." He waited for a response, then added, "Our guys from Gjirokaster are on their way, and also a car from Lapardha."

"Well, that's good, at least." Bega pulled out his phone and saw his driver had left a message. He played back the wavering voice, clearly still in shock. *Padron, we were hit by a big red SUV that badly damaged the car. I am very sorry to tell you the American was taken. We need help, will call Victor.*

Bega thought through several scenarios, most of which he discarded. Finally, he looked up. "Okay, first, I want our police contacts to look out for a red vehicle and ask everyone here if they saw one hanging around." He thought back to the driver's description. "Ardy thought it was an SUV, but I want any red vehicle south of Tirana to be looked at for damage. As for our vehicle, someone else can see to it. Let's get Ardy back here. I want to talk to him when he gets in."

"You think he fucked up?"

"Not good to speculate, but let's talk to him, find out everything. Maybe he saw more than he's saying." Bega liked his driver but knew how people reacted under fire. "He's a good driver, not a shooter. Was he conscious when they took the American?"

"That's a good point."

"I think they'll go north as fast as they can. We might catch them in Fier if you can get the police to cooperate."

Victor smiled. "It was the first call I made after getting our guys out to Ardy and the car."

"Good. One more thing—let's try and contact that Serb with the long-distance equipment. We'll need a specialist for this."

"The sniper?" His voice was loud, and there were others in hearing distance. He looked over to them, and lowered his voice as they turned away. "Don't you think they'll head for the border if they can't get through Fier? Would we still want the Serb if they're out of the country?"

"How would they do that?" Bega tried to think about the possible routes they'd take. "There aren't many options they can take between here and Fier, but we need to be prepared." For a minute he wondered if they might circle back and try to cross into Greece, but realised that would be foolhardy, taking any southern route right through Bega's territory. Unless they thought Bega wouldn't expect it. "We need to tell our friends on the Greek border crossings to be on the lookout."

"Sure." Victor still looked uncertain. "Weren't there some problems with the Serb's last job?"

Bega had heard that, but also that there had been extenuating circumstances. They needed someone quickly, and he knew the man was available. They could make a final decision after meeting him. "He'll have something to prove then, won't he?"

The big Albanian was a man who planned things out in detail, looking at any possibilities that might come up—maybe the Serb wasn't up to the task, but there were other matters to look into, once they managed to deal with the American and his rescuers. He only had contacts in Tirana, no operational abilities to deal with possible loose ends, thanks to all the EU interference. His connections would likely be good enough to find out who else might be involved with the American. The hard part would be getting something done about it, when his power base was restricted to the south of the country.

16

THE BRIGHT, WARM day made up for having to get up early on a Sunday, and I was quite impressed by the ruins at Butrint, even though I hadn't had a coffee. My dad had said we could get some breakfast before we went into the site, but he was wrong—there was still no power. Not having electricity was a pain, but the locals were probably used to it. Maybe they didn't have many electric gadgets, other than coffee makers and cell phones. We settled for fresh buns from a shop that must use charcoal or gas. Then we found soft drinks and bread crisps, a Balkan specialty and surprisingly tasty, on the hilltop above the ruins. By that time, I'd seen enough Roman baths, statues, and columns to last for the whole trip, but the double-headed eagle flag on top of the citadel reminded me of the carving on one of the Theresianum doors. It was attached at just the right height to allow you to grab hold of one of the two heads to slam the big door, like when you were angry, or sometimes just because you felt like it—something I started doing when I used the stairs. Then one of my least favourite Austrian supervisors caught me doing it and made it into a big deal.

It wasn't long after I got to the Theresianum that Giselle first showed me some of the old palace's neat features, including the door with the carving that was near the top of a wide set of really neat stairs. The stairs were once part of the main entrance, but they used to change everything around every few hundred years, so the stairs were now closer to the back. Best thing about this was I could come and go without being seen if I used them, so that's what I'd been doing for my meetings with Malik.

It was unusual to see anyone on the back stairs, so I was surprised to meet a teacher that day. Prune-face had looked up from below as I became the princess and swirled down the dusty staircase's beautiful spiral to where the wicked witch was waiting. She grabbed my arm when I got down and spoke in a voice that could have come from a bad movie before marching me to our boarding supervisor, who was told of the "incident." I understood that the *auslander*, meaning me, the foreigner, had tried to destroy a part of the Austrian nation's cultural heritage.

My supervisor listened to this wild story while I thought about the teacher's expression. The Viennese were really good at doing these horrible faces when they didn't like something, but loads of them were always scowling, probably so they wouldn't have to smile. Of course, Giselle and I practised making these faces for hours in front of the mirror, but we just couldn't hold them long enough and ended up killing ourselves laughing. I was really looking forward to telling Giselle about prune-face's latest, and waited as she finished her report. There was silence as she looked from my supervisor to me and turned to leave, but not before she

PETER J. MEEHAN

tossed a final look my way, meaning her colleague had better deal with this *kriminelle Aktivitäten*.

My housemistress was hesitant. "Michaela . . ." She stopped, waiting for her colleague to be out of hearing distance. "I know you don't think much of the other teachers, but you are very fortunate to be staying here as a boarder. It is a former imperial palace, and you really must remember that the furnishings and decorations are historically very important, even if they are no longer in as good a condition as they once were." She gave me a long stare that slowly softened, but I remained quiet. "I know it must be hard living in a strange city and having to go elsewhere for your classes, but is there something bothering you right now, in particular?"

For a moment, because she wasn't really Viennese, I almost blurted out the whole truth right there—everything about Malik and meeting him, and then how strange Albania was and that Hitler was really Austrian, but nobody here knew that, or if they did, they pretended it wasn't true . . . I didn't though, knowing she really was Viennese and that it could mean waaay too much trouble for everyone, maybe even Giselle. For some reason, I almost started crying, and then I said I was sorry and told her I wouldn't do anything like that again, though I wasn't sure which part I meant. I wasn't going to change, just maybe take more care with the Austrian heritage stuff.

At Butrint, after I mentioned how much the Albanian and Austro-Hungarian eagles looked the same, my father prattled on for a while about it and made a bad joke. Maybe he was trying to educate us by taking us to unusual places and showing us things, but he often talked too much, or thought he was witty. I'd started to see he wasn't funny, even if he could make my younger brothers and sister laugh. My mother had been ignoring his bad jokes for a while.

I found the castle in Gjirokaster to be massively creepy, unlike Butrint. It didn't help that it was cloudy when we arrived, but it was more than that. With its mix of old guns, an American jet that didn't have an engine, broken concrete statues, and weird monuments that didn't look right, it struck me as a broken mishmash of stuff that didn't seem to be part of the real world. My dad said the concrete statues and monuments were built by communism. This "socialist art" was just big, ugly, and stupid looking. The old castle was like a big dungeon with dark corners. We went inside a museum under the main entry but I left right away because it was cold and smelly. So much for this historical monument—I stayed outside and the sun came out and warmed me up.

As I was sitting there, a group of teenagers my age walked by, and one of the boys looked back at me. They were dressed like Italians: expensive clothes, snazzy leather shoes that were pointy-toed, and the girls had short skirts and heels and were wearing lots of jewellery and makeup. They were like some of the rich kids I'd see in Vienna at school, kind of loud and pointing at each other, except these guys were laughing and better dressed. I wondered if their fathers were in the mafia or the government, or if there might even be another way to get money in this poor country.

My phone buzzed and I saw that it was one of my Albanian friends. I'd met her through one of the guys in my class when I went to school in Tirana. She wanted to know if I'd be back in time for the party that she'd invited me to.

The family was still in the castle, so I texted her that I'd be there. My phone buzzed again, just as the Albanian teenagers came back along the path on top of the citadel's walls. Even though this time they weren't making any noise, I glanced up because I could feel someone looking at me, and saw that same guy staring at me the whole time they walked by. It went on for so long that one of the girls pushed him hard to knock him off balance, and then she looked at me as if to say, *He's mine!* Or maybe I was imagining it. Still, it made me feel good that he was looking at me, and then I read the text, another one from my Albanian friend—she had someone she wanted me to meet at the party. I looked up and out over the old town, and the sunshine made it look friendlier, and by the time my family came walking up the pathway, everything seemed a lot better.

The road back to Tirana was mostly smooth so we were able to go fast, but one car nearly crashed into us as it went by, and my dad slowed down, which was good because there were a lot of corners after that.

17

I DROVE MORE carefully through the hills on the winding road south of Fier. We joined the coastal route again in
the city after passing by our favourite gas station, but nobody
wanted to stop—the novelty of the fabled clean public toilet had worn off, and stopping just meant another delay in
getting back home. As we entered the city, we were waved
through a police checkpoint, as usual, as were nearly all the
vehicles, and then through another one being erected at the
main intersection. On the roadside, a policeman was talking
to a man leaning out of the window of his bright red Ford
transit van, while a multihued delivery truck with garish orange and pink advertising waited behind. From here we continued north, retracing our Saturday route towards Durrës.

We passed unmarked historical sites where the Romans
had fought some of their civil war battles, but I thought everyone had had enough of Albania's checkered past, so I kept
quiet, and the plain where Pompey enjoyed his only victory
over Caesar went unnoticed by the vehicle's other passengers.
The roadside was dotted with more than the usual number
of small concrete bunkers that also littered the shoreline and

nearby hills; they were often piled together, partially buried or painted as red polka-dotted mushrooms. On one particular stretch of road near the coast, several lined the cliff and more had toppled into the sea. The entire country had come together to build these symbols of a broken society. They were difficult to get rid of—only a very hot fire could weaken the hard rock surface enough to break them up. There were a few piles of blackened and broken concrete where this had been attempted, symbolising the ruin and failure of broken ideas like nothing else could.

We stopped for a leg stretch on the extensive beach south of Durrës—I'd noticed the two boys had stopped reading their books, which probably meant they were starting to feel car sick, though they would never admit it. The coast here was open and fresh, and looked to be a garbage-free spot, except for the small ridge near the sea's high-water mark. The crest was only noticeable when we stepped over it, a linear overgrown hump separating the windswept sand from the cars parked amid tall shade trees. I'd seen the same thing several times on other trips to the beach before poking at it with a stick and realising it was mainly plastic refuse gathered and compacted by winter storms on this section of the coast; it had been accumulating since capitalism's entry into the country.

Before commercial business or foreign aid arrived, there had been no water bottles, or excess glass, plastic bags, or other consumer by-products that would produce nonbiodegradable waste—plastic and metal garbage was unheard of in Hoxha's utopian nightmare. A few consumer goods might have been trickling in as the postwar boom started in

Western Europe, but when communism collapsed, the cultural shock to Albania's inhabitants must have been overwhelming—to go from a totally isolated, tightly controlled Stalinist "economy" to capitalism. Even assuming some minor smuggling was going on near the sealed Greek border and across the Adriatic from Italy, the government's demise and the resulting opening of borders would have exposed the country to the Western world of rampant consumerism. This onslaught might have contributed to the political and economic upheavals that occurred throughout the nineties, during Albania's needed adjustment period that was much longer than most of Eastern Europe's. A major change in attitude was still needed to manage the increasing influx of garbage.

While Michaela, my wife, and I ambled along the sunny shore, enjoying the lovely Mediterranean weather that can uplift a November outing, the other children kept running off and then flying back around us until our youngest daughter fell and needed attention. Then she joined us, and the four of us walked more closely together after a gust of wind scattered the sand in front of us. The two boys came back around us and gave a whoop of excitement as they ran to chase the wind, and were soon followed by their youngest sister, now fully recovered. The sun was warm and the family was just as cosy.

As we started back for the car, Michaela, who had been chattering away to her mother, grew quiet. She was nearly a young woman now—I could see the way she was carrying herself as she walked—but one who had experienced more lifestyle changes than others her age. I thought she was probably missing her older friend from Vienna, and my heart went out to her. Maybe it was a good thing she had met this young man. Despite my reservations, it could be an enjoyable evening out with him and my daughter.

Back on the highway, I opted for the old road east between the coast and Tirana, rather than the new autostrada. It had been a while since I'd been on it and was curious if there'd been any changes. We passed derelict factories and vandalised farm collectives from old five-year plans, and small villages where children were playing in the dirt. They looked up and waved as we drove past. Entire fields of smashed greenhouses evidenced the country's break with its communist past. During the periods of mayhem since the end of Hoxha's regime, the modernising of Albania's agriculture had been shattered in a mistaken attempt to restart the economy. Along with the greenhouses, all the orchards had been destroyed and other communist-led agrarian efforts ended. With the exception of the traditional Mediterranean olive groves, which needed decades to develop, there was a general belief that capitalism was the answer but needed to begin with a clean slate. This belief encouraged the population to dismantle and destroy anything tainted by the former communist government.

Near the airport road junction, we finally joined the main highway, which would take us back into Tirana in time for an evening meal. A downed power line crossing the highway had delayed traffic, but by the time we got to the spot, a quick fix had been rigged, and a pole with a cross at the top held the power line above the traffic flow. As we approached, I considered not going under the live wire in case it fell, but justified continuing—we'd have to backtrack several hours to avoid the spot. I also reasoned that our rubber tires would prevent any electrical conduction. That was *almost certainly* true, but I knew that I was gradually making these kinds of reckless decisions more frequently. My justifications of foolhardy behaviour like this should have warned me that my former rational thinking process was being undermined by frequent exposure to local solutions to potentially dangerous occurrences—in other words, everyone else was making a less-than-ideal solution work, so why would I continue to be the only one inconvenienced?

Michaela was breathless when we got back to our apartment, announcing she only needed a few minutes to get ready for her party. Everyone else was tired. Looking expectant, she appeared in front of me just as I sat down to relax. I stood, thinking she wanted me to drive her.

Michaela rolled her eyes and shook her head. "No, Dad. It's just around the corner." She turned towards her mother, who was still busy in the kitchen setting out something to eat on the counter. In an exasperated tone Michaela said, "Well, what do you think?"

"Honey, you look great," my wife answered. Looking again, I saw Michaela had completely changed her outfit and she did look more mature. "Should one of us walk you over?" her mother added, looking at me as I sat down again.

"That would be nice, *Mom*."

Good, I thought, taking her reply to mean that I didn't need to go. I had some thinking to do about work the next day and how best to find out more about Mr. Brown and his plans. I wanted more background information from the consulate on why they had contacted me prior to our week-end jaunt.

My wife was back a short time later. "I'm not so sure about that party. Michaela didn't want me to come in, but it seemed really loud. I don't think there were any parents there. I told her not to be late."

"There's probably an adult there who doesn't mind the noise." My reassurance was really to keep her from worrying, but I also knew from experience that loud music was regarded as a necessary part of a celebration by everyone in the former communist states. Indoor or outdoor gatherings were accompanied by noisy sound, often unrecognisable as music because of the level of distortion caused by cheap speakers. The new capitalists had yet to realise the difference between quality and quantity.

Michaela arrived back late, after we had all gone to bed. She stuck her head in our room breathing heavily with excitement, but I was nearly asleep.

18

"TONY." MY BOSS motioned me into his office with one hand, distracted by the phone conversation he was having.

"Was? Was meinst du damit Sie nicht können?" He listened, looked up at me in exasperation, and then attempted to calm down before giving the caller instructions. He eventually put his hand over the phone and turned his attention to me.

"We need to do the following," he said, and gave me a series of tasks from his mental checklist, using project management jargon. These "essential" steps were likely to ensure our asses were covered, his more than mine. He then turned back to his phone, a sign that he would ignore any questions or response I might have. It was an accepted Austrian method of communication, but not a recognised MBO (management by objectives) approach, as the company mistakenly supposed.

Back in my office, I got started on the list. When I needed a break, I called my cousin in Vienna. As I waited for the call to connect, a slight odour of tobacco drifted into my office through the open window. Ariyan had tried hiding on the balcony since arriving to avoid our general manager, but I'd told him what we needed. The secretary would have signalled him that there was responsibility coming with a special lift of the eyebrows towards her boss's office. I knew because she did the same with me, but I usually ignored it.

"Celine, it's Tony." The phone line was very clear for a Monday morning.

"Tony, how was the trip?" She sounded bright and breezy. Vienna coffee worked wonders for clearing weekend residue from the mind. "Is Butrint as good as they say?"

"Fine, Celine, but I wanted to ask you about your friend."

There was a hesitation. "My *friend?*"

I didn't say anything, knowing that silence would be more effective than "reminding" her about something she wouldn't have forgotten.

Her voice was guarded when she eventually spoke. "Well, actually . . . listen, Tony, are you on your cell?" She cut me off before I could answer. "It doesn't matter. I'll call you back in an hour on your office line."

I looked out of my window to the street below and started counting cars. Seven of the ten vehicles passing by were Mercedes, but none of them had flat-red paint. It was telling that the favourite German cars were Mercedes, not BMWs. Nearly all the cars were more than ten years old, some more than twenty; this country was filled with historical remnants. The numbers recorded a past in which the best German cars were Mercs, not the new upstarts from Bavaria. I started counting again, wondering how long it would take for something new to surpass the Merc, but then my boss was at my door.

"Did you call them? What did they say?"

"They aren't aware of any problems, but Ariyan is going to the ministry to confirm."

He stepped inside and closed the door. "I know we committed to the survey, but we have to postpone this new project and cancel the Croatian contract work. The embassy is sure the border will close. When that happens, the real problems will start." He gazed past me, out of the window to the outdoor scene, pale in the November light. When he looked back at me, I knew a decision had been made. "You need to put together an evacuation plan for our contractors there." Then he was gone.

Yeah, sure. I'll call the marines and have them stand by. He'd probably put something together himself and then look at my plan and say it was useless. How could I put together a plan to evacuate the mountains of Albania?

I looked at the time and called the consular office in Tirana. The consul wasn't available, so I got back to the original list and made some headway. The evacuation plan could wait. I'd learned that changes in direction were often reversed, so I would postpone the work until I was asked again about it. There was a good chance it would disappear.

The phone rang.

"Tony? Is this a secure line?" Celine sounded conspiratorial. I nearly expected her to start whispering.

"Yes." I said. *It might be.*

"First of all, this isn't official."

Whatever she was about to say, I'd have to keep it to myself if I ever wanted her assistance again, though I was now thinking back to other times she'd contacted me and beginning to wonder if I'd always given her more than I'd received.

"Okay."

She took a deep breath and plunged forward, speaking quickly as though to get it over with. "So we were approached when submitting our budgets for Eastern Europe. Mr. Brown was waiting in Vienna when I finished up with the budget meeting, and he had the ambassador's representative with him, which normally meant approval for whatever undertaking he had in mind."

I interjected. "So did you confirm that?"

Hesitation, and finally, "Indirectly, diplomacy being what it is—and the ambassador was out of the office."

Yes, I almost said, *getting a straight answer from a diplomat is nearly impossible*, but listened instead. Her admitting the shortcomings of diplomacy was unexpected.

"The ambassador's rep introduced Mr. Brown and left us to discuss various issues concerning the Balkans. Mr. Brown had a particular interest in Albania, wondering how far the 9/11 connection might go."

So even Mr. Brown had discussed a 9/11 link in the country. Was it the al-Qaeda financier Ariyan mentioned, or was this a ruse to allow Brown sympathy for better access to in-country resources he didn't have? There had been a worldwide outpouring of compassion for the victims and the US government in the aftermath of the attacks.

"It seemed feasible to me," Celine continued, "and afterwards I checked our database on the country's majority Muslim population and what financial ties there were to Saudi Arabia." She paused. "Thinking it over now, I'm not so sure of his motives, but it was all very rushed. Anyway, there are several Islamic NGOs funded through the Saudis, though most are registered outside Albania's borders, in Kosovo. Not sure what their status is right now. As you know, that border is hardly secure. The area has traditionally been an unofficial extension of Albanian territory for the locals. And the KLA has been active since the NATO airstrikes in Serbia pushed back support for the Serbian minority in Kosovo. But I'm getting off the subject at hand—Brown just *knew* we would be very willing to help in any way we could, as was everyone after the September attacks on American soil. I just can't believe he would take advantage of a terrorist incident to advance his own agenda."

"What was his agenda?" I asked, but she didn't reply. She must have believed here was an opportunity to get ahead, but I sensed she was almost telling me too much—she had to be under a lot of strain. It seemed helping Mr. Brown had hardly been authorized but she had run with it and now realised she had no backup for her actions. And she'd tried to rope me in!

What about the possible terrorist ties according to Brown? That would require an Islamic base in the country. The KLA were mostly ethnic Albanians in Kosovo whom Serbia viewed as terrorists, though Ariyan said real terrorists had been joining them. The NGOs were nongovernment organisations that helped with social and local financial assistance—but providing cover for terrorists? I'd heard all sorts of theories and rumours about Albanian connections to 9/11 since Ariyan first mentioned the financier's ties to al-Qaeda. I still had problems with that assumption, since

PETER J. MEEHAN

the Americans and likely the CIA had stepped up security after helping apprehend and extradite the Egyptian terrorists in 1998.

"Celine, in spite of the published ethnic statistics, the 'Muslims' here whom I've met and talked to aren't practising Islam, and even less true believers in the prophet and the Koran. It's different when you get into the mountains, where families are more isolated, or across the border into Kosovo, where Hoxha's decrees against religion had much less effect. The only Saudi Arabian connection here is money for building mosques that no one attends." I knew Celine was listening to me when she didn't interrupt, so I continued. "They tried setting up schools to indoctrinate the young, but that didn't go over well with the locals, according to my sources." Ariyan had said older Albanians no longer had the respect or knowledge the Saudis needed, and there were no Arabs who had learned Albanian, though it might be different in Kosovo if foreign jihadists were involved. "And how much of the money was actually used in the buildings? I'll bet a lot went into the locals' pockets. Is that the sign of true believers?" I let her think that over without mentioning Ariyan's story about the unfinished building behind our office or the Albanian money man who had disappeared shortly before 9/11—I needed to get our conversation refocused on the mystery man, even if there could be some connection in Kosovo to al-Qaeda. "So whom does Mr. Brown work for? And what do you think his motives are?"

She skirted around my question. "When I met with Mr. Brown, he told me that NATO's focus on the north of the country had put a lot of pressure on the local mafia,

150

or whatever you want to call them, so they moved underground or went elsewhere. He wanted to know where they had gone—his best guess was south. Vlora seems the obvious choice, but the death toll from human smuggling on those flimsy Zodiacs forced the European Union to step in and crack down, threatening to withhold additional development money until the trafficking from Vlora to Italy stopped. So he thought there was too much surveillance in Vlora for much to be going on. Then he asked about our contacts elsewhere in the country—people who were travelling around and able to see, firsthand, what was really happening in the south, closer to the Greek border. He doesn't have much regard for the official EU reports."

Well! So someone had noticed my registering with the consulate for the trip down to Butrint for the weekend. "So you volunteered me?" I asked.

"Not really, but I mentioned you were here, enjoying yourself in Tirana, and often travelled around the country as part of your job. You were obviously willing to take risks when you moved there, since no Western embassies were sending families."

How did that excuse her from using me without telling me the whole story? And enjoying myself in Tirana—is that what she thought? I was only willing to take an acceptable level of risk for myself—it was a lot different if my family was involved. I tried to keep the anger out of my voice when I asked, "Why didn't Brown use his own embassy for contacts?"

Again, she avoided answering the question directly. "I understood it would be a simple recon for you, but the next thing I know, he calls me to say they're arriving in Saranda and that he's going to try meeting you there. That was not part of the plan." I had to try and understand what she was telling me over my anger, because a minute later she added, "And I hope that isn't the problem."

"WHAT problem?" There was a long pause, or the line had gone dead. Had she hung up because I'd almost shouted? "Celine?"

"Well, don't get so upset. And *problem* might be overstating things. Mr. Brown told me he'd call me back this morning and he hasn't, that's all." Then she quickly added, "But that's not unusual."

"You've worked with him before?"

"No, but considering what he does . . ."

So he was some kind of secret-agent operative, and now she was getting nervous about possible consequences.

"What about the other embassy staff who met him in Vienna?"

"It was passed on to my desk by the ambassador's representative, who hinted there would be no official record. I'm even wondering if the ambassador knew about it." She had lowered her voice with the last comment. "Well, thank you very much," she said brightly, and hung up. Someone must have come into her office.

19

REBY STARTED THE engine so the heater would warm him up while he waited—it was cold here in Macedonia, even in the valley near the lake. As he looked out through the windshield, his gaze was drawn back to a spot under the hood where the windshield wipers were recessed—there was a trace of the former red paint that the new dark blue hadn't completely covered. He and his boss had rented two rooms in Ohrid, the town on the east side of the lake that traversed the Albania-Macedonia border. His vehicle was definitely less noticeable, now mingling with many other similar-coloured cars and trucks—he'd even looked for the familiar red colour that morning in the hotel lot. In the middle of his sudden panic, thinking his car had been stolen, he remembered the visit to the garage and the requirement that the vehicle remain overnight in the heated shop for the paint to set properly.

What was wrong with him? Maybe a decent coffee would help to get his wits sorted, not the shit they served here. He was about to turn off the motor to save his fuel when he saw the American exit the hotel. He moved the car forward, then leaned over and opened the door. He'd been delayed at the garage to the point where his boss had texted him. Then the American had kept him waiting in the cold. Was his passenger trying to show Reby he was the boss, or was he still not completely recovered?

"Someone found a business opportunity," his passenger said as they drove to the appointment the American had made that morning. "It's close to the border, so ideal location before import or after export. Reby, we need to encourage the same kind of thinking. Always be looking for that next possibility, so don't be afraid to make a proposal, even if the idea sounds wild," he said, turning to his driver. "We can talk it through—see if there's anything in it. Right?"

Reby nodded, hoping there were still some drugs in the American's system to explain his rambling like that, and parked. His passenger got out, saying, "I'll be just a minute." Reby hoped he wouldn't be long. He'd never been to the lake town, much less visited these mountains so late in the year, and he was unprepared for the cold. Running the car used a lot of gasoline, and he didn't want to buy any here—what was the quality like in a place that was this cold? Besides, he hadn't seen any premium, just diesel and regular benzene. He'd enjoyed the lake's tasty, famous fish the night before, but he'd be glad when they got back to the warmer weather near the coast. They would have to go back over the mountains, but in daylight. It had been a harrowing drive east from Elbasan through heavy weather to get here, but the news report on the television in his room had shown sun symbols and temperatures above zero. The bright young announcer had smiled and babbled in the local Slavic tongue, while meaningless Cyrillic letters slid below her on the screen. Good thing most locals could also speak Albanian. And the warmer forecast meant there would be very little snow on the roads.

He sat up as he saw his boss coming out of the building and hurry over to the car. The rear passenger door still squeaked slightly when the American opened it, but minor repairs had been less important than the paint job and engine look over. And it seemed like they were on their way if he was sitting in the back.

"Okay, let's go!" said his passenger eagerly. What passed for a full day's rest for him had flushed most of the drugs out of his system, even though he had spent much of the previous afternoon calling various contacts from his bedroom.

Reby was aware of the need to overcome any impression that the disastrous foray into Bega's territory had stopped their ongoing plans. He knew a different course of action was in the works after being woken by his boss's rambling that first morning in Macedonia. The American had fought off sleep while giving one-sided pep talks about needing to get back into business "right now—right fucking now!" And Reby had heard some of the phone conversations in the afternoon.

"Elbasan?" asked Reby as he prepared to turn onto the road that headed north and would circle west to the border. With a little American cash and the purchase of a temporary insurance green card, they had overcome the minor difficulty with the border agent two nights before, when first crossing into Macedonia. It would likely be easier returning, since their insurance and registration were now valid—car colour

— 155 —

was down near the bottom of the customs checklist, and unlikely to be an issue.

"Yes," said the American. "I've arranged for two associates to meet us there this evening. They're going to organise a dinner with our partners for tomorrow night, so the others will have enough time to join us from Tirana. Apparently our friend has been making enquiries about us in the capital, so we'll make Elbasan a temporary base for operations until we find out more." His face set as he added, "We'll keep our heads down and ears open."

Reby's skill at getting the American away and out of the country had yet to be acknowledged, but the driver was not one to expect much from his superior. As they started off his passenger asked, "So Reby, why the FYROM? Why didn't you try to get us to Tirana?"

The driver looked at him in the rear-view mirror, finally remembering that FYROM was Macedonia. "Bega would expect Tirana, maybe not this border." Reby wondered how it would have gone if he'd tried for Tirana—*probably not good*, he thought. He'd heard about the garage operation in Ohrid a month before, from a second cousin who'd mentioned they did great work and no records were kept. It was a chance to give the car a good looking over after the action north of Gjirokaster, and anything done outside the country was unlikely to filter back to Bega. Reby's family had been hinting lately that a regular mechanic's job was a good career for the future, seeing that he was no longer making the big bucks as a driver. But things had changed pretty quickly with the American back. The two of them together made quite a team, and the next time they met Bega—well, his boss had said he'd have Reby right there to deal with any problems. That had been part of a new arrangement: Reby would always be at his side when there were any meetings or negotiations, at least when it was possible, but Reby knew he'd be reluctant to have anyone even park his car after all the work he'd put into it.

"Good thinking." It was all the American said for the next while.

Reby glanced back at his passenger after a few minutes, happy that he had quieted and that he looked like he would soon be asleep. Maybe customs and border control wouldn't disturb him in the back seat. Reby still had all their documents up front and was looking forward to getting across the border and onto the good tarmac leading into Elbasan. He liked to be moving, not sitting around waiting. Driving was his refuge, an escape from the everyday boredom of normal life—he liked to think of himself as a man of action. In the dark, driving to Macedonia, the weather and the unknown state of the road had forced him to go slowly, even to stay within the speed limits on occasion. He'd seen that the major construction work between Elbasan and the border was nearly finished, so the return drive would be more interesting. There were a few stretches where he'd be able to check that the supercharger still had the acceleration punch that he'd worked so hard to perfect. In Ohrid, the mechanic had been quite impressed by some of the engine modifications. When Reby picked up the car, the owner took the time over his cash register to talk to him about motors, Mercedes in particular. Finally, once the euros had been handed over, he'd said, "If you're ever looking for a job . . ."

Reby had glossed over his discussion at the garage when the American, who had been waiting back at the hotel, had asked about the delay. He needed to keep a few things to himself.

—————=((•))=—————

It had been nearly two days and the reports were all in: the results of the roadblocks, the presence of a red Mercedes in the hotel lot during the party and its subsequent disappearance, and Bega's driver's detailed description of the interception of their SUV and the prisoner's abduction. Bega and Victor were finalising their options for a way forward, when the big man glanced at his cell as it buzzed on the table—he knew it might be significant. Bega held up his hand to excuse the interruption and then reached for it.

"*Po?*" His expression changed as he listened.

When the call ended, Victor waited as Bega digested the information. "And?"

"They'll be in Elbasan. A big meeting is planned for tomorrow, so he's likely staying a few days longer."

Both men knew finding out about Elbasan was a lucky break. They'd have to act quickly before the American moved on, likely before the weekend, which meant three days at most, and finding the American in the old city would not be easy. The communists had turned it into an industrial centre. Producing concrete and extracting the chromium ore for refinement had been one of the country's best hard-currency earners. Most of those factories were now in ruin but offered many places in which to hide for someone on the run.

"We're going to need him to stay longer to get our man there." Victor had told Bega he'd made contact with the Serbian, but the ex-Cobra marksman wasn't in the country.

When Bega didn't answer, Victor spoke again. "I can notify the Serb, but it needs to be soon."

"Yes, we don't have much time." said Bega. "Let's try meeting him in Shkodër, tomorrow. I'd like to brief him personally, see if he's up to the task."

Shkodër was the first northern Albanian town of any significance near the coast en route south from the Republic of Montenegro. The Serb would have to cross the border with the former province of the Yugoslavian state—flying was not an option, as he wanted to bring his own equipment. Victor had agreed to this, despite the extra time needed, since their organisation no longer had access to the American kit available through Kosovo. He'd last spoken to the marksman in Dubrovnik, which was the best example of a preserved Eastern Europe that tourist companies had found. Dubrovnik was actually in another country—Croatia was also a former province of Yugoslavia—but it was only a few hours' drive from the Montenegro-Albania border.

Both men realised it would be a tight schedule if their meeting was tomorrow—they'd be leaving as soon as the Serb was contacted and would have to do some night driving. Bega could see Victor was concerned that they were getting directly involved with the operation.

20

THE CONSUL RETURNED my call on Monday afternoon but didn't answer my questions. Instead, she asked, "Are you free for coffee Wednesday morning, say 10:00 at the Italian bakery? We can catch up."

"Yes, of course." *Catching up* seemed odd, given what I assumed we would be discussing, so I replied in the same vein, "Looking forward to it."

The rest of the day and Tuesday shot by more quickly than usual. Ariyan went out into the field to get a firsthand look at the status of our new operation while I dealt with my superior. The Austrian ambassador had strongly suggested to him that the border would close, but this had yet to happen. The Austrians had good contacts in the country, going back to when the Austro-Hungarian Empire had given conditional support for an independent Albania in 1911. They had yet to make any official announcement, but as the days passed, it looked as though things were quieting down, so our survey might still go ahead.

Wednesday morning arrived and I juggled my schedule to be able to meet the consul. The boss had called another "final" meeting at 8:30 to discuss formalising his evacuation plans. He'd not reacted when I got up to leave, so he might have remembered I'd told him that I had an appointment. As I closed the door, the finance manager looked up from the detailed plan. I got the distinct impression that he envied my escape.

The consul was already at the bakery when I walked in. "Sorry I'm late," I said, and sat down across from her near the back corner, where she had a good view of the entrance. She had ordered a cappuccino and a few pastries, and offered me the plate.

"No problem, Mr. McAtee. I'm sure the situation in the north is keeping you busy dealing with your company's operation, which is so close to the action, so to speak."

It was refreshing to hear her take on the situation. My employer had always insisted that we were far away from the trouble spot, but distance is a relative thing. I'd been repeating the company's line for so long that even I'd started to believe it. After all, why would we be considering withdrawing if we were really far enough away from the disturbances?

"We've had updates coming in all week," she said, "and I've had to postpone the consulate's routine schedule, but there's a good chance now it will all blow over."

If she was busy, why was she here with me? What had she to say that was so important? I waited for her to speak first and hoped my questions on the American would be answered.

She looked to the entrance and then back to me. "Well, the reason I wanted to meet, other than to keep in touch, of course . . ." She paused. "Has your survey started? It's important that the consulate has some idea how our nationals are doing."

Okay, she needed to cut through the small talk.

She saw my frustration and said, "Sorry, I'm still not *absolutely* certain about this, but the visitor who came to Tirana with your cousin last Friday ... well, I believe he was misrepresenting himself." She could see my immediate interest and hesitated before asking, "Has something happened?"

"I don't think so, at least not that I know of." *Other than that he didn't show up at the Saranda hotel.* "Why?"

"Well it was highly unusual, the way he hinted at security issues and secrecy, and insinuated it might be related to the World Trade Center attacks." She looked directly at me for the first time and continued. "I do have to be careful in what I'm telling you, but I know you'll keep this confidential. Unfortunately, I haven't heard back yet from the ambassador's office for official permission, or I'd be able to tell you more about what KFOR believes the situation to be in your survey area."

Great! If she could tell me what was going on, it would make my job a lot easier. She noticed my reaction.

"I'll likely hear back later today, but let's be clear—you shouldn't get involved with anything that might compromise your safety in the country. I've already talked to Celine this morning, and she feels the same way."

Celine must be shitting bricks—or maybe not. If something had gone wrong as a result of her collusion with the American, at least now she wouldn't be in it alone. The consul was obviously having regrets about her small part in getting me involved with him.

"Anyway, I thought I recognised him when I first met him but later decided it was just one of those things, someone reminding you of someone else. Then over the weekend I was out at the market when I distinctly remembered where I'd seen him, right in the middle of buying tomatoes. I don't need to go into the details, but I can tell you that he is not currently associated with any national embassy, and certainly not the U.S embassy here. I was remiss in not looking closer at his identification. I'm nearly sure he's the same man who was dismissed after having been involved in some illegal Kosovo business a few years back."

"Really?" That opened up a lot of possibilities as to why he had come into the country, including his now obvious plan to attend the big-shot party in Saranda. He wanted to get back into the action, though he must have changed his mind about meeting me. But that didn't quite answer all my questions. The consul was still talking and I tried to refocus on what she was saying.

"Yes, I think he was completely misrepresenting himself when he arrived in Tirana last week. And to think that I went along with the ruse, saying I had to make a call so that he could talk to you and Celine alone. I hope you didn't agree to anything?"

"Not at all." I wondered what Celine had told her.

"Well that's good. I'm sending in a report to Vienna. He might still be in the country. We really have to be more careful. Perhaps we should have had this meeting in the office, but we've got some NATO military in town now, a last-minute visit, and it was just easier to stick with the original time and place."

"Well this is just fine with me," I said, as I picked up the last pastry and smiled. The coffee and desserts were quite tasty, but she hadn't said why she'd wanted to meet out of the office to start with. I assumed she didn't want anything official to be reported, and she might have been unsure of how I would react, if I had gotten involved with Mr. Brown. At least here she could just have gotten up and walked out.

But I hadn't gotten involved because he hadn't shown up. I guess I'd been lucky. It wouldn't have gone well if the Albanian mafia guy had seen us together. Would I be sitting here now?

On the way back to the office, it struck me that the NATO group's presence at the consulate was how she knew what KFOR's opinion was on the Kosovo situation and how that might affect my area of interest. I wondered if it was worth talking to Celine again. She might tell me more, even if the ambassador didn't sanction going public. Celine knew I'd keep it to myself. At the very least, I'd be sure to bring it up the next time we got together. I should probably try to see her if she was still in Vienna on the weekend.

Ariyan called me on his cell later in the afternoon from our field operation. "Tony, I talked with the contractor. Very nervous man, but he's Croatian. One minute, locals tell him he better leave, border is very dangerous, problems are coming. Next day head man says 'no problem.' Very strange."

"When did he meet the head man?" I asked, thinking my boss had heard something similar from the Austrian embassy: *The border is going to close! Well, maybe not.* Even the consul thought things would now "blow over."

Ariyan started talking to someone away from his phone,

and I thought about the changes in the border situation. He came back on the line. "They met yesterday, but Sunday the contractor sure we cancel."

"There's a big penalty if we cancel the survey, Ariyan. That's why you're there. Try to find out what's going on." I wanted him to find out directly from the head man, and to talk to the locals. The decision to use a Croatian contractor might be one we would come to regret. They were experienced in the area but had their own bias and might not be able to give us an accurate picture of the situation. "Can you meet the head man?" I sensed Ariyan just wanted to leave.

"Okay, Tony. I try the best."

By late afternoon, after mulling everything over, I knew I needed to talk to Celine. There was too much uncertainty in having Ariyan stay with the contractor if it was going to be dangerous. He was a good man, and I had developed a strong attachment to him. I would even consider him a friend, which would mean a lot more if we were somewhere else. Celine might be able to give me something I could use to help decide whether to continue the survey. And if we continued, I'd have to treat the evacuation plan seriously, just in case.

21

"CAN I COUNT on your support?"

They were meeting in Elbasan, in a new restaurant behind the fortifications that dated back to the Romans. The Ottomans had strengthened the defensive walls when they'd expanded west of Thessaloniki, the Greek city they captured in 1439 after breaking through to the European side of the Bosporus. Resettling the main Roman garrison on the Via Egnatia was another step in bringing the culture and mentality of the east to Europe—and using the ancient Roman route had gotten them one step closer to the Adriatic, across which the Italian peninsula and Rome had beckoned.

Reby was sitting back from the table, where he could keep an eye on the proceedings. He'd seen the American looking over his guests throughout the meal and had watched them closely as the man stood up and welcomed them officially before making his speech. En route from the eastern border with Macedonia, his boss had talked about how he'd had to use all his persuasive skills when he'd called each of them— and nearly all of them had come to Elbasan. They were now leaning back in their chairs—safe behind the remains of ancient walls and relaxed after enjoying the first meal prepared from a new and modern kitchen.

The first meeting, in the Tirana hotel's garden, had been very successful in getting initial support and encouragement from these local chiefs, all of whom resented Bega's success in the south. But now, realism and caution had come into play, and it would take a miracle to show that the American was still the man to take charge after his botched venture into Bega's territory.

Gashi, the American's former deputy in the north before the KFOR crackdown, was the first to reply. Convincing him was critical. Gashi had re-established some control on the northern border after his former boss had been forced out of the country.

"We thank you for calling this meeting and for the opportunity to have a frank exchange of views. I say this because, as you saw in Saranda"—the American's eyes hardened—"it is not an easy thing to begin again when others have consolidated their positions. I think we have all made efforts since our last meeting. *Some* of us have made progress." He let the words sink in before continuing. "Many of my supporters in the north had agreed to negotiate for a share of future transport 'work' in areas of mutual interest, so expectations were raised. Unfortunately your promised success with Bega did not happen, and I've had to inform my men to be patient and postpone any actions." It was clear he had lost face with the locals in his area. "Tonight you made it clear you want us to resume the original undertaking, even though nothing has changed—if anything, it would seem you have made an enemy, and one who remains ambitious, despite all that he

PETER J. MEEHAN

has accomplished." The table shared muted agreement—by now most of them had heard of the gathering in Saranda. "We need strong leadership if we are to join together against this adversary. Only then can we support a united effort to grow our trade and transport routes throughout the country." He sat down, having made his point.

Many voices spoke up as Gashi finished. He had said what the others had been thinking. Reby looked around the room, watching for any sudden movements, but the group was simply voicing their concerns—loudly, in the Mediterranean way.

Belushi, a small-time player who had been invited because of his contacts to the east of Gashi's area of operation, managed to make himself heard above the din. "Yes, we were all prepared to step up, but we had to backtrack and say, 'Sorry, we made a mistake.'" The other voices quieted as he spoke. "What kind of game are we playing? If we are going to do something, let's do it, not one minute 'Go!' the next minute 'Stop!'"

"Gentlemen!" The American stood as the volume rose again. It was clear that talk and promises wouldn't work anymore—something quite drastic was needed. Reby wondered if it would be something foolish, sensing his boss had nothing to lose. The American looked out over the table and said, "Very well. We will meet again in Tirana next week, in the same garden as before. I will expect your support, but let me make it clear: those who are still not committed on that day will not have another opportunity."

22

I ARRIVED AT our favourite coffee house and waved when I saw Giselle already at a table on the far side of the room. It was difficult not to run over. We hugged for longer than I expected—she was such a good friend, and I needed someone to share with.

"Giselle, it's so good to see you," I said, and I knew she felt the same. She had returned earlier this morning from a longer than usual visit with her parents, but I'd already left my room in the Theresianum for class at the lycée.

"You missed me! How was it?" she asked, but the waiter arrived just then and took my order for a hot chocolate.

When he left I took a deep breath and said, "It was a really great weekend. We drove down the coast and saw these really amazing old ruins, you know, but not just the usual Roman stuff—these walls were so impressive, made of huge blocks, and a Byzantine castle on the top looking out over the sea." We often talked about how we always had to go and see ruins and museums with our families, and she rolled her eyes, a bit surprised that I had liked Butrint. "I think it had a lot to do with the weather, which was fantastic!" Seeing that she still had the bored look on her face, I asked, "And what about your weekend in Zagreb, or did you get to the coast?" I waited for her answer, even though I just wanted to tell her more about what happened—when we got back to Tirana Sunday night.

"Same old story." Giselle sounded kinda frustrated. For the first time since arriving I wondered if something had happened to change her. Even when we had problems, we had always been close, but her bored look and frustration were new. "We were supposed to get to Dubrovnik, but my dad had to go into work, so there wasn't enough time ... and the weather! And it's the same here." She nodded towards the window. "It's really starting to get to me." There was a hitch in her voice. Why was she was getting so upset?

The Vienna weather was pretty dreary, but I hadn't paid it too much attention. I was still running on the good feelings from the trip. It had been a more than welcome visit with the family, even my dad—the whole weekend had been an adventure. And then there'd been the party. "That's too bad," I said. "Any shopping?"

"We tried, but how many Croatian party dresses can I buy? Even my mother was kind of down with the shitty weather."

My hot chocolate arrived, and I tried a bit of gossip to get her spirits up as the light in the café faded. Eventually the staff turned up the table lamps and overhead chandeliers. I listened to her, but she seemed unhappy about everything, so I was only half listening. The brightened room's faded wallpaper and paint fit the weather and her mood, but a little glitter from the dusty overhead crystal was enough to add a bit of sparkle for me.

It was nearly time to get going but I still hadn't mentioned my news. I didn't want to make too much of it considering her weekend, but finally I just had to tell her about the party—it might even lift her out of whatever she was in, at least a little bit.

"There was a party Sunday night after we got back to Tirana."

"Oh? Meet anyone interesting?" she asked, but all of a sudden I got the impression she was just being polite. Maybe she didn't want to know I'd had fun.

"I wasn't expecting much," I began, wondering if I had to watch what I said, but then not caring. "But I kept thinking about the party when we were driving towards Tirana because my Albanian friend had texted me that she wanted me to meet someone there."

"Someone from Albania?" she asked, with a bit more curiosity

"I didn't know, but I saw this good-looking Albanian guy when we stopped earlier in Gjirokaster, and he kept looking at me and I started imagining meeting him at the party. He would be staring at me from across the room, but when he finally came over, some other guy would tell him that I was *with him*."

"Really?" she said, but I could tell she was back to being in the dumps, and bored with what I was saying.

"Giselle! I was just imagining that, but when we got back and I really did go over, I had a great time. I didn't know that there were so many interesting guys in Tirana! From the time I arrived until I had to leave, I was totally surrounded.

My friend Fiona—it was her party—introduced me to the group. It's the first time I've been to a party where everyone wanted to meet me. ME! Imagine that, Giselle, they all wanted to meet me! There was one really good-looking Albanian, Agron. I could go on and on . . ."

"Really?" she said again, but this time she didn't even try to seem interested.

I stopped talking and looked at her for a minute wondering what had happened since we'd last met, or maybe she just envied my weekend. Then I had a great idea. "Giselle, listen—why don't you come with me next time?" Her expression changed, though she said nothing, and I wondered if she was concerned that her parents might not allow it—or was it something else?

"Would you come, Giselle? It could be a lot of fun." I knew my parents would love to have her over, after all the times her parents had taken me along to places when they visited Vienna. "My dad is coming on Friday, so I'll ask him when we meet. He can even call your dad, if you want. If there isn't a party, we can hang out with some of my other friends, and my dad always, always, takes us to the sea at least once on the weekend—just a walk on the beach or even in the water, just wading to our ankles if it's warm enough." One time we went and it had rained the whole time, but we just went to a restaurant and looked out over the beach. "It seems that it's nearly summer when we go, rather than November."

We got up to leave a short time later, but she still hadn't really said anything about wanting to come. It was overcast and damp as we hurried along outside, and the early twilight made me want to feel closer to her. I guess I was a little too excited about the party and all the attention I'd had. I was still sure Giselle would have a good time with me—she just needed to think about it some more.

Just before I fell asleep that night I remembered Malik. I realised I hadn't really thought about him since coming back. And Giselle hadn't said anything more about his visit to the school. I guess I really didn't care that much. I mean he was a nice guy and everything, except when he kinda lost it, getting angry. And the way he left the last time I saw him—that wasn't nice at all, it was just rude. If I saw him again, I'd still be nice to him and even thank him for the fun times we had. It had been fun, for a while. But it was time to do something different and see other people—Agron, the guy from the party, for instance!

My dad was still expecting to meet Malik, but now he'd be glad to find out that I wasn't seeing him anymore. I'd think of something to tell him—maybe like we both decided our age difference was starting to be waaay too obvious, like at the restaurant, and it was better to stop seeing each other.

23

BEGA SAT IN the passenger seat of Victor's older Mercedes. They were driving up the long hill to the Rozafa Fortress just south of Shkodër. He looked out over the old city and north to the lake that marked the border with Montenegro. He had insisted on accompanying Victor to the meeting with the Serb. The big Albanian was aware that Victor had wanted him to stay behind, but Bega had overridden his objections and the drive north had been long and tiring, but uneventful, with little conversation.

He'll get over it, thought Bega.

"We need to keep this tight, my friend," Bega had said. "No one else should know about this arrangement, and you know we don't have much time. There can be no slip-ups on this one. We'll go together to meet and brief him once he crosses the border—that way he can go directly to Elbasan with no delays. If we're successful, there'll probably be trouble for all of us, depending on whom the American has reconnected with, but I doubt his embassy will get involved unless this gets really messy. At the worst I think we'll have to limit our activities for a while, and keep our heads down."

Bega knew this was wishful thinking. The worst case could mean stopping all his operations for some time, but he needed to take care of the problem quickly before it mushroomed into something he'd not be able to control. There had already been problems with the first development proposal for the resort on the Vlora-Saranda coast road. He didn't want more attention on his revised plans, or even any delays. The reality was that if the American had succeeded in getting enough support, Bega's planned expansion of his operations would have to be curtailed, even cancelled. But if he was lucky, Bega thought that the Elbasan action might be far enough away from their base in the south to go largely unnoticed—if they could hit the American in the old Ottoman city quickly, a clean in and out, they might get away with it. Repercussions might be confined to the north, where the authorities would focus on the American's former centre of operations, and when his earlier criminal activities were again disclosed, that might be the end of it.

Might be. The problem was that the Europeans were insisting the country be as clean as possible, in order for investments to continue.

Victor was approaching the main gate, through which they'd proceed to the parking area. The Serb was to meet them there, near a kiosk, at three o'clock. As Victor pulled into the end of a row of cars, Bega saw their man. He looked away from the kiosk. "There he is. Right beside the water cooler."

A short, casually dressed figure was lounging beside the sandwich stand. He looked like a father waiting for his family. Kids were running around everywhere, hyper from the soft drinks and chocolate bars.

"I know," said Bega, when he saw Victor looking over to the kiosk, "but that's him. It's probably helped him stay alive, not looking anything like an ex-Cobra. Just don't underestimate him, even if those rumours have some truth—it's a tough business." As they got out, Bega glanced towards the kiosk again. The former military police specialist was leaving. "He's seen us," he said to Victor. "Let's wander over. He'll be back."

They bought two coffees at the kiosk and sat back from a cheap table where spilled ice cream had attracted a few wasps. Victor scowled as he took a sip of the watery instant coffee. "So how will this work?" he asked. "Will we decide whether to use him after this meeting?"

Bega didn't answer. He had a feeling something wasn't right, but breathed deeply to calm himself. Was it because he was back near his old home turf and close to the border? He looked around without being too obvious, knowing the Serb was watching them, then finally answered Victor. "That would be best. Let me do the talking when he comes."

There was movement from behind a tree, and the Serb sauntered over. He was walking past them when he paused and took a seat at a table next to them. After a minute, he leaned slightly back and, without looking at them, said, "Give me your keys and meet me in your car in five minutes."

Victor looked at Bega, who barely nodded, and then got up and moved towards the WC. The keys dropped out of the bottom of his trousers as he passed the other table. Bega watched the Serb pretend to stretch and then retrieve the keys as he moved his chair back. The Serb stood and walked away from the kiosk and the parking lot, but Bega knew he was circling the area to ensure he and Victor were alone.

When Victor returned, Bega looked at his watch and got up to accompany him to the parking lot. As they approached their car, it was difficult to see if anyone was in it, but the doors were unlocked, and they were getting in when a voice said, "Don't look back here, just start the car—keys are in the ignition—and drive down the hill slowly."

Victor backed up and turned the vehicle towards the main entry. As they passed under the stone walls and started down the steep incline, the Serb spoke again. "So the target is in Elbasan? I need a photograph." Bega passed a photo back without looking over his shoulder. A few moments passed, and the car rolled slowly down the hill, bumping unevenly over the cobblestone track. "This man is English?" he asked, finally.

"No, American," Bega said.

"That might be a problem. No one wants the Americans coming for them."

"With him there will be no problem." Bega wanted to guarantee this, but he knew that wasn't possible. Maybe it was the Serb's way of asking for more money. He leaned over to adjust the rear-view mirror to see the back seat, but the Serb was behind him, near the window. He could see another car coming up behind them. *They're driving too quickly,* he thought. *What's the rush?*

"How to be sure?" asked the man in the back seat. "Easy to say, *no problem.*"

They were approaching the bottom of the hill, but Bega still hadn't answered the Serb's question as he continued to watch the car behind them, and then he put his hand lightly on Victor's arm, ready to warn him if the car didn't slow down soon.

The back-seat passenger continued looking at the photo and asked, "What knowledge of his location in the old city?" Neither of the front seat occupants answered.

Bega's hand started to grip the driver's arm as the car behind them continued to close the distance. The car was dark, but he couldn't make out the driver in the sunlight glaring off the oncoming windshield. He saw that it was going to hit them, and he barked a warning to Victor, and scrambled for his hidden weapon, the access made difficult by the seat belt. The back-seat passenger reacted to this, ducking low and reaching for a small pistol attached to his leg.

Victor glanced into his side-view mirror then stomped on the gas pedal, and they shot onto the main road through a small break in traffic that he'd spotted. There was a massive transport speeding towards Shkodër that was closing the gap. The two passengers flew back into their worn seats, losing sight of the oncoming traffic on the main road. Bega felt the pressure of the old bent seat springs against his thigh as the truck veered at them with its horn blaring—airbrakes hissed and tires screeched as the old Mercedes continued on across the centre line towards the far lane to avoid the north bearing truck. There was a loud *bang!* as the transport clipped the car's back bumper, causing it to spin around. The next vehicle coming from the direction of Shkodër hit the driver's side full on. Traffic from both directions came to a noisy stop on both sides of the accident scene.

It was a small Ford that hit them, but Victor hadn't done

his seat belt up, and the old-style airbag only partially protected his head. He slumped over the steering wheel when the bag deflated. Bega and the sniper leapt out of opposite sides of the Mercedes, glaring at each other, as a hubcap from one of the cars rolled into a spiral and finally stopped. In the momentary silence that followed, both men stood watching the other, their small calibre weapons held discreetly at their sides.

A crowd of onlookers gathered as other drivers got out of their vehicles, but the driver of the Ford remained in his car, slumping down into his seat and yelling into his cell phone after watching the two men emerge angrily from the vehicle he'd just hit. The truck driver cursed and wiped his forehead with a handkerchief, but then reached over and locked his doors after seeing the two figures jump out of the Mercedes directly below him.

Bega waited for the other passenger to act but saw that the man was looking indecisive and hadn't looked back to the side road, where his accomplices might be waiting. He quickly glanced over to the road going up to the fortress, but the other car was gone. *This was not his doing*, Bega thought.

He concealed his weapon, and the shorter man did the same. Bega watched as the specialist looked around and turned back to him saying, "I can't stay here." He came around the vehicle, and as he passed the Albanian he said, "Later, Hotel de Paris, six o'clock."

Bega watched him walk calmly away and went around to Victor's door, trying to see him better. Blood was trickling onto the floor. As he tried to look through the cracked windshield, a policeman appeared waving his traffic paddle at the observers.

"This is not a football match! Everyone back, give us room. I want everyone to move on, but any witnesses to this collision must remain until I say they can leave!"

The crowd dispersed immediately, and slowly the road around the scene cleared, leaving the policeman standing alone with Bega beside the big truck, the small Ford, and the Mercedes. The big Albanian was still attempting to see how much Victor was hurt.

Later in the afternoon, the ex-Cobra operative met with his accomplice for the upcoming operation. Both had served together in the Cobra unit as weapons specialists, so a kind of trust had been established, more or less. The meeting in a small, dirty café was short, and he arrived at the Hotel de Paris at five. He casually surveyed the entire bar, restaurant, and lobby before going across the street to wait and watch for any sign that there might be a risk in meeting the Albanian.

This job was not one he had particularly wanted to take. He had been to Elbasan before but didn't like it—only one road passing through for access and escape, and too many Albanians. The incident at the base of the fortress only confirmed that this would not be a straightforward job. The specialist knew he could walk away from this matter before it became serious, but his reputation was at stake after the failure to follow through with the last job. He liked to think of it as *complications*, but the result was the same—he hadn't completed the contract.

Prior to that, he'd had nearly a perfect record since leaving the Serbian military police, getting enough difficult work to become known as a reliable specialist. But even before the last assignment, the operations had become less lucrative as the region stabilised with the end of hostilities amongst the former constituent states, following the breakup of Yugoslavia. Albania and its borders had become the main area of his activities, but even this would only be temporary. He'd directed his best efforts to find work further east in the former Soviet republics without success. He knew that the chance of getting employment in the east had substantially lessened after the last contract, and he needed to prove that he hadn't lost his technique—this next job was probably more important than any he'd had in a long time.

The last contract had interrupted a visit to his older brother at the family home in Montenegro, where business was similarly dependent on Albanian money. When the war had ended with NATO's intervention in the former Yugoslavia, the brother had returned to Montenegro to open a restaurant in their coastal hometown—the family had reclaimed the land and the earthquake-damaged ruins that overlooked the natural harbour of the old town after communist rule ended—but there had been a problem. Though Montenegro had remained untouched by any military action, the route to their coast had been cut off for the wealthier northern Europeans during the hostilities, and the Germans and Scandinavians hadn't returned since the Yugoslav war ended. His customers were now mainly gangsters, the rich ones who came north with their new black cars and designer tracksuits. His brother's efforts—working as a waiter to learn the languages in Europe and England during the dark times, then using all his hard currency to transform their family holdings into a restaurant and small hotel—had produced little of substance since most of the customers were Albanians with too much blood money. And nearly nobody came before May or after mid-September, even though there was still stretches of good weather for weeks.

His brother had even talked of leaving the country if things didn't improve—"Anyone, just not the Albanian mafia," he'd said, but his brother talked too much, and had even asked him to come and help when he'd first started the new enterprise and was optimistic about the future. It wasn't an option for someone with military instincts and background, though—he couldn't see himself serving food and drinks to rich Europeans, much less Albanian gangsters.

⸻ ◈ ⸻

Bega arrived at five thirty and performed the same surveying ritual as the man he was to meet. As he came out onto the street from the agreed meeting point in the hotel, the Serb waved him over. The big man hesitated, realising that he was on his own now that Victor was in the hospital recovering from a severe concussion. But then he smiled. There hadn't been any sign, as yet, that the ex-Cobra wasn't up to the planned operation—he'd handled himself pretty well that morning at the fortress and in the aftermath of the traffic incident. Bega still hadn't decided if the "accident" had been planned, and if so, by whom. He crossed the street and took the seat offered at the outdoor table.

The Serb watched closely as he asked, "Well, my friend, a coffee or something a little stronger?" Without waiting for a reply, the specialist signalled to the waiter and ordered two coffees and two rakis. Both men kept a careful watch on the street and nearby buildings until the drinks were delivered.

Bega held up his raki until the other man did the same. "*Gazuar!*" They toasted each other and downed the small glasses of plum brandy. The Albanian would make his next move based on what the other said, and waited for the Serb to speak.

The specialist put down his glass. "First, let me tell you something about myself. My family is from Montenegro, not Serbia, and we are a proud people."

Bega was aware that the small country was the only Balkan state not conquered by the Ottomans. *Interesting detail, but what's your point?* he thought, and waited for something else.

"After my first successful job, I became known as 'the Serb.' It does sound more menacing than 'the Montenegrin,' no? Outside our corner of the world, who even knows where Montenegro is?"

Bega could see that the Serb was trying to gain his trust by sharing small truths. He liked this approach. Perhaps the accident had been the result of locals noticing this man at the fortress that morning—locals who resented his invading their territory? Or maybe it really had been just an accident. Who could know? With Victor out of the picture, he'd have to rely on his instincts and resist the urge to call in others for help.

The operation to take out the American needed to go ahead, and if the plan was to succeed, it must be kept close. After its completion? Perhaps this Serbian, or Montenegrin, would not get back home—but that was in the future, a place where the unknown always waited.

"My family is from Kosovo," said Bega, "which means we are the true Albanians, independent and fiercely loyal to our kin, never to Hoxha's craziness or some bureaucrat in Tirana. We kept our traditions, even the blood feud, though that part may be regrettable." He'd said more than he'd planned, but it was true, all of it, and he felt the pride of his heritage flow as he talked to this stranger.

"Good," said the specialist, and now he looked at Bega carefully as he continued. "Unfortunately, *we* have a problem."

Bega's face showed no emotion, but he wondered if the Serb knew more about the traffic incident, or was still concerned about taking down an American? Maybe whatever had transpired on his last job had followed him here?

"My spotter recognised the target as an American operative." He hesitated slightly before adding, "He has withdrawn." His former partner had pushed back from their table after being shown the photograph, and had warned him of the unacceptable risk involved before leaving the Serb sitting alone in the café.

When the Albanian didn't react, the specialist continued. "I realise that the security of this operation is critical to its success, but don't worry, I will deal with my colleague later."

Bega was not convinced, but forced himself to plough

ahead with the arrangement. "And he was necessary?" he asked, wondering if knowing the target was the real reason for the withdrawal—did this former colleague know something more about the circumstances of the Serb's last job? Despite this development, Bega remained comfortable talking to this man, away from Victor and his minders, in the street and taunting danger. "You cannot take this opportunity we have discussed without your colleague?"

The sniper became more formal. "I did not say he was necessary, but the short timetable without a spotter—most importantly, a reliable one—increases the risk of failure." He waited for this comment to sink in before adding, "But if we can find someone who knows the target on sight and is familiar with the area of the operation . . ."

Bega's only thought was, *When was I last in Elbasan?*

24

I STOPPED IN at head office in Vienna Friday morning and met Michaela at the lycée in the afternoon. Unlike other times, when she thought I was just checking up on her, she wasn't unhappy to see me, but there was no sign of her friend. "He's not coming," she said finally as we walked. "I think he had something else on."

This news was quite annoying to me, particularly after an encounter I'd had at headquarters that morning. I overheard some reaction to the Albanian progress report I'd given, in which I played down some of the concerns in the north. I was feeling pretty good about the presentation, particularly in handling questions on the northern block issues—being too open about the situation might give the impression that the Tirana office couldn't cope with the operation, something my general manager would immediately be called to account on. If that happened, I'd lose all his support and be unable to finish the job. It was a fine line between being too candid and hiding our current issues, since my Vienna colleagues expected me to reveal any problems. I'd seen other managers at my level get squeezed between head office and branch office, and suspected that our head office wouldn't do much anyway, unless things really deteriorated. The branch office was supposed to find solutions to local problems, not pass them on. And I wasn't about to have my Tirana general manager be told he was inept, something his competing colleagues would relish.

I returned to pick up my briefcase in the meeting room after some discussion with the senior presiding manager in the hallway. The room was nearly vacant, but I walked in on two managers who were in the middle of discussing the company's involvement in Albania.

". . . well if Italy is the slag heap of history, then Albania must be the cesspool!" One of the managers turned to me when he saw his colleague look up at my entrance. "Right, Tony?" He was arrogant, even for a Viennese, and not afraid to speak his mind, provided senior management wasn't around—the blame culture that had typified the company in the past was being discouraged, and attempts to replace it with Western management practices were progressing, but slowly. "How about telling us what's really happening in the north?" he said, then laughed and added, "What a shithole!" as he exited the room, closely followed by his associate.

He must have a source in our Tirana office, and was likely getting updates on our daily activity. So what? I could live with disapproval from someone for whom I had little respect. It did add difficulty to the situation, but it was hardly news. I should have expected it from the company culture. And I wondered if Ariyan could be the leak, playing favourites, despite our close working relationship. He did have to look at the longer term, while I was involved with the company for a few years, at most.

The incident occupied my thoughts as I went to meet my daughter. I wasn't so concerned that some of my colleagues suspected things weren't going as well as I reported—it was more the attitude towards the country. How many others thought Albania was a cesspool? I felt unusually defensive about a place that I had been critical of only a few months before, almost like I had adopted it. As an expat, I encountered "Where are you from?" frequently on meeting new people, but it was a question I needed to qualify before answering. Was the speaker asking about my place of birth, longest residency, or current address? It dawned on me that I would probably answer "Albania" without hesitation. Though it was somewhat misleading, I felt a strong sense of pride in being able to make this association.

Michaela saw that I wasn't too pleased with her news, and tried to move on to how well things were going at school, but I persisted. "Well, Michaela, I thought we had agreed to meet with him?"

"Oh, Dad, don't go on about it. I won't be seeing him again, and that's it. He was nice to meet and talk to." A hesitation. "But he is kind of old for me."

The complete change in her attitude was surprising, but I continued walking beside her in silence. She was in a great mood, despite my displeasure—nearly skipping along. I should be taking advantage of the atmosphere. I said with a slow smile, "Okay, well what's the movie?"

She told me and smiled back. I thought that she must be looking forward to getting away from cafeteria food—and that the movie might be really good. The restaurant was just up the road, a nice place that we'd found on one of our previous outings. Though the food was expensive, I enjoyed being able to treat her to a good meal. She hadn't really appreciated it last time, but now she seemed to be in a much better frame of mind.

As a parent, I couldn't quite let go of the boyfriend, yet. I waited until we were nearly at our destination. "So he's not coming back to Vienna?" I asked, still a bit troubled by not meeting him. "You've said goodbye?"

"Yes." She replied a bit too quickly, looking away and then back at me. I looked at her with a raised eyebrow. At least she wasn't getting angry.

"Well, Dad . . . we got together, ah . . . on Wednesday, and I kind of said that he was a nice guy, but, well he *is* old."

"What did he say?"

"Not much. He was sort of quiet when he left me back at the lycée. We shook hands and I thanked him."

"He was happy with that?" I looked at her. "Shook hands, eh?" There was something more to this than she was saying, but we were at the restaurant.

We walked into the dark entryway. Michaela took off her coat and made a point of holding it out to the maître d' when he approached. I was surprised he took it, and she continued with this presumptuous attitude throughout the rest of the meal. She refrained from smiling too much and ordered confidently for both of us in German.

"Michaela, are you all right?"

"Perfectly fine, Father," she said rather haughtily. "Why do you ask?"

Following her German instructions, our waiter was a

model of Austrian efficiency, as had been the maître d', who, after taking our coats, had whisked us to one of the better tables. There was something to be said for their immediate response and curt acknowledgement of our new status, but was this all because of the manner in which Michaela had carried herself into the restaurant and instructed our waiter? Evidently she was capable of Austrian curtness when required. Her attitude and something about the way she looked at certain moments in the restaurant light reminded me of her mother—when we were younger and the world seemed ours for the taking. Several times during our meal, my daughter reverted to her old attitude towards me, but then she'd lighten up and I could see that she was trying her best. It helped that I didn't mention the boyfriend again. We talked about the Butrint trip and the possibility of another drive south, maybe to Greece. Even when she had her moments of being slightly negative, her eyes shone with a humour I hadn't seen since she was younger, before she'd developed the teenage attitude towards me.

Her no-nonsense manner continued until we'd been given our coats and escorted to the entrance, with much fanfare and hearty wishes for our return. As I stepped onto the sidewalk, I finally asked, "Well, that was interesting. Are you like that all the time now when you go out?"

Michaela smiled. "Mostly when service is involved. I've watched the Viennese, and learned that when in Rome, do as the Romans. All the Austrians are into status, so the waiters and workers want to be treated *properly*. You know, depending on their job level. I've learned some of it from school here, and I've seen how Giselle's father is when we go out.

The Viennese will be snobbish if you're not formal enough to them, and being uncertain is a no-no."

She was right; they had basically ignored me and given her all their attention, respecting her evident authority. It was probably a holdover from the old empire where the class system was based on rank, and politeness was regarded as a weakness. The Theresianum and lycée were working out better than I had hoped for, if this was part of the curriculum—as long as she didn't practice it at home. As we walked towards the movie theatre, she appeared more relaxed. We needed to talk about her next visit to Tirana, and she was keen on discussing it.

"I'm really looking forward to it. There's supposed to be another party at Fiona's on the Friday I get in."

"Another party?" I had to be careful, wanting her new attitude towards me to last. It was so nice having my old daughter back.

"Oh, Dad, it's just a party, nothing bad will be going on. I met some really nice people last Sunday. I was also thinking of maybe having Giselle come with me to stay for the weekend with us."

"Well that might be an idea. I mean her parents have taken you out in Vienna, right? And I suppose the party is your reason for wanting to invite Giselle?" Could that be why she was being so nice? "You didn't tell me too much about the last one when I was driving you to the airport."

"I know, but that was . . . before. And it isn't just the party—she'd like the country and the weather." I was thinking about our "new understanding" when she stopped in her tracks and nearly squealed, "Can we go for a picnic at the beach?"

More of my little girl, but it was confusing: the switching back and forth. She'd had an attitude like a policewoman in a bad mood for so long that the change to gleeful child was a bit unnerving.

She continued in a normal voice. "Of course I know she'd like the party, too, and she might meet a nice Albanian. I know you'd like the guy I met."

An Albanian boyfriend would make for a great conversation with her father, I thought, but let the comment go, saying instead, "Yes, we should have him over for supper when Giselle is here." At least he lived in the country and I could meet him, though he probably smoked and drank.

But I was getting ahead of myself, and before I made too many assumptions, I decided I would actually meet him and then evaluate his character. Well, provided Michaela didn't change her mind.

She enjoyed the movie, but I wasn't able to focus on the storyline, wondering how things would develop at work once I got back to Tirana. I had switched my flight to Saturday morning, deciding not to stay for the weekend due to all the ongoing issues on our northern acreage. Celine had already left Vienna, and I hadn't been able to contact her. In any case, Ariyan was also returning Saturday morning and I needed to find out from him firsthand about the situation in the north.

25

THE SPECIALIST HAD acquired a vehicle of sorts, a very old Renault with Tirana licence plates, to get them to Elbasan. It had been a reliable car when Eastern Europe first opened up a decade before. The legal importation of vehicles had caused a flood of various models, particularly Mercedes, but the Renault had an advantage. The gearshift's location on the dashboard, rather than the floor, provided more room for the sniper's rifle, tripod, and scope under the seats in the front. Bega could feel the concealed gear when attempting to adjust his position better for driving, but his new partner had insisted his equipment would remain as it was, accessible if needed. The sniper reached back for several blankets that would help smooth out the seat's lumpy base. Bega found he was barely able to fit into the now higher driver's seat, with his shoulder confined by the window. He looked even more oversized in the small car, but accepted his appearance as the clichéd overly large East European squeezed into the freedom of the open road.

Bega thought his passenger's specialised gear indicated that the sniper had smuggled himself into Albania, probably near the coast or by boat, in order to take in his weapon. The fact that he hadn't wanted to be questioned at the scene of the accident likely confirmed his illegal status in the country. Unfortunately, Bega was now officially known to be visiting Shkodër after accompanying Victor to the hospital.

"The purpose of your visit?" the policeman had asked while they waited for transport. Though he appeared to be a dumb traffic cop, his manner and efficiency with the "ambulance" attendants was effective. And he insisted on interviewing the other two drivers, despite their reluctance. Bega thought he might be one of the new breed needed to advance the country's prospects—good, provided he stayed north and didn't interfere with Bega's southern area of operation.

"Business and possibly pleasure," Bega had answered, hinting at the typical entertainment available in cities throughout the world for harmless businessmen like himself and Victor. It was unfortunate they'd had to show their papers, though the policeman didn't seem to know who they really were. Bega did have other, bogus, ID, but didn't think it was worth the risk with this man, and it might be possible to have this record expunged before any investigation got underway, assuming success in Elbasan.

The previous night, he and the sniper had agreed on a plan to proceed to the Ottoman city and try to meet with Bega's contact there before finalising the course of action. He'd gotten a good night's rest, considering they needed to be on the road before dawn. Now the Albanian was driving, enjoying his new freedom on the road to Elbasan and thinking it was a great day to be on the move. It had been some time since he enjoyed this kind of excitement. He tried to focus on the operation ahead, remembering to pass on any information he recalled that might help the marksman when they located the target. There would be time later to decide what to do about the ex-Cobra's accomplice—despite his reassurance, could the specialist be relied on to do what was necessary? The sniper must realise that his former colleague would later be tempted to come forward if a reward was offered for information on the hit, particularly since he hadn't been involved.

They drove along the wide Shkumbin River valley and entered the outskirts of the city in the middle of the afternoon. There had been little obvious evidence of environmental pollution in the valley, but the absence of farmland and older trees said much about the damage from the attempt at Stalinist heavy industry—the remnants of the huge steel and metallurgical compound built by Hoxha with Chinese investment appeared just outside the western limits. The main road deteriorated as it meandered around the largest industrial complex, most of which was blackened and broken near the collapsed central concrete structure—a lone brick smokestack poked out from an impassable swamp of rusted metal and slag away from the potholed tarmac.

"We'll drive past the citadel, then turn back." Bega remembered the main street from years before, now a wide grassy boulevard. "That's where the American was originally having his meetings. But I don't know if he is staying there or if he's holed up elsewhere."

People were out and about as the sun shone on the streets, and a fresh cool breeze overcame the lingering industrial odour that hinted faintly of burnt tires. They drove east, past the blackened walls marking the south perimeter of the old town, where the Romans had built a small fortress to defend their main easterly route, the Via Egnatia. The walls had once been higher, but gradually, floods and wind had deposited enough soil to raise the ground level considerably. The castle's battlements were no longer as imposing as they'd been when the Ottomans constructed the massive defensive structure five hundred years before, on top of the Roman camp. They'd built their fortress town to ward off the last, and greatest, of all Albanian heroes—Gjergj Kastrioti Skanderbeg. Known as George Skanderbeg by the West, the great fifteenth-century defender of Christian Europe had successfully halted the Turkish armies and stalled their rapid advance here in the Shkumbin River valley. This military containment endured for some time after Skanderbeg's death from old age in his fortress at Kruje, to the west. Eventually his successors were betrayed, allowing the Ottomans and their vassals to break out of the valley and overrun the country that they would rule for nearly four hundred years.

The Renault circled back by the citadel's northern flank, moving along the narrower back street adjacent to what was originally a moat, though the walls on this side were largely dismantled and the moat was only a slight depression. There was a narrow street entry into the citadel that they passed, built across a low section of wall for deliveries and transporting building materials inside the castle. Further along, a newly completed café and restaurant were inside the grounds, visible from this northern vantage. The outdoor section of the café appeared to have several levels that dropped down against the southern and western walls. Only the upper two

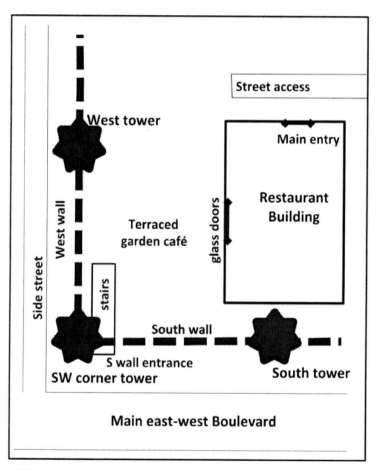

Elbasan: SW corner of citadel showing towers, café/restaurant and terraced garden (not to scale)

terraces were visible from the vehicle. At the end of the street they turned south, following the well-preserved west wall that was dominated by a squat tower midway along it. Bega saw his passenger scanning this carefully, likely judging whether it provided a long, clear view. It was high, but what about hiding places and escape routes? There were two other squat towers in the walls: one at the southwest corner and the other midway along the south wall. These were better fortified, and stronger because of their circular shape, than the intervening walls that had needed repairing over the years—uneven stones had been inserted into weakened sections between the older linear blocks. Two of the three towers directly overlooked the outdoor café, but even the third and furthest away might have an acceptable vantage point.

"Can we stop and have a look at this? Maybe have a coffee?"

Bega considered this, then said, "I can stop on a side street and you can go and have a quick look." He turned at the next street and pulled over into the shade of a building. "Don't be long—we can't risk being seen here. Better if we return after dark." He knew he would stand out, particularly to any of the American's men who might be monitoring traffic.

The specialist hopped out and was back while Bega was still trying to phone his contact in the old city. As he got back in the car the sniper said, "We might have a good spot, but I need to have a better look."

"Well that's some good news," said Bega, but he was only half listening. He'd been texting and calling his contact, but there had been no response. He wondered if they would have to change plans. There was so much that could go wrong—maybe the American had already left the city. "Let's check into a hotel and you can come back alone."

The Albanian started the car and drove back around the walls, leaving the city for a hotel not far from the eastern perimeter, on the new road to Macedonia. While the "Serbian" scouted the area in detail, Bega needed to make contact with the man who had called him in Saranda. He'd known the man's father in the old days, so his northern connections were still useful, but he suspected his contact was only positioning himself in case Bega's influence and success moved north. So not entirely reliable.

———— •«◊»• ————

The sniper drove back into the city and found an obscure place to park not far from the southwest corner tower of the citadel, from which he presumed the new café and restaurant could be reached through an entry point. He walked over and found the entrance in the south wall and, after pushing open the untended door, had a look through to the café terrace below. The new restaurant building was on the other side of the garden café.

A guard coming up the stairs must have heard the heavy door's hinges squeak and was looking up to see who had pushed it open. "No entry, is closed," he wheezed, stopping halfway up the steep incline while continuing to breathe heavily.

The specialist continued his scan of the fortress interior from his vantage point as he said, "Sorry, looking for the new restaurant." He studied the garden below him that was terraced down to the bases of the earliest blocks in the walls, noticing sculptures in the sunken garden that looked like unearthed artifacts, some appearing to be ancient busts. The digging out of the walls had uncovered a number of nooks and crannies, though how long these small alcoves could remain without the support of the earth on the inside wall was anyone's guess.

The guard on the stairs appeared to be getting impatient. "Tonight is grand opening. Maybe you come back with invitation."

As the marksman turned to go, he looked up at the towers and confirmed that they would provide an excellent position from which to see over most of the grounds. They would likely also provide good cover on the top level, as the uppermost walls were built to shelter archers and riflemen. Based on his police experience, he suspected that they would be guarded only if trouble was anticipated. Based on what he'd seen of the "guard" and the lack of a security detail, the towers might only be locked at their base entry points.

The sniper returned to the hotel and told Bega about his reconnaissance. "The location is nearly ideal if our man is staying in the citadel—better if his meeting point is the new restaurant and perfect if he sits outside at the adjoining café." He tipped his water glass and used his finger to trace a wet outline of the fortress on the small table where Bega was having an afternoon coffee. "It looks like the owner has dug out the old fortifications, so there are long lines of sight from the three towers in the walls, despite all the foliage that's been planted in the garden. The entrance, here, has a guard, but security isn't a serious threat, though it might be upgraded for special events—there's a grand opening this evening."

It might be good news, but Bega had been unable to confirm the American's presence in the town, or where he was staying, and they were running out of time.

———⊙———

Reby had sat in his car long enough. They'd be leaving for Tirana in the morning, but a few final arrangements had to be completed that evening, and later they'd need something to eat. He got out and walked across to the park outside the old city wall and found a shady tree.

After Wednesday night's disappointing meeting, the American had spent Thursday on the phone scheduling appointments with his remaining supporters. Reby had joined him for some of these gatherings but found them boring, and had gone back to his car between sessions. He'd be glad once the drive to Tirana was underway. He was planning on taking the old high road north into the capital. It snaked down to the Shkumbin River valley and joined the ancient east-west route from Elbasan to the coast on the valley's north flank, just west of the industrial complex outside the city. The northern route had yet to be fully improved, and still had dangerous corners as it climbed up to a linear ridge. There were sheer drops as it switched from one side of the ridge's crest to the other. The final section of road was a series of winding switchbacks that dropped down into the valley of Tirana—nothing like the mountain road down from

Llogara Pass to the coast in the south, but the blind corners and straight stretches offered plenty of challenge. Just before the outskirts of Tirana was a small hilltop crowned by ruins of a castle that had belonged to Skanderbeg's sister. Reby had always wanted to stop at the castle, which was now being developed into a restaurant with a 360-degree view of the countryside around Tirana.

Reby was feeling very much like just another employee of his American boss. So much for the new arrangement they'd talked about after he'd rescued the American from Bega's men. To avoid a recurrence of the Saranda incident, Reby was supposed to accompany his boss everywhere, but that appeared to have been forgotten as well. He didn't really mind—he wasn't one for business and meetings.

After Wednesday's attempt to rally support, Reby had been curious to know what was planned before the next supporter meeting in Tirana the following week. "What have you got in mind?" he'd asked. "Are we arranging anything special?" An appropriate demonstration of the American's ability to take action would require time and careful planning.

The American had taken a moment to reply. "It'll have to be something up north, won't it?" But he'd said it in a way that had ended the conversation.

Reby suspected that the arrangement, whatever it might be, wasn't going as well as was necessary.

26

BEGA FINALLY GOT a message from his contact in El-basan—a young chauffeur from Tirana with big ambitions. He'd had to call the young man's father when the expected call didn't materialise. The big man had suggested to the father there'd be serious opportunities for the son if he'd follow through on some information about the American. Half an hour later he'd received a text.

Dinner planned late tonight. New restaurant inside castle.

He'd called the number back immediately to get more details, but there was no answer. Bega considered but decided against texting. Maybe they had enough information to go on. He stepped over to the specialist's room and let him know they'd be going back into town at 6:30 p.m., when it would be dark in this region of hills and valleys. He wanted to ensure they'd be positioned for any changes in plans the American might make.

<hr/>

The sniper went outside for a walk to compose himself and prepare for the evening's assignment. He returned to tell Bega he was going to take their vehicle and make a final check on his equipment. He found a sheltered spot further up the valley from the hotel, close to the river, where thick growth provided cover and would absorb at least some of the sound. He needed to confirm that the rifle's telescopic sighting was adjusted correctly. His viewpoint at the top of the stairs had allowed him to estimate the likely target distances from any of the towers to the restaurant—he always set the scope for the furthest distance expected, as it was easier to compensate should the target be closer. As he loaded and fired off several rounds, he remembered his training and what his seasoned instructor had insisted was the most important lesson for effective shooting:

A bullet crosses the line of sight twice—the first after exiting the muzzle, and the second at the adjusted sighting distance, when the projectile drops because of gravity. A rifle sighted dead-on for a target at a hundred metres will probably miss at two hundred metres, while a rifle sighted to hit slightly high at a hundred metres will almost certainly hit the target at both distances.

⸺◉⸺

They were nearing the dark line of the castle walls by 7:00 p.m. Bega was still uncomfortable in the driver's seat, even though the Montenegrin's equipment had been moved to the trunk. He hadn't bothered to readjust his position, and he was hunched forward as the worn-out seat was too low.

It would have been a minor irritant normally, but they were running a bit late and his call to Victor before leaving the hotel had put him on edge. He'd justified contacting Victor, thinking they should get something done about erasing the record of their involvement in the Shkodër accident. It was true that it would be better if nothing tied either of them to an appearance outside their normal territory, but the underlying reason for the call was that Bega was getting nervous and wanted to let Victor know the situation. Many things could happen to alter the planned outcome.

Victor had been livid. "Everyone's been called in and is out looking for you! We've even been making some peripheral approaches to the authorities. How can you expose yourself like this? You've worked to build up everything and now you're risking it all!"

The big Albanian had tried to shrug off the criticism while knowing his second-in-command was right. "Listen, Victor. I'm proceeding with the only way we have to stop this threat, and it's too late now to be concerned about how this might play out. I have no intention of being apprehended. If something goes wrong, I have the car and can get away." But he knew their organisation would suffer, and the future would hardly be rosy for either of them if the sniper failed, or identified his employer if caught. He brought the call to an end before Victor could say too much more. "I've got to go! See you soon."

Bega continued driving down the nearly empty boulevard and tried to focus on the present action. The dark road was dimly lit in spots by the occasional working streetlight that flickered overhead.

The Montenegrin put a hand gently on his arm and said, "Drop me anywhere around here." Bega's passenger continued checking outside the car as the Albanian pulled into an empty lot and switched off the headlights. The sniper was wearing dark clothes, a black baseball cap, and a longish raincoat, presumably to conceal the weapon. The car stopped and Bega looked over at him.

The specialist leaned closer and spoke quickly and calmly. "A final check. You've got your cell?" Bega patted his pocket. "Good, I'll make my way to a position and wait for your confirmation that our man has arrived. Short texts only. Park the car near the north side of the fortress, where you can see the café. You might have to leave the car to find a better vantage point. We'll rendezvous at the car right after." He had opened the door, and gave Bega a final nod.

"Good luck," Bega said, as the man went around to the trunk. There were some muffled noises after the lid opened. It closed, followed by a gentle hand thump, and Bega started off, only turning the headlights on when he emerged onto the boulevard. By then, there was no sign of his passenger.

———⊙———

It was after midnight, and Bega slapped his arms together against his chest to keep warm, thinking it would be better to be in the car with the insulative blankets. He'd forgotten how cold it could get away from the coast as November advanced towards the winter. The American had arrived about an hour before, but the restaurant opening had been long over and any remaining guests had moved inside. Bega had texted his colleague when a car had gone around back to the delivery entrance to get inside the castle walls and then arrived in front of the restaurant at the only direct street entrance to the building. Because the street terminated at the restaurant, the driver had turned the car around, parked it against the curb, and stayed in the vehicle. If the Montenegrin had been in the west tower, he might have had a clear line when the American had gone quickly from the car to the interior of the building, but no shot meant he was likely in the south wall tower, possibly the corner if no one was guarding it. In his text, Bega had advised switching location to have a view of the street entrance and the American's vehicle, but it would take time for the sniper to move to the west tower and not be noticed. If the American went out to his car now, before the Montenegrin repositioned, they'd have to follow him in their vehicle, lights out, and look for another opportunity. Bega didn't want to be driving in the dark, but at least the car would be warm.

Then Bega saw a door open on the side of the restaurant's lit interior, and several men came outside and huddled. Flashes of light as cigarettes were lit. The marksman might be looking these men over with his night scope. It was puzzling that they had come outside to smoke until he remembered the American didn't allow the use of tobacco in his vicinity. The smokers therefore told him two things: the target was still inside, and these were likely his supporters if they'd obliged him and come outside.

Once the smokers had returned inside, Bega hurried back to the car and manoeuvred it in the dark to face the restaurant and garden, glad they had thought to disable the interior lights earlier before leaving their hotel. The car's new position meant that in the driver's seat he had a line of sight on the restaurant's street entrance, but he couldn't quite see the American's car or the garden's lower terraces. As his colleague had said when they first saw the restaurant, getting the American in the open was the key, but how to get him outside without raising suspicions? Bega still had the element of surprise in his favour—they wouldn't expect a sniper—but was it worth the risk of showing himself if it meant giving the Montenegrin a clear shot?

———•《◎》•———

The Montenegrin waited in the west tower. He was crouched on the old stone floor, and shifted every half hour to ease cramping while scanning the area below over the low wall. He'd moved from the corner tower earlier after hearing from Bega that the target's car had arrived out of his line of sight. He was thinking back to other times when he'd been cold, more often in the vague daylight of winter. Back then he'd have been well prepared with thick woollen socks and a good warm coat if there was to be an operation in the mountains of the former Yugoslavia. As the hours ticked by his thoughts drifted to other jobs and inevitably, his last outing came to mind. He'd been over the events again and again.

27

THE VISIT TO his family home on the southwest coast of Montenegro had started well enough, even though his brother's business was going through a difficult time. He was on holiday; a time to see his extended family, marvel at how all the nieces and nephews had grown, and generally relax after having made a name for himself. It would be perfect if the call to go east would materialise, but the best time for this would be after he'd rested up enough and had seen all the old familiar places and faces.

One evening he went down to the restaurant to find a family lingering after their meal—his brother's wife had joined them, taking a break to chat with the young wife, a local girl home for a visit. He sat down at his usual spot to enjoy his soup, and when his niece came with the fish, he looked up to see that two young children had wandered over from their table to inspect him from a safe distance.

"So here you are, bothering another guest," said their father, returning from the toilets in the back. "Come along now," he said, acknowledging the lone diner with a nod.

The Montenegrin, charmed by their appearance and

quiet behaviour, said, "Actually they've been no trouble at all—quite the opposite, in fact." He occasionally dreamed of possibilities, knowing a family was just a fantasy for quiet moments.

The two women at the only other occupied table had turned at the sound of voices and saw the father returning with the children. The Montenegrin's sister-in law waved towards him. "Come and join us," she said, as she turned to her companion and explained, "He's family."

"Of course," said the father arriving at the table, "but I think we need more wine."

Introductions were made and slowly the conversation turned to politics and Montenegro's possible future as a country separate from Serbia. Eventually the young wife excused herself to put the children to bed, and the sister-in-law had to see to the kitchen closing. The two men were left alone at the table that looked out over the bay.

They grew silent as the moon rose gradually over the Adriatic and a single small boat moved slowly out beyond the pier, its wake glistening in the moonlight. The Montenegrin wondered how many times he'd see something as peaceful as the glittering harbour below. The family man finally spoke. "My wife should be here to see this, but she's probably fallen asleep with the children."

That night was the first of several sessions between the two men. Being similar in age and having grown up in the same region, they had much to talk about. But equally as much to avoid discussing.

After a few days of this new lifestyle, the Montenegrin received a call from his principal contact indicating a contract was available, but the reality of returning to work was an un-welcome development. "This one should be no problem, just an Albanian getting to think he's important. The payment is generous for someone without protection. He's just small time. No need for a spotter, I think." The details with timing and location would come through on the following day, when he would need to indicate his interest in the assignment.

The next day he got an early call. "Okay, a small hiccup, they're still trying to pin down the exact location." The delay was a relief, of sorts, to the Montenegrin. "His last sighting was near the Albanian border, so he's likely still in your area." His contact was very reassuring. "Should be no problem when you don't have to go far. I'll forward a picture by the usual means. If you want to do some legwork yourself, there's a bonus to confirm his location. There aren't many towns big enough, and he's likely on the coast."

Doing a job close to home was not something the spe-cialist really wanted, particularly since he was getting very comfortable in his hometown. If he refused the assignment, it would be a first. His reliability was one of the reasons he was still active, despite the decreasing number of opportunities.

Military discipline reasserted itself, and he decided to proceed to the next stage. The target's picture would be sent to the local post office to avoid any possible interception of an electronic image. On his way to retrieve the package, a new Mercedes with Albanian plates roared past him in the street and made a dusty turn down towards the harbour, where it parked. He waited until he saw the track-suited figure emerge and walk away from the boats, towards the beach and sunbathers, before he went into the post office.

The counter clerk told him his package had been delayed en route, but it would be there the following morning.

He made his way to where the Albanian's vehicle was still parked. A quick scan of the seaside indicated Mr. Track Suit was likely at the only restaurant on the beach, a partially completed glassed expanse with an extensive deck, beside the sunbathers. As he climbed the stairs to the patio, he spotted the Albanian, and sat down nearby to order a late morning coffee. He watched discreetly as a local small-time hustler joined the visitor, who proceeded to loudly order an extensive early lunch. The Montenegrin left when he was familiar with the man's gestures and was confident that he could identify him at any distance.

His contact called that evening, having heard of the postal delay, but was pleased when the Montenegrin accepted the assignment, though he didn't confirm he'd found the target—better to wait for the photo validation. "Good! I knew you'd come through. And no location confirmation yet, so you can still get the bonus when you find him."

The next morning, he returned from the post office with the nondescript brown envelope and went into his brother's empty office to study the picture. It was black-and-white, but good quality considering it was likely taken from a distance. He could see the man was sitting at a café. There was a small espresso in his hand as he talked to someone outside the picture frame. The Montenegrin looked in disbelief at the side profile, and then saw the wedding ring that confirmed the target was the family man staying at his brother's hotel.

He's Albanian? he thought, and looked around the office for the registry of guests. He found the black-lined record book and quickly scanned the few clients for that month. He saw the family's name carefully inscribed in black pen. The listing indicated the young wife held a Montenegrin passport, but the husband and two children were Albanian citizens. *But why the secrecy?* he wondered. They had talked *a little* about how visiting Albanian thugs were ruining the chance for legitimate tourists from the south to be open about their nationality. He likely had voiced his anti-Albanian prejudice a little too strongly.

When he'd accepted the assignment, he'd planned to do it quickly, so he'd still have some holiday time left to enjoy the family visit. He didn't know when he might be called to travel to the former Soviet republics. Two days went by before he received another call from his contact.

"I hope you got the photo."

"I did."

"Have you found him?"

"I think I know where he is."

"Good. Call me when it's done"

Three days passed before his contact called again.

"Our friends are wondering if there's a problem."

"I've lost him."

"Not good. I'll request a few more days. We've been consistent, so it might be all right if you can find him again and finish it."

The Montenegrin twice prepared himself and made plans to follow through on the contract, but both times he stopped at the last minute. It wasn't just that he enjoyed the man's company and admired his family—they were also guests at his brother's hotel. The Montenegrin tradition of hospitality was something that his brother took seriously, particularly with a family. If his guest disappeared, his brother would surely ask him to help find out what had happened, knowing he was something of a specialist. The Montenegrin had never told him he was operating freelance, and his brother would assume he could still use his military contacts in most of the former Yugoslavian states.

The specialist had been avoiding his former acquaintance at the hotel, but came down one morning and saw that the family was preparing to leave.

"Where have you been hiding, my friend?" asked the family man as his wife and children exchanged tearful goodbyes with the Montenegrin's sister-in-law. "Maybe you found out I'm Albanian?" he joked.

The Montenegrin stood by awkwardly as the man produced his business card and said, "Next time you're in Shkodër, look me up and I can show you the town. There's been a lot going on." The man extended his hand in farewell and the Montenegrin gripped it strongly enough to cause a questioning look from the Albanian.

"Be careful," said the specialist, but before the other man could respond, his children distracted him. When the young wife wished him the best for his future, the Montenegrin nearly followed them out to their vehicle.

He left his brother's hotel that afternoon saying he'd been called up. Later, when he managed to re-establish that he was still operating, he heard from his new coordinator that the Albanian family never made it back home.

28

I WOKE EARLY Saturday morning not having slept very well at all. Telling him a little lie wouldn't normally bug me, but I'd enjoyed the evening out with my dad. So saying that I'd already said goodbye to Malik had started to nag at me while we were watching the movie, and I'd kept thinking about it as we walked back to the Theresianum.

"Did you have a good time?" he asked.

"I did, Dad." We *were* getting along better. "I think it's because we're away from home."

"You may be right," he said. "You enjoyed the trip last weekend, though."

It was true, but maybe I was already ruining this new feeling. Okay! Now or never. "Uh, one thing I should tell you . . ." He looked up, waiting. "I, uh . . . need you to book my flight for my next visit." *Telling Malik first would be better*, I thought. I'd tell my dad after that.

He'd looked at me, and I'd gotten the feeling he knew more than he was letting on. "I'll do that when you know whether Giselle has gotten her parents' permission to visit."

Preparing breakfast helped take my mind off the problem,

PETER J. MEEHAN

and I had plenty of homework to do. The best thing would be to contact Malik, meet him somewhere, and do what I told my father I'd already done.

By late afternoon I was really pissed off with myself for letting my lie bother me so much. I knew I had to do something about it or I'd be awake all night, and trying to do any work on Sunday would be a total waste of time. Giselle was in her room, working to catch up on the days she'd been away in Croatia, so I stopped by her door and eventually she looked up.

"Working hard?" I asked. "Ready for a break?"

"One minute," she said. She was getting on her coat when I returned, and shortly, afterwards, we were walking towards another little spot we'd found. It was a *Konditorei* we knew would be nearly empty—a typical Viennese pastry shop that did most of its business in the morning.

Giselle was in a better mood than on our last outing, and quite talkative. I still hadn't told her that my dad thought her coming for a visit to Albania was a good idea. Today would be a good time to tell her.

"Well, I'm glad you wanted a break," she said. "I needed one after doing all that catching up, and—" She stopped talking in midsentence.

I looked over at her as we walked along, thinking it was rare she was at a loss for words. English was her second language, but she spoke it nearly as well as her Québécois French, particularly now after all the conversations in English we'd had. Sometimes she helped me with my French homework, but we nearly always spoke in English.

She looked at me. "I just remembered something that

Papa found out about Malik that I wanted to tell you."

I was glad she had brought him up. I needed to talk to someone my own age about him. I hadn't told her much about the restaurant outing with him, though she knew it hadn't been perfect, or I would have said more. We reached the pastry place, which was nearly empty.

We went to the counter and chose our favourites with hot chocolate to drink. I preferred the lightly flaky chocolate-decorated croissants, and Giselle was a whipped cream fanatic, usually on top of a chocolate dessert. The cream was real, a bit yellowy, and the desserts would be set out only for a day, but there were no reduced prices, even though the extra would be thrown away later.

We sat down and she continued. "My father called me last night. You know, he was quite interested in Malik's story, having gone to the same university, and all that old-boy stuff. Papa had said he wanted to contact him again, so he's gotten in touch with the embassy and the university. And Michaela," she was grinning now, "he also thought that we were more than a little interested in Malik, so he felt it was only right that he should look into his background—for our sake." Her voice became a little more serious. "So Papa confirmed that Malik was an engineer in training—but he's nearly sure Malik is *working* in Vienna."

That was interesting. "You mean he isn't just taking courses here?" I asked. "What about his trips to Romania?"

"Papa wasn't really sure about all the details, but he did say Malik has been to Romania—that's where they operate the machines and stuff—but only once or twice." She could see I was wondering what was really going on, and tried

— 217 —

again. "Papa found out that there's an agreement between governments to help the engineers in Romania. To keep the costs down they needed a student engineer who wanted work experience as part of his degree. His assignment was going to be mainly in Vienna because it's the closest centre to Eastern Europe. They might move the assignment to Romania if it continues, but right now it's still in Vienna until Romania joins the EU. I think Papa did the same work experience thing when he was getting his degree, but it was back home."

Was it important that Malik had told me he was on courses here when maybe he wasn't? I wasn't really sure, but why not tell me the truth? When I thought about it, I remembered he had often been vague on the dates when telling me about his schedule in Vienna, so I had a strong feeling what she was telling me was true. He'd also changed the weekends that he'd said he was going to be here or away several times on me when we were talking on the phone, telling me the course had been shortened or cancelled that week. I hadn't really thought much about it, being a little nervous talking to him, and believed whatever he'd said. Why would I think he was making it up?

"That's okay," I said. "We didn't really have a good time at the restaurant, and when we left each other that night, he didn't seem really interested in seeing me again soon. And I was getting the feeling that maybe he wasn't quite the person I thought he was, so maybe we weren't all that well suited, you know?" Something else had been bugging me about him. Where did he get the money to go to fancy restaurants if he was only a student? What was the whole story?

Giselle was waiting for me to say more, but she didn't

look very sorry for me. Was I missing something? I decided not to say too much more, but added, "And then I guess he came over looking for me when I was away?"

She was digging into her chocolate and looked up. "Yes, he was acting a bit odd when he came here. He wasn't really looking for you, though."

"Oh, I thought you said he wanted to know when I'd be back?"

Giselle wiped her face with a napkin and said, "Yes, that's true, but he almost sounded like he knew that already."

"Well I had told him I'd be away." I took another bite of my croissant. The flakes went everywhere as I leaned over the plate. "What else did he say?" Thinking back, I was starting to realise that he really had been quite dishonest with me on other things, like telling me how lonely he was out in Romania. Was he just looking for sympathy? And now I knew he must have been in Vienna for long periods when he'd told me he was in Romania.

"Well, he asked me if I wanted to get a coffee with him."

"Trying to find out more stuff about me, I guess," I said, looking over at her, but Giselle was finishing her pastry, getting the last few bits on her fork. "What about Maria?" I asked. She was the younger student we were friendly with.

Giselle looked up. "Maria? Well she could see that Malik wanted to talk to me in private."

"Really?" I said, giving her a laugh, but Giselle didn't join in.

The server behind the counter had gotten up and was making a big show of rattling the keys, so we drank the last of our chocolate and went out into the damp Vienna evening.

The weather was the usual: depressing, though I hadn't noticed it so much when we'd left the Theresianum. Maybe the Viennese had a reason not to smile, but Christmas was coming and there were advent lights in some of the window displays. I was starting to see how coloured lights made a difference at this dreary time of year. What would it be like here without Christmas coming? I had a quick thought about the sunshine that was nearly always waiting for me in Albania.

Neither of us spoke very much on the way back. There was a lot to think about, and I had to contact Malik first thing in the morning to arrange a meeting and say so long. Then I'd feel better—and I owed my father that much. After I was in my bed, I realised I'd totally forgotten to tell Giselle that she needed to find out if her parents would let her come to Albania with me.

29

REBY OPENED HIS eyes and was surprised to see that the first hints of violet were appearing to the east against the dark night. He tossed the warm blanket into the back seat and texted his boss. *Ready?*

After a few minutes, the reply beeped through. *Come for coffee.*

He needed no more encouragement as the car was quite cold, and he would need to be sharp for the drive ahead. He left the vehicle and hurried over and up the restaurant path. If Reby had looked back towards the northern perimeter wall of the citadel before entering the building, he would have seen the door to an older car open and a large man emerge.

The figure moved quickly towards Reby's car in the still dark street and circled around the vehicle, looking towards the restaurant door. Then he crouched down next to the driver's side front wheel before quickly retracing his steps back to his car.

———※《①》※———

"So? What do you think?" the owner asked. The opening of the restaurant on the previous night had drawn only a small local crowd despite the elaborate preparations.

His guest remained noncommittal. "Let me try your coffee first—I'll let you know after that."

Reby entered to the sounds and smells of coffee being noisily prepared behind the bar. He saw his boss sitting with the restaurant owner, who'd been good enough to offer the American his only guest room for the night, though he suspected his boss had spent most of his time in the restaurant building's small conference room meeting with various local clan heads and had used the guest room for only a few hours' sleep. The owner got up as Reby came over, nodded a greeting, and then went over to fetch their coffees while resuming nonstop promotion for the unique opportunity to invest in his business.

Since when is opening a restaurant no risk? Reby thought as he joined the American. The owner looked familiar to him, possibly from past exploits. He'd settled down to run his own business here. Reby knew his boss was only listening to him because the American needed support, and this man had already succeeded in becoming influential in the region.

"You maybe want to know it all, I think. How much this place cost." He was back at their table, and set the cups down one at a time. "It was difficult, I tell you, but was worth every lek." Reby exchanged a look with his boss. He knew the owner was trying to become legitimate but doubted he'd solved his difficulties through lawful channels. "Big plans for Christmas, my friend, big plans. This castle very old, no news about that, but we find many old things: Ottoman coins, nothing special, but also Roman statues. Only one complete, but marble everywhere. This will be popular place. People already come to Elbasan to see other Roman things, but this totally new. You must see garden. Finish coffee, then I take you personal. You too, Reby—very educational."

The American had nearly finished his small espresso. Reby put his cup down, refreshed, and raised an eyebrow at his boss. They needed to get going.

"Maybe next time." The American got up and Reby followed, going around him to open the main entry door.

"Look, come this way, only two minutes, you'll see." The owner switched on the outside lights and slid open one of the glass doors that led down to the garden outside. The lights revealed the details of the lower terraces, where the statuary was visible.

The American turned and glimpsed the lower sections of the unearthed wall, clearly a different and more ancient construction than the repaired Ottoman section above. He moved closer, towards the opened terrace door to better see what remained of the Roman structure as Reby waited.

"You see? Is very unique, sheltered from hustle of traffic. Great for coffee or private meetings in garden, and cool when summer day too hot. Beautiful and warm any time, when sun shine." The outdoor heaters would be installed when the funds were available.

The American moved closer for a better view of the garden.

———«◉»———

There was a figure at the terrace's glass doors, but through the rifle scope, the Montenegrin could see that it wasn't his man. In the background, another figure looked to be approaching, but the outside lights had been switched on and his features weren't clearly defined in the bright reflection now shining off the doors—if he moved just a bit closer his face would move out of the reflected light. More movement and the glass door was suddenly pulled open. Voices carried out towards the walls. The marksman took a deep breath and held it, waiting to exhale if the target appeared.

———«◉»———

"Look, very good stonework just like walls; and tables are good quality—no rusting, guaranteed! What could be better? It's great opportunity." He stepped out onto the terrace.

Reby, watching the owner and his boss from the main entrance, had started over when he sensed that they were going to go outside. He quickly stepped in front of the American just before the jagged hole in the glass appeared, and he felt the pain in his arm from the force that swung him around.

"Down!" he shouted.

Another muffled *crack* and there was a grunt from the American, who'd hesitated after the first shot before stepping back, and he collapsed backward, away from the door. A third bullet cut through the air, shattering the glass in the

doors completely, and gouged chunks out of the newly finished Italian granite floor. The busboy and waiter looked up
from the bar while the two guards who'd just sat down for
their coffee reacted by going into a crouch from their chairs,
backing away from their table beside the doors to the terrace.
They both drew their weapons as they looked toward the
garden. Only the owner remained standing, out on the terrace, mouth open and speechless, as he looked around before
comprehending the danger.

Reby had moved quickly despite his injury, jumping over
his boss and pulling the slumped American completely inside and away from the door with his good arm. Then he
scanned the top of the Ottoman walls. The shots appeared
to have come from straight across the terrace, from the high
side of the wall near the tower. He'd been hit in the arm, but
the American's wound looked more serious. Blood smears
outlined a path from where he'd fallen, and his unconscious
face was ashen. Reby would have to staunch the bleeding and
get him to Tirana as quickly as possible.

30

THE SNIPER WAS already down and running along the outside wall towards the car. *Three fucking shots!* He'd had three shots and still he wasn't certain—he'd taken a chance, shooting through the glass when he was nearly sure of the target, in case the man didn't step outside. He'd had him dead in his sights; a head shot that instead had hit someone who'd stepped forward. His second shot had been just a little too quick, and he'd hit the target in the chest. He'd hesitated on the third to be sure, and then just missed him when the man dropped as he pulled the trigger. The shot might have creased his shoulder?

"Fuck!" His leg cramped as he ran. He'd been crouched in the cold all night—waiting. It had been a relief to get down from the southwest tower after Bega's message, and he'd warmed with the exertion of getting back up to the western location. He was breathing heavily now, rounding the end of the wall, and looked for the car. He knew he might be seen in the early light, and he was carrying the rifle. He searched back and forth. Where was the fucking car? A big figure appeared from the other direction and signalled to him.

———— •((◉))• ————

Bega pointed the Montenegrin in the direction of the car, which was up against some bushes, lodged in a spot that had provided the best overview of the citadel's interior. He ran the few feet to the car and got in as the sniper threw his rifle in the trunk and opened the passenger door.

"You got him? Great, let's go!"

The Albanian turned the key, but the car barely turned over. The glove compartment was open. They'd forgotten to remove the small dim light and it must have drained most of the battery's power. Bega wondered how he could have left it open, then panicked to think someone had been in the car while he was over deflating one of the target's tires. He looked to his passenger, who appeared calm. The man's composed features had a reassuring effect, and he realised he had probably knocked the glove compartment open when he was getting out. Just then the car's engine caught and he over-revved the motor. His sweaty palm slipped on the gearshift causing the transmission to grind noisily as he forced it into reverse. He backed up then started forward and was turning onto the side avenue as the one street light along the narrow road flickered and went out.

"What about the rifle? We need to dump it!"

No reply.

They swung past the corner tower of the old walls without slowing, the tires screeching slightly and the suspension making an ominous *crack* that affected the handling as Bega tried keeping the car steady. They reached the outskirts in a few minutes as there were no other vehicles on the road. It would have been busier on a weekday. The rough section around the old factory came up, and Bega made the wrong turn at an intersection, onto a road that ended in a fetid pool of dark liquid that enveloped an overgrown structure. "Fuck!" He jammed to a stop and slammed the gearshift into reverse, nervously backing all the way to the turnoff, nearly going off the track and overcorrecting, but there was still no traffic. The car almost stalled as his foot slipped on the clutch, then jumped forward as he started off and raced through the gears, straining the old French motor. Once beyond the outskirts, he swerved north at the last minute, onto the mountain road to Tirana, catching his passenger unprepared. The Montenegrin lurched into him and straightened up without a word as they started up the incline that would take them around the back way into the Albanian capital. The smell of hot lubricants grew slowly as the car's engine began overheating—it was being pushed to its limits and burning off grease and grime accumulated over years of use and abuse.

Bega had made a snap decision at the turnoff, but he thought this route might be a better way. He hadn't planned to go into Tirana but now felt it was the safer option, assuming the authorities would soon be aware of the shooting—they'd set up checkpoints on the main road west first, not this back way into the capital, and Tirana was big enough to find a safe haven until he got in touch with Victor. As the old car gradually climbed its way back and forth up the narrow switchbacks of the short, steep ridge to the crest and on to the Tirana valley, he risked looking over at his passenger, who had yet to say a word. *Understandable in the circumstances*, he thought. This route was shorter, but the road was not good—several corners were known to have claimed vehicles whose rusted and twisted frames had yet to be hauled up from the deep ravines far below. It could work to their advantage though; the first in a series of sharp corners was coming up, and he could pull over and get rid of the rifle, and add it to all the other garbage that had been dumped into the gorge over the years. Then he could slow down, or else the old engine might give out. He wondered about the brakes on their descent into Tirana—one step at a time. He heart was racing and the excitement was nearly too much to handle.

———————

Reby risked running out to the car and driving it closer to the restaurant's entrance. There was a very good chance the shooter was long gone, now that other guards were running around trying to look unafraid and important. They had checked along the wall, in all three towers, and in the nearby alleys for any sign of the marksman and his support. Let them—Reby needed to get his boss to a hospital, and quickly. There was no facility here in Elbasan that could help.

The American had been shot in the upper chest, and his breath was rattling, a bad sign. All the blood had come from a shallow wound as a result of the third shot, which had nicked his shoulder and removed a flap of skin. That had been patched by the owner, who had quickly taken charge of the situation once he overcame his initial shock. Now the man's brother was waiting at the entrance with the American, who was on a makeshift stretcher. Reby's arm hurt—the bullet had gone straight through his forearm—but at least the steel cigarette lighter he carried in his inside jacket pocket had deflected the projectile. There was a bad bruise, and it hurt like hell, but the heavy stainless steel had prevented any real damage to his chest. The owner had insisted on wrapping his arm using military-grade dressing, and then gave him some penicillin tablets, which Reby suspected were past their expiration date.

Reby backed the car up to the restaurant door at the base of the steps, then got out to help carry his boss into the vehicle. The restaurant owner's brother got in the back seat, and he and Reby laid the American so that his head was up on the other passenger's lap. The three of them were out of the city in minutes, Reby glancing into the rear-view mirror to the back seat often and wondering if internal bleeding was further damaging his wounded passenger. One of the front tires felt like it was low in air pressure, but he wasn't overly concerned—he had equipped the car with the best run-flat tires he could afford. A short time later, he turned north onto the shorter mountain road to Tirana and accelerated loudly up the first straight stretch, automatically doing up his seat belt as he came out of the first corner.

At the first right-hand switchback, after throttling down, he felt the car drift slightly in its turn, a definite sloppiness in the wheels. He hadn't checked the tires since yesterday, but a low-pressure tire was clearly affecting the handling. On the next bend in the other direction, the car tracked better, but there was still a spongy feel. He'd never actually tested the claims that run-flat tires could be driven without air pressure, but he was reasonably sure the tire wasn't totally flat. Even if he stopped now to look, what could he do? There was no time to change a tire. Reby considered calling the embassy—the Americans must have a helicopter on standby for medical emergencies—but there'd be red tape to talk through and he wasn't sure he'd be convincing. He'd try calling only if they got stuck somewhere.

They were barrelling along the top of the mountain ridge now, and he was going as fast as he felt his car's poor handling would permit. He was trying to recall the recommended speed for the maximum range on the run-flat wheels—excessive wear occurred with low pressure in the tires, but driving normal speeds should be safe enough, provided the road was straight and the tarmac even. He knew there'd be enough of a safety margin to be able to exceed the recommendations for speed and distance, but by how much? And for how long? He'd been looking forward to the series of sharp bends coming up, but not now, not under these conditions. He wanted a cigarette badly, but quickly cut off the thought, as well as others on how dangerous it was to be driving on this mountain road with a bad tire. Instead, he tried to focus on his driving skills. He was being tested, and his confidence returned as he prepared for the upcoming bend, slowing marginally as the curve came into view.

<hr />

Bega had pulled over as far as he could on the wide shoulder, just after the sharp bend. The view southeast towards

Elbasan was wide open in the early sunlight, and across the ravine some distance in front, he could see the road continuing back around the far side of the ridge. He looked up when the muffled sound of a big diesel transport truck changed to a clear tone. He saw the vehicle slowly trudging around one of the tight bends. It would be picking up speed on the wide inside curve and soon be passing their position. They needed to get moving.

They were opening the trunk to retrieve the weapon when they heard another vehicle coming up behind them. "Hold on," Bega said, just as his colleague was reaching into the trunk. They'd have to wait now until both vehicles were out of view before dumping the weapon. The Montenegrin's head emerged just as a dark blue Mercedes screeched around the bend and continued on past them. Bega, who had expected to see another truck, watched in surprise as the car disappeared around the winding curve. "Shit!" he yelled, thinking about earlier that morning when he'd tried to cripple the target's vehicle—he should have deflated all the tires.

He reacted quickly and reached into the trunk for the rifle, looking hard at the Montenegrin. "Get ready for when he comes back around the bend over there!" He pointed to the far side of the ravine. "That was the target's car! Finish your job!" He knew they only had a minute before the car would reappear and then be gone. Their car would never catch up to the Mercedes.

The Montenegrin turned slowly to the big man who was yelling angrily, and he wondered what had happened. The words sunk in slowly, and then it was clear—he was going to have a second chance. The uncertainty vanished as his training took over. He straightened up, took the rifle and tripod from Bega, and looked across the gully at the road where it was exposed on the sharp bend, before it disappeared around the far corner. Closing the trunk, he leaned over it while adjusting the position of the tripod. The roar of the super-charged AMG Mercedes echoed from the wide inside curve of the ridge face that was hidden from their view. He flexed his shoulders and looked down the scope to where the road emerged from trees on the far side of the ravine. He moved his eye out of the scope view to look once more across the gully, in order to estimate the distance to the other side.

And now the hard part, he thought. He would have to hit the driver of a rapidly moving vehicle with a scope that was set for a much shorter distance. A bead of sweat started to form above his sighting eye, but he simply wiped it away. He couldn't let the difficulty of the shot become an obstacle.

Okay, he thought, *but the car has to slow for the bend. And rounding the inside curve of the highway will actually bring the car closer as it circles around the ravine . . .*

Time slowed as he calmed his breathing and looked back down the scope to focus on the world of magnified light, where the crosshairs wavered on green, yellow, and grey in the hazy distance. He did his best to readjust the scope but could hardly make out the windshield, much less the driver's position, as the vehicle moved through the scattered tree branches and leaves. The sun sparkled off the chrome wheel and drew him to the larger target. He could hit any part of the tire for the shot to be effective, but not dead centre.

Group your shots when you have a moving target. He could hear his instructor repeating what was important.

In a trance, he tracked the emerging shape as it fully materialised from the line of trees, a dark form advancing silently along the line of the mountain road and nearing the far bend. The marksman sighted high for the distance and in advance of the target's front tire for the speed, then gently squeezed until he felt the kick; then once again, but a touch lower; and a third bracketing shot to be sure, but he knew already, and looked up before the big man beside him reacted to what had been an amazing shot.

The big transport's air brakes hissed sharply in slowing for the corner, jolting the shooter back to a world of sound, and he looked up to see a startled driver looking down on him and the rifle spread out across the car trunk, but it was only for an instant, as the wide stare quickly disappeared around the bend and the smell of hot brake lining and dust wafted over them.

The sniper stood up from the car trunk, reached for the rifle and tripod, and stepped towards the drop-off on the edge of the shoulder. He rotated like a shot putter to heave the equipment far out into the gully and watched it spin slowly down as it crashed into the thick foliage. Only then did he finally relax.

31

"SO, ARIYAN, HOW was the trip?" I'd gone straight to the office from the airport.

He stubbed out his cigarette hurriedly and rushed through the balcony doorway into his office to shake my hand. He looked apologetic with a half smile as he said, "Tony, I never go to visit this place again. They are crazy. One old man, he must be smoking hashish, wild looks and pull his knife out!"

"He threatened you with a knife?"

"We talk to locals like you ask. This man walking along and look up at our car, then start crazy talk, holding a knife. He was drug addict, for sure."

I found this hard to believe, but I hadn't been there and would have to think about his story—maybe talk with the other managers at our weekly meeting. I'd heard that Albania had major marijuana-growing operations in the nearly inaccessible mountain areas, but could I ever be sure about what I was told here? This was still a culture of hiding the truth so as not to offend or cause negative reactions. It was understandable, but difficult to accept in my position—my relationship with the country and its changing traditions was getting better, but it was challenging work, like getting to know a strange new friend. Albanian customs and behaviour were becoming more familiar but retained a sense of mystery that I found somehow appealing.

"You stayed in the car?" Had he met someone mentally ill or had this person simply been caught by surprise? As a manager making decisions, I needed to get the facts straight.

"Of course! He was crazy dangerous! No more trips to north for me."

"But Ariyan, did you talk to the head man? What about the contractor?"

"Look Tony, I met both like you ask. Head man was very nervous. I think he not sure who I am, even with contractor explaining things. Contractor's better now, slowly getting preparations going, but head man nearly run away from me at the end, like I'm ready to hurt him. Contractor says he always like that." Ariyan's cell phone tinkled and he went back outside, lighting another cigarette.

I was getting two different messages from his story. The contractor appeared to believe things were going ahead, but the head man's reaction suggested otherwise, unless he was simply burned out from all the problems he'd faced over the years. I could hear Ariyan's excited voice outside, probably reliving his experience of meeting a crazy old man in bandit territory. If we went ahead with the survey he'd have to go back. Part of me suspected he might be exaggerating the incident to try to avoid going next time.

Meeting Malik was easier than I thought it would be. I just called him on Sunday, and he said the Prater was good later in the afternoon. It was the big amusement park where tourists and everyone else went on the weekends, so out in the open, nothing too quiet. His voice sounded nearly bored, so it seemed he was no longer trying to be a *special* friend.

Giselle was in the kitchen when I walked in, and I told her the news after we'd nodded good morning to each other.

She seemed surprised but didn't look at me or stop what she was doing. "I got the impression that it was all over between you?"

"It is for me," I said, wondering again if she'd become interested in him. I'd thought about it after our outing the previous day, and I'd woken early and been thinking it over. She hadn't stopped moving around as we spoke, fixing toast and opening the fridge.

"Giselle," I said, really hoping she was listening to me, "I don't think there ever was much from Malik's side." I was going to say more but didn't. Neither of us seemed to be in the right mood for talking.

It dawned on me overnight that I really was quite stupid, but it was a lesson I would remember. And it was also possible Giselle might have lied about Malik's actions if she was interested in him. I wasn't going to accuse Malik of anything when we met in the afternoon. I'd wait and see if he'd act like the jerk he'd been when we'd last seen each other. And I was unsure now how I would act with him, after all this thinking.

There had been a hint of his uppity side on the phone, but maybe I was just reading more into what he was saying, now that I'd stepped back and was seeing him waaay differently.

"That's too bad," she answered, but I couldn't tell if she meant it.

The day was beautiful and sunny for late November, and I left a bit early to be sure of getting to the Prater on time. As I walked along, I decided I really didn't want to take Giselle with me to Albania for a visit, and she probably wouldn't want to come either.

The subway was crowded as fewer trains ran on Sunday. My "friends" at the subway station were all hanging around, more of them than usual, but the attractive guy didn't notice me walk by. I might have tried my German on him, but he was too busy trying to convince two younger girls to come over and hang with their crowd. I guess I'd missed my chance.

The park was quite pretty in the weak afternoon sun. Though all of the trees had lost their leaves, quite a few flower stalls were open around the walking paths, and there were lots of lights going up onto Christmas arrangements at the major corners of the walkways.

We were to meet near the giant Ferris wheel that was the centre of the park for most families, and then I saw him in the distance. As I got closer, Malik looked down at a bench he was standing beside and said something to the person sitting there. She stood up as I slowed, and smiled in my direction. Malik extended his hand to shake mine and said, "So glad you could make it. I'd like you to meet Stephanie."

Her smile continued as he said, "Stephanie, this is Michaela, my friend I was telling you about. She's a big rugby fan, too."

So that's what I was! I had to bite my lip and remember I wasn't going to make a scene—I had kind of made up a few things when we'd first met at the rugby match, but that wasn't the same as his total bullshit lies. Was anything he'd said true? What a jerk! Did he think I was that stupid? Still, I wasn't going to show that I was angry, especially in front of his new friend. Whatever he'd told her about me, I wanted to be much more than that.

Time passed as we walked along, and I eventually calmed myself as Stephanie and I began chatting about our mutual interests. She really was quite a nice young woman, British, and maybe a year or two older than I. Malik didn't say much. Apparently the asshole was enjoying the outing. At one point, the jerk referred to our evening out at the Austrian restaurant, telling Stephanie, "The experience was wonderful. It's so nice to know they have efficient waiters here when the service is so difficult in the south." Did he mean southern Europe or where he was from? The stupid twat.

Eventually I offered my regrets to fuckface and his new girlfriend, saying that I had to be getting back. "I really enjoyed talking with you," I said to Stephanie, and it was true. "You're really much nicer than what Malik told me, but you must know he does exaggerate . . ." I gave a little laugh and could see him slowly start to react—he really was slow-witted. Then I added, "A lot!"

"Now, Malik," I said, smiling as delightfully as I could as I faced him, "it's been a particularly enlightening afternoon. But don't forget to send me my money." The money part had just popped into my head. What would she think? I walked away.

32

UNLIKE HIS CAR, which was a total write-off, Reby counted himself lucky as he gradually got free of the mangled vehicle. The smell of oil hung heavily in the tangle of vegetation and boulders at the bottom of the ravine, but the car's self-sealing gas tank had prevented much fuel from leaking. Slipping and staggering his way up the slope through the rock scree and prickly vines, his mind began to clear as the initial shock subsided, and finally he managed to scramble the last few difficult feet to the roadside embankment.

Reby looked both ways along the road as he crouched, exhausted from the climb. There was no sense in going on to Tirana. There wasn't much for him here in Albania, anywhere, now. Having chosen the wrong side, he wouldn't be employable for a while, even with his driving skills. And these would be in question once it was known he'd been the driver of this wreckage. North to Montenegro or Kosovo, near his home, was one possibility, but there was the opportunity in Macedonia, at the lakeside town where he was nearly sure to find a mechanic's job. Better to go where he could lose himself and forget about what could have been rather than have to listen to his family.

There had been the sounds of a few vehicles passing overhead as he made his ascent up the steep slope. He tried to stand up, thinking he'd flag down the first vehicle going south, but it was a major effort, and to avoid the temptation to sit back down, he started to backtrack along the road, to a place where there'd be more room for anyone stopping to pull over. His arm was starting to ache from the wound and would only get worse. A rusted signpost offered a place to lean for a minute as he thought back to the difficult race up the mountain with his wounded passenger, and then the sudden loss of control before hitting the trees—had it only been a few hours before?

It must have been around here, he thought, and with an effort pushed away from the road marker to find the spot where the car had gone off the highway. Reby searched down the steep slope, trying to see signs of damage in the undergrowth, and then remembered the car had been airborne because of the speed, and scanned further out to where snapped treetops and broken white cores of larger branches revealed themselves. He started shaking slightly as he stood, and suddenly he could feel the weightless arc of the car's plunge, could hear the sound of the snapping trees, shattering windows, and screeching metal as the vehicle tumbled against rocks and boulders before jarring to a dead stop against the base of a massive trunk. It had all gone quiet then, except for the ticks of the cooling engine. The cautious call of a bird, and then another, finally broke the silence, and Reby overcame his bewilderment by slowly working himself free of the seat belt and out of the driver's-side window and crushed door. By the time he'd reached around the deadfall and broken vehicle to check on his passengers, both partially hanging out of the windows on either side of the car, neither man showed any sign of a pulse.

Thank God the gorge into which they'd crashed wasn't that deep. The bigger drop-off was at the bend on the end of the straight stretch of road. There the floor of the ravine was several hundred metres deeper. For that, Reby was grateful. If the tire had blown out on that turn, he would be in much worse shape, possibly trapped within his crushed mausoleum until he died of thirst. And he'd been a fool to believe the hype on run-flat tires!

The muted sound of a vehicle approaching got Reby moving again—it would soon come around the bend. He crossed quickly back over to the inside lane to signal the driver. An old van came into view and slowed to pull over. As he hobbled towards his ride, the late afternoon sun shone on metal below the van's opened door, and he scooped up the piece, thinking it had fallen from the vehicle.

"*Faleminderit*," he said, climbing in. The aged driver looked him over before turning back to the steering wheel to resume the journey.

Reby sat in the worn seat, his head down. He was looking at the surface of the road as it slipped by, visible though a jagged hole in the floor, and then the image shifted to another scene—his mind replayed the moments in the car just before the morning's accident. He'd been compensating for the low tire pressure on his side of the vehicle, while using all his skill to push the car's speed to the absolute limit of safety, and then the front tire had blown out. He'd lost control almost immediately, veering off the road. At first the bright blue sky had filled his view through the windshield, and then the vehicle had tilted forward . . .

"ELBASAN?" the driver shouted.

Reby turned to the man, whose raised voice he could only just hear over the road and engine noise. "YES, THE BUS STATION." He glanced into the side mirror through his window and could see the corner of a badly scratched and dirty face staring back. He looked at his hands and felt his wounded arm throbbing. At least his torn and muddied clothes weren't out of place on the grimy seat. He had thought to give an explanation for his appearance, but the driver was staring forward, all his concentration on the road. He was probably old enough to have seen worse, and Reby was content to sit and try to relax. The vehicle's din receded into the background.

They were coming up to the other sharp bend, having circled around the ravine. Reby looked over to the view where the old fortress town could be seen far in the distance, but his thoughts were elsewhere as his gaze came to rest on the wide shoulder of the curve he'd driven past that morning. It seemed different. He continued looking at the roadside spot closely, as the driver steered the van around the corner, until it disappeared behind them.

His mind turned to the loss of his passengers. It was no surprise that the wounded American hadn't survived the ordeal, but the death of the other man forced Reby to think about the need to tell his brother in Elbasan. It was a task he felt strongly about, part of the Albanian code of family. But stopping to tell him would delay getting away, now that he'd nearly decided to continue on to Ohrid. He thought about the two possibilities a while longer, but knew it would be better to go straight to Macedonia—he'd return later to Elbasan. Having to admit being responsible for what happened to the restaurant owner's brother made him uncomfortable—how would the owner react? Perhaps the dead man had a wife and children?

He was becoming more confident that he could find a job at the garage in Ohrid where they'd had the paint changed on his car. The owner had been impressed by Reby's car, and he spoke Albanian well, so they'd talked for a while about the best modifications for various engines. The Macedonian had been looking for a Mercedes mechanic. Reby knew he'd be good at the work and he could lose himself in the complexities of patching up newer vehicles, sorting out the electronics, and figuring ways around the high-tech software installs. He'd eventually be able to earn enough to put together an older model and fix it up in his spare time. It was a plan to start again, at least. And he could get used to the colder climate. It needn't be forever ...

The loss of his mentor was a major blow, and just when he'd gotten used to having him around again. His future prospects had radically reversed—it would take time for him to accept the American was gone—now that the hectic lifestyle was over. Even during his boss's exile, Reby had believed he'd return. Now it *really* was finished.

At least he was alive. He counted himself lucky to have survived the accident. How many of his former colleagues were still around? The American was now just another number to add to all those he'd lost over the years. He thought back to their meeting again at the Tirana airport, and the trip south to Saranda. In many ways, the events of the last few days had revealed a harsher reality of his former boss, showing him to be a desperate man capable of nearly anything to advance his own self-serving agenda. Reby recalled someone quite different when they'd first met, a foreigner who'd helped him become more skillful and self-sufficient. There had been times when a cold-hearted indifference had been visible, but that was a rarity sometimes necessary for the lead man in their operations. The American's recent failure in Saranda had revealed a more troubling character, not much different from what he'd been told about Bega. And he had seemed to be out of touch on their route south, even before their arrival in Saranda. All of this now made him question whether the big Albanian was as bad as Reby had been led to believe? Had Bega really cheated his partner out of their original agreement to become successful in the south? It was what Reby had been told, and always accepted.

He closed his eyes to the sights and sounds around him as the van swayed back and forth on its worn suspension. He thought about his wrecked car at the bottom of the gully while they made their way down the mountain road and on towards Elbasan. The broken Mercedes was only just visible through the bare trees near the bottom, but only if someone knew where to look and what to look for. It might be spotted eventually, but it would be nearly invisible with the coming of leaves in the spring. If someone saw it, Reby hoped he'd be long gone before the bodies were discovered and the car was dragged up the slope. Of course if the restaurant owner found out, recovering his brother's body and the car would

PETER J. MEEHAN

be the first thing he'd do. Reby's head leaned forward as he drifted off, his thoughts slowing—too tired to wonder why the image of the big man he'd seen going into the hotel in Saranda hovered in his dreams . . .

A horn sounded, and Reby snapped awake to bright daylight and the sight of the blackened factories outside Elbasan. The van was quieter now that they were slowing at the outskirts of the city, too slow for a new BMW sedan that had shot past them on the narrow road. The bus station was on the other side of the citadel, and they were nearly passed the fortress' walls when Reby turned to the driver. "I know I said the bus station, but can you let me out here?" he asked.

———◦《◉》◦———

Reby waited inside the restaurant for the owner to return, and signalled to the waiter at the bar, who'd been looking over at him and talking to the barman. Workmen were already repairing the glass doors, but the Italian granite floor would require special attention—it might be some time before it was completely restored. He'd gone into the WC to make himself a bit more presentable, but realised as he looked in the mirror that he'd need to buy new clothes. He'd just have to give the owner the bad news as he was. He'd managed to get some painkillers for his arm, but something more would be needed. There was no sign of infection, yet.

The waiter arrived and said, "The boss shouldn't be much longer, but I'll get you a coffee—maybe a raki? You look like you need it." He received no reply.

"How's our friend doing?" Still no answer. The waiter returned to the bar.

Reby sat at the table and smoked, trying to think about the best way to deliver the news. The waiter returned with his coffee and a good-sized raki, but remained standing beside him until Reby looked up, bothered by his proximity.

"Look at this," the waiter said, holding out his hand to reveal a bullet. "The police have one, but this one was harder to find."

Reby glanced at the slug of metal, then looked more closely, studying it in detail. "May I?" he asked, reaching for the bullet, which he put on the table. Then he searched in his pockets, until he found the metal piece he'd picked off the road near the scene of the accident. They were different shapes: the one from the restaurant looked like a bullet, though the colour was unusual—it must be a special make. The other piece was smaller and deformed, but side by side, it was clear they were the same colour and made of the same metal compound. The smaller one could be a piece of a bullet the same size as the one from the restaurant.

Reby stared at them. *Fine, but how did that piece end up on the road?* The other bullet had gone clean through his arm. Could it have been trapped after hitting his lighter? Did it fall out later? It seemed very unlikely, but how else to explain its presence? It didn't seem to make much sense. He picked both of them up from the table, one in each hand, but felt his eyes closing—he was completely exhausted.

"Fuck!" Reby exclaimed, standing abruptly. The driver's side tire hadn't blown out. It was the passenger side! He'd felt the dip and heard the metal wheel rim scrape the tarmac on the side closest to the ravine! His chair fell over, and the waiter slowly backed away from the table, leaving the souvenir with the driver.

Reby thought it all over as he heard the main door open and the owner arrive. The low pressure run flat tire wasn't the problem—it was the passenger tire that exploded when hit by the bullet. There had been a car on the first corner of the ravine, and he remembered now that the trunk was open. It was also the only car they'd seen while driving from Elbasan. Then he remembered the big figure standing beside the vehicle on that first bend that morning.

Bega! But he was no shooter—he must have had someone else with him.

33

THE MONDAY REPORT from our Croat contractor on the northern block was positive. They'd completed the first survey line, so regardless of any issues brewing with the locals, the work was going ahead without incident. By Tuesday, the Austrians had downgraded the risk, according to my general manager.

"Tony, I hope you've got the surveyors working full speed. The Austrian embassy is nearly ready to issue a green light on any planned activity in the northeast. By Friday, latest. Frankly, I think we've been worrying too much, and a lot of this is because of your personnel in the field. I was of the opinion that there wouldn't be any *real* difficulties. You need to keep in mind that we are in the Balkans, after all, and this . . . *Diese Schwierigkeiten sind normal.*"

I thought about apologising to him in overly polite Germanic phrases, but he wouldn't be in the mood for sarcasm and I needed to keep on his good side—to have my contract renewed or extended when the two-year term expired. He'd previously threatened me—"it will go on your record!"—over some minor breach of Hapsburg etiquette.

PETER J. MEEHAN

It was during my first month on the job, but I was a long-term consultant, not an Austrian employee concerned about his personnel file. There was still much I wanted to see in Albania, so I'd need to be more careful. Like not mentioning the war or signing off with *Seig Heil!* anymore in my emails to friends back home. It was childish, but had made me laugh and deal with the stress, until I'd unintentionally attached these to a Vienna email and spent two days worrying how best to get the Austrian recipient to remove the incriminating Nazi references without drawing attention to them—luckily they were buried in a long boring message and I'd heard nothing more about it.

I was thinking about taking a family trip to northern Greece, possibly visiting Corfu from the Greek side, when Michaela was back on her next break. I'd talked to her Monday night and she'd said she was looking forward to the trip.

"Dad," she'd said, "you do remember I'll be going to a party on the Friday, after I get in, right?"

"Yes, I remember that."

"Oh, and Giselle can't make it," she'd added.

"That's too bad." But I'd guessed this was the case when she hadn't said anything more after bringing it up the first time. I hoped there hadn't been any real problems with her friend, knowing that teenagers often had fallings in and out with one another.

I was looking forward to seeing northern Greece now that the border would be much less difficult to cross, even with Albanian licence plates. Work had apparently resumed on the highway bridges south of Gjirokaster, so the drive should take less time. It would also be familiar to all of us, now that we were growing accustomed to travelling in the country. We'd take the inland route rather than the coast, but just to get there faster. Would I consider coming back on the coast if we had time? Would northern Greece have anything like the Venetian fortress? Perhaps sometime down the road I'd venture down Llogara Pass to the fort—best to bypass the causeway slowly, and have a look to see if my buddies were there or if things had changed.

———— »«(()»«———

"Are you absolutely sure that's how it happened?"

The restaurant owner sat with Reby outside on the terrace continuing another session of questions. The driver knew the owner would keep talking to him alone until he was sure Reby hadn't missed any of the details. Reby had learned that his other passenger was the owner's only brother when all the sisters had arrived to discuss what had to be done. He could see some of them now over his interrogator's shoulder, sitting at a table inside, waiting to hear what the head of the family had decided.

The man sitting across from him had transformed over the last two days, ever since Reby told him about the incident on the mountain road. This wasn't just a grieving brother he faced—the owner was now a very determined investigator, nothing like the friendly promoter on the morning of the shooting. Reby was reminded of his "interview" with the KFOR police regarding his former boss's operations on the Kosovo border. There had been no emotion in the questions from the American officer, who had been strictly polite and formal, but they were relentlessly repeated. The owner was not so polite. The driver now wished he'd followed his original plan and continued on to Ohrid. But he hadn't, and he had no idea how long his "guest" status at the restaurant would go on for. It would be for the head of the family to decide when he was free to go.

"Yes!" Reby said, and pointed to the table where the bullet from the restaurant and the piece from the road lay side by side. He'd already told the owner what he thought had happened, but the man wanted to hear it again. Reby picked up the metal piece he'd found on the road and said, "This piece of metal is from a bullet. I know this because the bullet that was found in the restaurant is made of metal that is very unique, not the normal armament that's used in Albania. Just look how they are both exactly the same colour and sheen." He put the fragment down beside the bullet and looked at the owner. "I found this piece," he said as he picked up the metal again, "right near where we went off the road. I originally thought the tire on my side blew out, but then I found this fragment and remembered it was the passenger side wheel that scraped the road. I also remember a car was parked right across the ravine from where we went off the road. We had already passed it, and I'm nearly sure Bega was standing beside the car. He must have had someone with him who could shoot out my tire, and this person waited until we came around the ravine so he could get a straight shot."

"You think Bega was involved directly?"

Reby knew the owner was skeptical that the biggest

operator in the south of the country would implicate himself in the shooting of the American. "I know it sounds crazy, but I've seen him before, and he stands out. He was probably helping the sniper get away when we passed them."

The owner took the bullet from the table and tapped it on his knee while he continued looking straight at Reby. The driver tried to look back straight into his black eyes but managed only to stare at the bridge of his nose.

Reby said, "Like I've already told you, the wheel can be checked when the car is hauled up and examined. Look at the passenger side!" He wondered if the police knew he was here in Elbasan. "Did you find the driver of the van that picked me up?

There was a knock at the glass doors and both men looked over to see one of the owner's men standing and motioning for him. The owner stood up and went into the restaurant, disappearing inside to talk with his man.

The driver sat in his chair and looked around at the garden and the tables set out in the sun. He wanted to be away from here. At least his arm had been patched up, but the "doctor" had said nothing to him when Reby questioned him—Reby suspected he was only a veterinarian, but his wound had stopped throbbing and the arm was feeling better.

He thought again about the owner's brother. What if he had still been alive after the crash? Reby hadn't felt a pulse, but it might have been very weak. The owner had sent his men to the site with a detailed sketch of the road: the inside curve between the sharp bends, and the gorge where the car was located. Reby hadn't heard anything about what they'd seen or done. The owner hadn't wanted him to go with his men, but Reby wasn't sure why. Were they wondering why Reby hadn't been the shooter's primary target instead of the car?

The glass door slid open, and the owner came back outside. "The marksman must have been quite a shot to make the car go off the road—unless you slowed down to help him."

Reby was about to protest when the owner sighed and reached out to put his hand on Reby's shoulder. "Relax. Your story checks out. The car was hauled up yesterday after the bodies were retrieved. The front passenger tire was completely destroyed, and there's a bullet hole in the passenger-side fender, above the wheel rim."

34

MY ATTEMPTS TO contact Celine finally paid off when she called me late Tuesday morning. After the usual chit-chat, she said, "Tony, I hear things may have quieted down again."

"You mean in the north? Are you confirming that? I was trying to get hold of you last week to get a better idea of whether I needed to plan a pullout."

"Yes, sorry," she said. "I had to tend to some business in one of my other areas of responsibility. You do know Eastern Europe isn't just Albania."

Yeah, thanks, Celine—or maybe it was just too difficult, so best not to say anything? I thought, but no sense in pissing her off. "Well, the consul was helpful. She told me a little of what she could about the situation and that she'd run it by you." I waited, wondering how she'd react to being involved.

"She told you that?"

"Yes, we're good buddies." No harm in a bit of exaggeration. "She was quite revealing about Mr. Brown, once she remembered him from his past exploits. I take it you know he was fired after his association with illegalities on the Kosovo border?" The consul hadn't quite confirmed that, but it was a safe bet it was true.

Celine was quiet for a moment before she said, "Well, it's unusual for her to be so frank, though I'm not sure we've been able to confirm that."

"It's just a matter of time though, right? I think she felt bad that the embassy had misled me about Mr. Brown," I said, wanting to push the matter and get a reaction from Celine. It wasn't really the consul who'd helped create the impression that Brown was legitimate.

"Well, Tony, I think you're reading too much into what she said. There was no deliberate attempt to mislead anyone, though we might have accepted him as legitimate . . ."

We might have? She was trying to convince me I hadn't been misled by the meeting at the consulate, but it was really she who had misled me, and I wanted her to know that.

"One thing I *can* tell you, Tony."

"Yes?" Good, she had put me in some danger, knowingly or not, and needed to be a bit more open about what had happened.

"They found a car wreck at the bottom of one of those ravines." There was silence as I waited. "There were two bodies."

"Is this significant?" I asked. Bad driving was normal here, and there were plenty of steep drops for old cars to drop off after brake failures or excessive speed.

"It is Tony, if you'd let me finish."

I'd hardly interrupted her but there was a momentary silence—she must be thinking through what she would reveal to me.

"One of the bodies *might be*, and I mean might be—it should be confirmed later this week, but you won't hear it from me ..."

Yeah, whatever, but let's just hear it! I was starting to get a wee bit impatient with my cousin.

"The Americans think it could be Mr. Brown." Her voice was rushed. "He still hasn't reappeared."

Aha! So she was worried! And now I had an explanation why he didn't show up outside the Saranda hotel. "Was it an accident? Where was the car found?"

"Don't know Tony, and I've got to go."

Just like that, when it was starting to get interesting. I put the receiver down. It could have been an accident, or had he been cornered at the hotel party, after he'd texted me about meeting him? It would be easy to make it look like an accident somewhere up the coast road, as though he'd never made it to Saranda. But Celine knew he'd arrived in Saranda from his call to her.

Or that's what he'd told her.

Well, that's what she'd told me—that he told her he was in Saranda—but she had no reason to mislead me about that, though he might have reason to lie to her.

I really didn't know anything with certainty, but I also realised that if it wasn't an accident the people involved may have checked his phone to see who else he'd been talking to—me, for instance. Though I'd recently agreed with my wife that we really needed to start communicating better—and no more secrets—I would certainly not be sharing this concern.

35

WEDNESDAY MORNING, THE general manager called me into his office all smiles. He had a great idea. "Tony! Sit down, please." I joined the finance manager, who was already sitting at his little conference table. He avoided looking at me—not good.

My boss took his time, talking about progress in our working areas, and then got to our northern block. "I think it's time to pay an official visit to show our support for the region. We need to demonstrate that the block is safe and secure. More importantly, you need to show that we are a capable operator—that we can handle any situation."

I knew he wanted to demonstrate to head office that any issues had been resolved—the "cesspool" comments I'd heard in Vienna were likely circulating at a higher level. It was also important that the Albanian authorities had confidence in our operation, so the trip made some sense.

He barely looked to me, but I knew I was expected to voice approval with the finance manager present, whose support was also important. When I remained silent the general manager continued. "All the reports are looking very good."

"Not quite all of them," I said, knowing I needed to be careful.

He ignored the comment and went on. "I have a call into the ministry for them to join us. We don't want to risk using their vehicle, so Ariyan will make the final arrangements." On the last official trip to one of our other blocks, two of the ministry vehicle's tires had gone flat—either slow leaks or punctures—this, with two hours of daylight on a back track somewhere east of Vlora. Now he looked at me, giving me his full attention. "*You* will take your Nissan and I'll take the two ministry officials in the Land Cruiser."

When the GM's new Toyota Land Cruiser arrived the previous week, I should have expected that he'd want an opportunity to show the flag (and his new SUV) to the Albanians. Could the new vehicle even be the driving force behind this morning's inspiration? No, I was being overly cynical, but the new Toyota model had undergone an attractive design change, and shone like a movie star compared to our older fleet (which included my Nissan Patrol). He'd use the company driver for his SUV. Ariyan and a couple of ministry technicians whom we dealt with day to day would accompany me.

Ariyan had qualms about the whole plan. His report on the north, which I'd heavily modified for head office, was less positive than the general manager would have liked. And that was after I'd toned down the language, made the English readable, and removed the hashish references. I was beginning to think Ariyan was prejudiced against the more active Muslim presence in the north. He identified Islam with Arab influence—fair enough—but to him that meant kif pipes everywhere. Had he seen any camels on his recent visit?

"Funny joke, Tony, but is serious business. This peoples almost Kosovars, very different from Tirana. Very backwards. Maybe they want camels, but too much snow?"

We turned inland after driving north from Tirana and passing Kruje. We were the lead car on the roads that were not good, as per usual, but then they became teeth-chatteringly potholed, so I slowed down. Ariyan was sitting in front with me. I noticed how he was wearing his "concerned" look as we drove carefully along. The new Toyota would be getting a workout—and the water-filled holes were going to make it dirty.

"Ariyan, I thought you said the road wasn't too bad?"

"Was good, Tony, like I said, but this way shorter."

"You mean this isn't the way you went?"

"No. But is shorter way."

"Ariyan, shorter distance doesn't always mean shorter time."

"Road good last time I'm here."

"How long ago was that?" I asked.

"Only three years," he said. We continued on for a bit. The Land Cruiser was falling behind us, and it flashed its lights. "Okay, Tony, maybe five, six years at most."

At least, I thought, and pulled over to wait for the Toyota to catch up.

Things improved once we got onto a wide gravel track that hadn't been used much since the fall of Hoxha's regime. Ariyan was quick to point out how good the road was. Then we gained elevation and saw that streams had washed out sections, but between these breaks the going was reasonable.

Ariyan had wanted to share the driving, and I finally let him once we joined up with the road he had taken on his previous visit. He wasn't a great driver, especially on winding roads—he didn't keep to our side when going around blind corners, despite my best attempts to explain the dangers.

"Don't worry, Tony. I already been here." The Toyota had moved in front on the gravel, not wanting to be in the dust, and had stayed there. "Land Cruiser will warn others," he said, just as a big ugly transport blared its horn and narrowly missed us, coming around the bend.

Ariyan looked over at me as he swerved to the right and shook his fist into the rear-view mirror. "Crazy people here, I tell you!"

It was surprising to see a big transport up here on these roads. It could have been a fuel truck, based on the rounded tanker shape I'd glimpsed before it disappeared in the dust. We had used a lot of helicopter time to fly in most of our diesel—money spent to avoid any unnecessary risk of accidents on the road.

Another thirty minutes went by and then Ariyan banged into a big pothole that shook the Nissan down to its heavy frame, so I asked him to stop. I didn't care if he lost face with the two ministry guys; I was going to resume driving. They had woken up with the jolt. One of them was much older than the other, and he looked momentarily terrified—bad memories from the past, I guessed. Ariyan tried ignoring my request, but I insisted he stop. When I got out, one of the tires was hissing out air and nearly flat. I hoped the final section of road was in good shape because it had started to rain. And we didn't have a second spare tire.

The two of us were removing the wheel when the Toyota showed up, having turned around. The ministry people stood watching while the general manager tried using his phone. Good luck. We should be close to our base, but there was no line of sight to our cell tower.

We got underway again and within twenty minutes had reached the edge of our block. A cloud of black smoke billowed up into the sky ahead of us as the rain subsided. The fire was nearly out when we arrived. Our Croat consultant came running over, looking nervous, but it appeared he had things under control.

"Just burning garbage," he said as I lowered my window. "They use too much diesel."

We all got out of the vehicles, and I wandered over to have a look at the smoking fire pit, but there wasn't one, just the burned materials. The contractor had started to follow me but turned back when he saw me going towards the burn. The rain had prevented the flames from spreading, but using too much diesel could have been dangerous without a pit or empty oil drum to contain the fire. I turned back to the vehicles, where Ariyan was standing smoking with a couple of workers, and caught sight of the big old fuel truck I'd overlooked on our arrival. It was parked just off to the side of the SUVs, and much too close to the crew's living quarters.

The contractor was talking to our general manager, between glances in my direction. They were discussing the operation and the Croat was involving the ministry officials, normally good for relations between us and the government.

I waited until everyone went into the kitchen hut for coffee and something to eat, and then approached the contractor and asked him to wait—just a few questions I wanted to ask.

"Didn't we have enough fuel flown in at the start? Why the fuel truck?"

The contractor smiled. "With all delays and cold weather we need more. Ariyan knows this. They drive up old truck and park. Good idea but bad road make leaks."

"The truck is leaking fuel?" I asked. "When did you notice?"

"After other fuel truck leaves. I see cook helper fill bucket to burn garbage from leak."

"Well first, the truck is parked much too close to the living quarters, but what about this other truck? When was it here? Did someone order more fuel?" It must have been the truck we'd met on the road.

"Today, maybe one, two hours, but leave before finish. Then I see leak. Look." As we walked over, the Croat explained the driver received a cell call and left. "Ariyan don't order diesel?"

On closer inspection, it appeared the stationary truck was in very bad shape. Two of the tires were covered with wet cardboard, which I lifted to have a better look. This revealed the rubber on one of the tires was shredded, nearly all were bald, and another was nearly flat. I climbed up to see how much fuel was on board. There was a very strong odour of gasoline, not diesel—I stopped in my tracks and carefully got back down, motioning the Croat to move away.

He was worried now. "Okay, sorry for tires, but is like this when they come. Is terrible, but what to do? Only after they park and leave do I see this . . ."

"The fuel is benzene—it's gasoline not diesel!" No wonder the garbage had burned so rapidly. With all the leaking gasoline and the strong vapour smell, it was a miracle there hadn't been an explosion. I ran up to the kitchen hut, which was further away from the tanker. It might be a safe distance, depending on how much gasoline was in the leaking truck.

The general manager looked up at my entry. He came over quickly and I filled him in. His face darkened and he was on his cell before I finished giving him the details. I went over to Ariyan and the others to get them outside while it was still wet from the rain. We pushed all the vehicles away from the tanker, while it continued to dribble its explosive fuel onto the ground. The SUVs needed to be far enough away from the fumes to avoid any possibility of a spark— from static electricity or any of the vehicles' electrics. And Ariyan had been smoking with the field crew near the truck when we'd arrived!

"What do you think?" I asked my boss. He had joined us outside to have a look for himself. The ministry people followed him and were jabbering away to each other.

"We'll isolate the truck until firefighting help arrives." He saw me wondering and said, "The embassy is arranging for an Italian helicopter with foam and personnel." And he walked away in disgust—so much for our health and safety training. These courses had been mandatory for everyone, including the contractor. I was impressed by the general manager's quick thinking. His contact to use the helicopter as a part of an evacuation scenario had now been put to good use.

36

THE FIELD SHUTDOWN was temporary, and once the helicopter arrived, we left Ariyan with the contractor to sort things out, and find out how the fuel had been ordered. The Croatian contractor was going to send me copies of any receipts or material he'd received from the company that had supplied the old truck and the latest delivery—he didn't find anything before I left the site with the general manager later in the afternoon.

I wondered if there was anything to find.

We arrived back in Tirana very late on Wednesday night after playing down the incident with the ministry officials. They seemed ready to accept sending gasoline instead of diesel as a simple, though very dangerous, mistake.

The general manager talked confidently in Albanian to the senior officials in the middle seats, while I sat up front. The driver was our most experienced local employee, but he remained quiet. All sides of the conversation would be passed on to Ariyan, once he returned.

Nothing was mentioned about the unknown source who had ordered the fuel, since the contractor had insisted to everyone that this information would be forthcoming.

At our management meeting on Thursday, I summarised the events, but any conclusions regarding responsibility would be postponed until I'd heard from the contractor.

An envelope addressed to me with an Albanian stamp was waiting on my desk on Friday morning. Despite the lack of a return address, I expected it to be something from the ministry, possibly something about the incident in the north. I had to smile when I saw it was an invitation to stay in the new Saranda hotel, free of charge.

An attached note from the management informed me that they were trying to encourage travellers from Tirana to make the trip south; the note was accompanied by two tickets for a harbour cruise, with the possibly of going further out for fishing, weather permitting. A Mr. Bega had signed the note, and included his warmest personal regards.

I put it aside for future reference. I wasn't sure that we'd go; after all, we'd been there, done that, though not the harbour cruise. And fishing? That seemed odd.

The rest of the day was slow. We all stepped outside for coffee in the warm November sun, and I looked forward to having a beer after work. We were going to finish early and enjoy the weather, courtesy of the general manager. For someone from the northern latitudes used to a long, cold winter, being able to sit outside on a late fall day and still be warm was heaven. Provided I could convince the rest of the family to stay, Albania was certain to remain interesting. And I thought this would help keep away my "impending" midlife crisis that my wife was becoming concerned about.

Epilogue

REBY EASED THE nose of the car forward as he carefully parked the Mercedes across from the restaurant inside the citadel. It was the first time he'd been left alone in the car since he'd been asked to drive the lead of two cars for the operation that would get underway very early the next morning. The owner would be one of his passengers, and they planned to drive south towards Gjirokaster and get as close as feasible to Bega's mountain stronghold at Lapardha before daylight, in order to avoid raising suspicions. They'd wait in the vehicles and try to get some rest somewhere well off the road during the day, while a local reconnaissance was undertaken to see how best to access Bega's hideout.

The owner had briefed Reby that afternoon on the terrace—the target was to be a close relative of Bega's. "I know he has no brothers, but I have learned that he has two daughters, and one of them has a son." The owner's eyes gleamed as he spoke. "She stays with her husband at Lapardha. We will find the husband and he will lead us to the family. They will pay for my brother." He got up to go, then added, "An eye for an eye."

As he sat in the car, Reby considered again about making a run for the border.

————)(()(————

The Montenegrin waited in the small shed used as an office beside the airfield—he was cold, even with the winter boots and parka. An adjutant opened the door and a senior military officer stepped inside, stamping his boots and shaking the snow from his thick coat. He looked at the sniper, his face registering some surprise from under the overly large peak of his Russian-style cap.

"So, you are the man we have been waiting for?"

The Montenegrin gave a smart salute and handed him his transit papers.

"No need for those formalities here." But the officer took the papers and scanned them briefly. "There will be no mistakes. You will board the aircraft in a few minutes with a small team of patriots. Their leader will give you the details of the target once you are airborne." He stepped closer to the sniper and looked down on him. "Listen to me closely now. The team will accompany you *at all times* and act as guides and spotters for the operation. Are we clear?"

There was a double knock on the shed door and the adjutant opened it and saluted. A big man came in, nodded to the officer, and looked towards the Montenegrin. He walked over and circled around the sniper. "Your reputation precedes you." He stopped in front of him and poked him in the shoulder, hard. "You will have *one* chance to prove it." He walked back out the door. The officer gestured for the sniper to follow.

As the turboprop Tupulev lifted into the air, the Montenegrin sat on the canvas-strapped bench and looked around at his fellow passengers along both sides of the aircraft's interior. The leader, sitting directly across from him, continued to stare at him, even as he withdrew an envelope and leaned over to shove it into the sniper's hand.

The Montenegrin extracted the photo and the sketch of the target's location, but his thoughts were elsewhere. He assumed they were somewhere in eastern Ukraine from what he'd pieced together of his transit. He'd arrived in Moscow two days before and been bundled aboard several aircraft over the following twenty-four hours. Then a half day to rest in an overheated bunkhouse, by himself.

Having finally gotten a chance to operate in the far east of Europe, where there might be lots of work, he did not regret his decision to accept the offer. But it might be a long time before he saw his brother again.

━━●((◉))●━━

By early January, we'd put the northern operation on hold for two or three months because of winter snow at those elevations. The gasoline cleanup had incurred additional delays and costs, but the surveying was completed quickly once it finally resumed. Costs to date had been within our contingency budget, so head office wasn't too concerned.

The mysterious fuel incident had been largely buried,

PETER J. MEEHAN

though my general manager had hinted that I was at least partially to blame. Ariyan agreed that the contractor had made him aware of the need for diesel on his solo trip in November, but he had forgotten to pass that request on to me. Not only had he not told the office, he'd also insisted he'd forgotten about it completely, so he wouldn't have requested the delivery.

So who did?

Everyone at the site would have known that fuel was needed, but no one would admit to contacting anyone requesting diesel delivery.

The only paper trail the contractor had found was a poor copy of a receipt for either one thousand or ten thousand litres of fuel from Gashi Transport Services. The ripped corner made the amount unclear, and there was no mention of fuel type. The company denied any knowledge of the delivery, insisting they would have wanted payment for any services rendered if they had made the delivery.

Was the gasoline a mistake? Who had paid for the fuel?

I had to remember that this was the Balkans. Maybe Ariyan would eventually tell me what he thought, even though this was unlikely to convince my boss.

And maybe I'd be able to drive the coast road from Llogara Pass to the Venetian fortress again, though not until Ariyan filled me in on what he knew about any new development—but probably best to avoid Saranda.

Acknowledgements and References

This work of fiction is based on residency in Albania—all locations are real and many are worth visiting. Albania has made great progress in the intervening fifteen years since the time when this novel takes place: primarily November, 2001. Even during the three and a half years that I resided in Tirana with my family, there were tremendous advances in safety, policing and infrastructure within the country, and multiple border points opened with Montenegro and Greece that I crossed with my wife and children.

Many of the incidents described are based on actual events that I witnessed, but many are also fiction used to move the plot forward, in particular the details of criminal activities of Bega, Victor, the Montenegrin and other illegalities. All characters are works of fiction.

I would like to thank all of my family for encouragement, especially my daughter, Sandra, who had to attend too many schools because of my line of work, and brother, Patrick. My editor, Rachel Small, has been of particular help in advancing a short travel piece on my family's weekend trip to Butrint in November, 2001. Beth Kallman Werner is my publicist, and helped guide me through the self-publishing warren.

The historical events described are true to the best of my knowledge, based on references (below) and long discussions with other expatriates, consular staff and locals. My former work colleague, Adrian Ballauri, was an Albanian friend and offered many insights into the country.

Albania and Kosovo Blue Guide, James Pettifer, A&C Black Ltd., 3rd edition (2001): General history and background, locations not always accurate. Numerous websites are listed, with links to http://reliefweb.int/report/albania/stability-pact-southeastern-europe and other NATO and KFOR websites.

Regarding al-Qaeda's connection to Albania and Kosovo, and a possible 9/11 link:

The Coming Balkan Caliphate: The Threat of Radical Islam to Europe and the West, Christopher Deliso, Greenwood Publishing Group (2007): Jihadist activities and reports they threatened a major attack on the US shortly before 9/11.

Arab News (Jan 23, 2002) and *Radio Free Europe's* website archive (Jan. 25, 2002): Arrest and deportation of five Middle East businessmen involved in money laundering for al-Qaeda.

CPSIA information can be obtained at www.ICGtesting.com
Printed in the USA
LVOW08s0511060816

499258LV00001B/1/P